For Herri....

von

mi freind Mattin B.

aka . Leo Kessler

am 10ᵗʰ Juni - 1997

THE BORMANN MISSION

THE BORMANN
MISSION

Leo Kessler

This first edition published in Great Britain 1997 by
SEVERN HOUSE PUBLISHERS LTD of
9–15 High Street, Sutton, Surrey SM1 1DF.
Originally published in 1980 in paperback format only
Under the title *The Phoenix Assault* and pseudonym *John Kerrigan*.
First published in the USA 1997 by
SEVERN HOUSE PUBLISHERS INC., of
595 Madison Avenue, New York, NY 10022.

British Library Cataloguing in Publication Data

Kessler, Leo, 1926-
      The Bormann Mission
      1.   World War, 1939-1945 - Fiction
      2.   War stories
      1. Title
      823.9'14 [F]

      ISBN 0-7278-5224-8

Typeset by Palimpsest Book Production Limited,
Polmont, Stirlingshire, Scotland.
Printed and bound in Great Britain by
Hartnolls Ltd, Bodmin, Cornwall.

Prologue

On the night of 1 May 1945, a fat man started running in Berlin. That terrifying night the undersized, forty-five-year-old German with the pugnacious chin and shoulders of a run-to-seed boxer started the greatest adventure of his long, bureaucratic life.

Against the blood-red, burning backdrop of a dying National Socialist Berlin, he scurried through the few streets left in German hands, running for his life. Dodging and twisting, his heart thumping painfully in his chest with the unaccustomed exercise, he tried to save himself from the terrible revenge the victors would take on him if he were ever captured.

Some said that he met his death at the hands of a Red Army patriot. Other reports suggested that, during that night of wild excess, he slunk away to freedom. But when, in November 1945, the trial of the guilty men of National Socialist Germany took place in the medieval city of Nuremberg, the running man was absent from the ranks of those twenty-one men who faced Allied justice.

For another quarter of a century he would be sighted in one or other of the five continents: in 1947 in Australia; three years later in Africa; in 1951 in South America; the year after that in Italy. Twenty years later he was back in South America and still running.

Now we know that he did not run far after all. The truth is far stranger. This is the story of what happened to the running man that terrifying night. And why....

The bad jokes of Fortune: village pierrots yesterday, arbiters of life and death today, tomorrow keepers of public latrines.

Juvenal

Acknowledgement

I should like to thank ex-Obersturmbannführer Heim, who was once the running man's secretary; ex-Standarten-führer Zander, his long-time military adjutant; his brother-in-law ex-Obersturmbannführer der Waffen S S Buch; as well as that lady in the Home Counties who was the last of the running man's staff to see him alive. Or was she?

One: The Mission

'I hope the bastard fries in hell!'
Hermann Goering, 1945

20 April 1945 turned out to be a fine spring day after all. By ten o'clock that morning the temperature stood at 18.2° C in Berlin-Dahlem. In the dusty bomb ruins of Zehlendorf and Wilmersdorf, the flowers bloomed. The Grunewald, now full of smooth-cheeked boys from the Hitler Youth flak units and S S men from half a dozen European nations, including Britain, was heavy with the heady scent of pine resin; and in the once famous *alleen* of the shattered Westend, cherry blossom flourished a bright, confident red and white.

It was what the Berliners had once called in other and better days, 'Führer weather'. But then that was as it should be, for today was, after all, Adolf Hitler's fifty-sixth birthday.

But the capital, now surrounded by the advancing Russians, showed little outward sign of celebrating the event this particular April morning. Overnight a large new poster in blood-red and black had appeared strung between two bomb ruins in the Lutzowplatz. It announced grandly : *We thank you for everything, our beloved Führer. . . . Dr Josef Goebbels.* But from the few beaten, yellow-faced shabby Berliners, who chanced to look up at it, there was little reaction save a curse or a raised, threatening fist. Close nearby in a bombed house near the Brandenburg Gate, the 'poison dwarf' as they called him, Reichspropagandaminister Dr Josef Goebbels, began his traditional birthday speech in praise of the 'saviour of the German Folk'. But when a Russian 105mm shell exploded nearby and shattered the remaining windows of the house, he soon gave up. Nobody was listening anyway.

Now with the 'sub-humans' of the Red Army, the 'Ivans', as the Germans called them, occupying virtually every Berlin suburb, life in the shattered city centre continued drably, dangerously. In Kreuzberg, a pregnant woman trundled her dead fiancé in a wheelbarrow to the local registry office so that she could be married to him. Afterwards the body was tossed carelessly into the nearest, lime-filled mass grave. In Friedrichshain, a deserter from the Armed S S, who had been on the run for three months now, prowled through the still smoking bomb debris with an enormous pair of pincers pulling out the gold teeth of the prosperous dead bourgeoisie to sell for food and drink on the black market. Nearby in Lichtenberg, a drunken fourteen-year-old from a Hitler Youth flak unit 'serviced' his sixth woman in the last twenty-four hours and told himself this kind of war could go on for ever. And in the shattered Unter den Linden, the dead bodies of the deserters, officers and common soldiers both, swung slightly in the faint warm spring breeze.

Soon the procession of the grey-camouflaged Horchs and Mercedes began to arrive outside the bunker, in which the 'Leader of the 1000 Year Reich' had hidden himself. The Prominenten were coming to pay their respects for the last time. Joachim von Ribbentrop, the Foreign Minister, once a salesman of cheap German champagne and former minister to the Court of St James, arrogance etched in every line of his stupid gaunt face, was one of the first. He was followed by a clutch of generals, their features dull and exhausted; they knew Germany had lost the war anyway. Reichsführer S S Heinrich Himmler appeared a little while later, his dark eyes revealing nothing of *his* plans for the future behind the rimless schoolmaster's pince-nez he affected. The 'Poison Dwarf' limped in on his monstrous club-foot a few moments afterwards, flashing confident looks at the gigantic S S bodyguards who obstinately lined

14

the entrance to the dripping dank bunker. Finally Reichs-marschall Hermann Goering eased his monstrous bulk out of his Mercedes and waved his jewel-encrusted marshal's baton at the bodyguards. In spite of their rigid position of attention, the S S men grinned. 'Fat Hermann' was always good for a laugh. Goering lived up to his reputation with the troops. 'Don't worry, lads,' he chortled, as he waddled by them, 'one blast from my secret cannon and we'll blow the whole Ivan pack back to Siberia!' He raised his fat right leg and gave them one of his celebrated juicy farts.

Finally they were all assembled for the last time in the gloomy, windowless, concrete room, uneasy and unusually silent for the important men that they once had been. Bormann, lounging in the corner and studying them with his greedy little pig's eyes, reflected that they looked like men who had made other plans. The rats were about to leave the sinking ship.

'*Meine Herren, unser Führer Adolf Hitler!*' Guensche, Hitler's massive S S adjutant, announced in his parade-ground voice.

The Prominenten clicked to attention as Adolf Hitler came slowly into the room, ashen-faced, his jacket apparently too large for him, his left hand, which Bormann knew suffered now from a convulsive tic, buried in his pocket in an attempt to hide his defect.

There was a strange silence, broken only by the sound of Hitler's shuffle, and then, as if the Prominenten remembered for one last time what was expected of them, the room exploded with the cry: '*Heil mein Führer!*'

Almost uncomprehendingly Hitler stared at them and then at the presents they had brought – the bust of a Roman emperor, a naval battle in oil, large deluxe art books and the rest – and then he began to struggle along the line of the Prominenten weakly shaking hands. An old, painfully old, hunched man.

The birthday party took its sombre course – the drinks, the over sweet, synthetic cakes, the measured words of

15

congratulation – until it was finally time for Hitler to speak. The Prominenten waited for him to say something until finally an embarrassed Goebbels, flashing an inquiring look at Bormann in the corner who shrugged carelessly by way of reply, said in that rasping Rhenish accent of his: 'The whole world will know that our Leader has decided to stand fast in Berlin at the head of those brave men fighting not only for Germany but for the whole of western culture!'

At last Hitler responded quietly. 'Yes, I shall remain here. The rest of you will go your various ways, but remember as the enemy advances he must find nothing but scorched earth. All factories, workshops, houses must be destroyed, not one stone must be left standing upon another. If our enemies desire total war we shall give it them.' There was no conviction in his voice and the Prominenten knew it; their master of these last twelve years, when for half of them he had ruled Europe from Russia to the English Channel, was finished.

Somehow Hitler seemed to sense their knowledge. His voice rose, a pathetic imitation of that tremendous guttural roar that had once made them shiver at the Party Rallies at Nuremberg: 'I will tell you one thing, *mein Herren*, Stalin will lose his teeth here in Berlin. He has bitten off too much. Berlin will be our Stalingrad. We shall beat him here.' His enthusiasm vanished as quickly as it had come. 'Go, gentlemen, Reichspropagandaminister Goebbels and Reichsleiter Bormann,' he nodded at the fat man in the corner, 'will stay with me here.'

Bormann's face feigned enthusiasm. He was hungry again and he thought of the sausage he had hidden in his cupboard. Before the Prominenten could begin to shuffle out, he cried: '*Mein Führer*, with your permission, I shall teleprint those words of yours throughout the Reich. They will give courage and hope to our hard-pressed Party members. *We shall beat him here.*' His fat red face glowed.

Hitler waved a weak hand at him. 'As you wish, Bormann.'

16

The 'General of the Teleprinters', as Bormann was called behind his back, clicked his heels together. A few moments later he was locked in his little room carving off great slices of the forbidden salami with his penknife and taking greedy gulps at the bottle of *Doppelkorn*. Outside the Russian artillery had begun to fire again, but now the sound of their guns no longer frightened him. His mind was full of the future.

> *'She'll be wearing khaki bloomers,*
> *When she comes.*
> *Oh, she'll be wearing khaki bloomers,*
> *When she comes. . .'*

The little camouflaged Bedford 15cwt pulled up and let the platoon of singing A T S girls swing down the hill, their full cheeks red with good health, their bodies held like guardsmen.

'I know what they ought to do with their khaki bloomers,' Mallory's driver said moodily and then turned off the little side road leading into Bletchley and started down the drive towards the ugly ornate Victorian mansion and the surrounding Nissen huts.

A sentry stepped into their path and a little to his surprise Mallory noted he wore the Italian and French campaign stars. Idly he wondered why a frontline soldier should be employed guarding this Home Counties establishment, which bore the vague title of Government Code and Cypher School, when the front was crying out for skilled infantrymen.

'Your pass, sir, please?' The sentry broke into his thoughts.

Major Mallory handed him it and the sentry scrutinized it at some length before clicking to attention, opening the gate and snapping, as if he were on the parade ground, 'You can pass now, sir!'

The little van moved forward and, as they turned right towards the tin huts, Mallory caught sight of the sign:

17

W D Property – Trespassers Will Be Shot. He frowned. Here, they were pushing it a bit much, he told himself, and his frown deepened; wandering about the lawns were bespectacled long-haired dons by the looks of them in battered tweed jackets with leather patches at the elbows and baggy flannels. There were even a couple of them playing, of all things, croquet! Hardly the kind of civilian who would warrant guarding by top-class soldiers, he thought, as the little van came to a halt outside the Nissen hut.

Fred was waiting for him. He hadn't changed much since Mallory had first met him in 1939 when he had joined Le Grand's D Section. He was still blond, though going a shade grey at the temples, and his narrow face was as keen as ever. But today, wearing the wing-commander's uniform of the Royal Flying Corps he had left in 1918, he was strangely formal – almost as if they had not been on christian name terms for six years. He did not ask Mallory to sit down. Instead he nodded to the waiting RAF squadron-leader, who wore a steel helmet, but whose chest was without wings or decorations.

The squadron-leader cleared his throat and said a little pompously, 'Major Mallory, we've asked you down here to swear an oath. I know you have already sworn an oath of loyalty to the King Emperor,' he added hastily as if he expected the man facing him to object, 'and signed the Official Secrets Act, but this is something different.'

At the desk, Fred drew his service .38 and laid it on the cleared surface in front of him. 'Carry on, Squadron-Leader,' he commanded, watching Mallory's face closely.

The squadron-leader cleared his throat again. 'In a moment I shall ask you, Major, to sign a statement that you will not reveal anything of what is said in this room. Otherwise the penalty will be' – he hesitated, with a hint of embarrassment – 'death.' Fred snapped and pressed the trigger of his .38. There was a click. The chamber was empty. Major Mallory jumped slightly all the same. Since Albania,

18

he told himself, his nerves were shot. 'I shall shoot you personally.'

With a hint of irritation, Mallory took the form and fountain pen the squadron-leader offered and signed with a flourish. 'All right, Fred,' he said sharply. 'What's all this bloody charade about, eh?'

Fred smiled, but the blue eyes were still wary. 'Charade, Mike? Perhaps, but believe you me, if you ever mention one word of what I'm going to tell you now, I *will* shoot you. Without compunction.' His voice lightened and this time his eyes smiled. 'Welcome back, Mike. Take a pew and have a cigarette.' He pushed an open packet of Senior Service towards the puzzled army officer. 'Now pin back your ears. Do you remember the month you joined Le Grand's section and you couldn't meet C – or the Deputy C, as he still was then?'

Mallory nodded wondering where all this ancient history was leading to.

'Well, he was over in Poland for us, obtaining a top-secret German coding machine from their Intelligence people. It's all very hush-hush – a thing called the Enigma which the Jerries use to encode all their top-level messages, military, naval and political. Well, thereafter for nearly a year our top boffins worked on it trying to come up with some way of decoding those messages almost as soon as they had been sent and by the spring of 1940, our chaps finally did it – *here.*'

Mallory stared at Fred. In his six years of fighting the secret war in Europe for C, Mike Mallory had encountered many strange things, but never anything like this. 'You mean . . . you mean to say that we've been able to read. . .'

'Yes. To read every top-level Jerry communication as soon as its official recipient,' Fred interrupted enthusiastically, obviously proud of the surprise he had been able to spring on Mallory. 'Quite something, eh?'

Mallory breathed out hard. 'All I can say then is we took a bloody long time to win. Besides, why did we swamp

Europe with agents when we knew all the time what the Jerries were up to. . . . Oh, come on, Fred, clue me in,' he broke off a little angrily. 'Why are you telling me all this now?'

Not answering immediately, Fred looked hard at Mallory, studying the other man's long lean face with the trim little moustache of the regular soldier, as if he were seeing it for the very first time, noting the contained nervousness of a superb athlete which contrasted with the somehow sad, slightly bewildered eyes. 'Why did you volunteer to go on ops again, Mike? After that Albanian thing we all thought you had perhaps done enough. I mean there was that mad-fool scheme of Le Grand's to blow up the Iron Gates on the Danube in '40, the Heydrich killing, Peenemunde a year later in '43, and then Albania – you've done more than your share.' Fred hesitated for just a fraction of a second. 'Mike, you don't want to go and get yourself killed because of Albania, do you?' His keen blue eyes bored into the other man's face, watching for a reaction.

Mallory gave little away, replying wryly, 'I see you know all about my little – er – accident, Fred.' He shrugged easily, the gesture of a man who had come to terms with himself. 'In the old days when I came back from an op, there'd be London, booze and those popsies C provided for blue-eyed boys like me. Now there's only the booze – and you can't get drunk all the time.' He looked down at his hands and noted automatically the slight tremble of his fingers which hadn't been there before the Albanian operation. 'So,' again the major shrugged easily, 'I might as well be on ops as drinking myself to death. Come on, Fred, what gives?'

Fred thought for a moment and made his decision. 'Have a look at this.' He handed Mallory a flimsy stamped with the bold yellow letters 'TOP SECRET U'. 'Our classification,' he added.

'U?' Mallory queried.

20

'Ultra – that's our code name for the info we get from the Enigma.'

'I see.' Mallory started to softly read out the message pencilled on the thin paper. *'I have considered your...'* There was a blank and another hand had filled in *'suggestion, offer?' ... 'very thoroughly. I am prepared to discuss ...'* Again there was a blank and the unknown hand had filled in *'at earliest convenience, soon, etc?' ... 'The Führer is prepared to stay. Reichspropmin too...'*

Mallory looked up at Fred who was watching him keenly with those bright blue eyes of his. 'Goebbels?' he queried.

Fred nodded.

Mallory looked down at the message again. *The rest are going to make a run for it. I remain and await your orders.* There was no signature, but an official hand had pencilled *transmitted 1800 hrs. 21.4.45* at the bottom of the message. He returned it to Fred and said, 'So?'

'So, do you know who that message was intended for, Mike?'

'No, but I think that you're going to tell me,' Mallory answered with a hint of affectionate mockery.

'For Uncle Joe!'

'Stalin?'

Fred nodded his head slowly. There was a heavy silence in the hut. Outside the muted sound of an Andrew Sisters record could be heard.

'And who sent it?' Mallory asked, already aware that he was getting into something that was bigger than anything he had ever tackled before.

Fred looked at him, studying those haggard hurt eyes and the lined topography of a long war of grief and exhaustion on the other man's once handsome face, and replied: 'I won't attempt to pre-empt C, Mike. You know how blasted fussy he is about playing top-dog these days. But I'll tell you this,' he paused, as if for effect, 'they're going to send you out there to kill the man who did!'

*   *   *

C picked up the red phone from the big gleaming desk that had once belonged to Nelson and said in a louder voice than normal, 'General Donovan's office, can we scramble — *now!*'

General Donovan's voice boomed across the 3000 miles of the Atlantic, as if he were speaking from next door in that discreet street off St James's Park and not in a sweltering office in Washington D C. 'Hi, Stew,' he said, full of Bostonian bonhomie, 'how you keeping?'

'Quite well, quite well,' the grey little man behind the big desk answered and after a moment's hesitation added the American's absurd nickname, 'Big Bill.'

'Fine, fine,' boomed the Head of the United States' newly fledged Intelligence service, the O S S. 'You had me worried for a while earlier this year with that ticker of yours, you know.'

'Thank you, Big Bill.' Having dispensed with the formalities, C was crisply businesslike. 'The reason for my call is that we have important news. They're after Big Six. It's official.'

'Well, the double-dealing Commie bastards!' the American general exploded. 'For the last two years they've been accusing us of trying to pull a deal with the Krauts ever since Allen Dulles took up with 'em in Berne. I kept telling F D R not to trust them. And now. . . . What do we do about it?'

'Our people have already made their decision at the top level. The F O and I believe your State Department have decided to take him out like we did with Heydrich back in '42.'

C could hear the slight gasp at the other end and smiled to himself. In spite of their tough talk, the Americans were always shocked when one mentioned murder so cold-bloodedly.

'Knock him off, Stew?'

'Yes, that's it. We've got a very good man lined up for the job here, been with us for years though he's had a bit

22

of bad luck lately on one of his ops. Now we want one of your boys. The politicos think it should be a joint effort with American participation. That way your new President – er – Truman will be compromised.'

'Helluva good idea, Stew,' Big Bill said enthusiastically. 'We don't want Harry to be taken for a ride by the Commies like F D R was at Yalta. If anything goes wrong, he'll land in the shit, too.'

C chuckled mirthlessly. 'Nothing will go wrong, Big Bill. This particular op will belong to the secret history of World War Two. It'll be buried so deep in S I S files that it'll take a brigade of miners to dig it up again. But I want your best man for this one, the absolute top class. None of your American college professors of modern languages either,' he added quickly.

Donovan laughed easily. 'Sure I know what you mean – Jewish scribblers from Harvard, as Goebbels called O S S back in '42. We're much more professional now.' He paused for a moment. 'I think I've got the very man for you. He's called Piludski, Captain Paddy Piludski. Came to us from the University of Pittsburg in '42 – instructor in German and Russian. But he's very definitely *not* the college prof type. He's a typical husky Pittsburg Polack, who played semi-pro ball after leaving college before taking his graduate course. Since then he's done three combat jumps behind the Kraut lines in Europe till he bought one last year in the fall when he dropped with Hemingway's son. The Krauts bagged young Hemingway but Piludski with a slug in both legs managed to get away. He virtually crawled his way back to Spain. He was in a bad way for a while, but now he's fighting fit again and raring to go.'

'How is he on Communism, Big Bill? You know how these intellectuals can be.'

'He's a Polack and a Catholic like myself, Stew. They hate the Commies like poison. Besides, he probably doesn't know the meaning of the word politics. Semi-pro ball, dames and action – those are Piludski's politics, but don't

23

get me wrong, Stew, he's smart, smart as a whip. He's your man. I'd put my arm in the fire for him.'

C considered for a moment. The sky behind the barrage balloon was growing dark; a storm was on the way. Then he said, almost as if he were speaking to himself, 'He'd better be, Big Bill, because if we fail this op, the Bolshies will be on the Channel coast within the year. It could mean World War Three.'

Big Bill Donovan breathed a sigh of infinite weariness. *'Christ on a crutch!'* he said.

'Swing them ruddy arms now. . . . Get them legs open, nothing's gonna fall out. . . . Bags o' swank there. . . . Come on now, you bunch of pregnant penguins . . . lef' right, lef' right. . . .' The tremendous voice echoed and re-echoed across the parade ground, sending the blackbirds rising from the trees in flapping, hoarse protest.

'We accept them as criminals, Major, and we return them to their units as soldiers,' the commandant of the Aldershot military prison said, standing at Mallory's side at the barred window and looking down. 'None of that modern rubbish, probing their backgrounds and finding out that they wet their beds when they were young or that their fathers didn't love them. Lot of old balls. Here we believe in drill, drill and yet more drill.'

Down below one of the 'staffs' was poking the ribs of a sweat-lathered young soldier, laden down in full field marching order, with his brass-pointed pacing stick. The boy stumbled and fell to his knees on the gravel. But a great whack across his skinny shoulders brought him to his feet again and back into the ranks of the marching men.

The camp commandant stroked his pencil-slim moustache and said, 'We don't believe in mollycoddling them either. Fifty-six days of misery most of them get here so that they're only too glad to get back to the front or wherever they've come from. This is no rest home. This is a military prison.'

24

'So I see,' Mallory commented drily, noting that the commandant's narrow chest was bare of any medal save the Territorial Decoration. He had probably never seen a shot fired in anger throughout the war. 'Which is Higgins?' he asked.

The commandant took his hand from his moustache and pointed at the rear rank of the nearest column on the drill square. 'There he is – the one with the badge of the Royal Artillery. Higgins 175, in person.'

Mallory stared at the tough, wiry soldier in his mid-thirties, whose muscular arms were tattooed with the badges of the half a dozen regiments through which he had progressed in his fifteen years in the army, being kicked out of each of them, until finally he had landed in Anti-Aircraft Command. He caught a glimpse of a smart, knowing Cockney face that was not even dampish with sweat in spite of the 60lb load of equipment he carried on his back and the tremendous pace that the 'staff' was forcing on to the military prisoners.

'A typical barrack-room lawyer,' the commandant commented, 'who went a little too far in the end. Now he's a murderer and for my money, he deserves the rope he should get at the trial.'

'Could I see him privately?' Mallory asked.

'*I* wouldn't trust him,' the commandant objected. 'Remember he did stab a comrade to death.'

'I'll take my chance,' Mallory answered, not attempting to disguise the contempt in his voice.

The other officer flushed. 'Be it on your own head then, Major.' He raised his voice. 'Sarnt-Major!'

Five minutes later Mallory was staring up at Bombardier Higgins, R A, from the commandant's own desk and knew instinctively that he was looking at a typical pre-war 'old sweat': one of the diminishing few from the old Regular Army, who had been everywhere, seen and done everything and had somehow survived six years of total war. All the same, Mallory was surprised to note the red, white and blue ribbon of the Military Medal on the little man's chest. His kind was usually too smart to allow themselves to be sent where there was any chance of serious action.

Higgins 175 noticed Mallory's look and smiled softly, his dark-brown eyes cunning and knowing. 'Unfortunate oversight, sir,' he said. 'Snaked the posting clerk's old lady and he found out. Next thing yours truly knew, he was in North Africa getting his sodding knees brown.'

Mallory was tempted to smile, but he restrained his impulse in time: the little Cockney had summed up his own career from the decorations for bravery on his chest and had guessed that that kind of remark would appeal to a fighting soldier like Mallory. Instead he said, 'Sit down and have a cigarette.' He offered the prisoner one from his silver cigarette case engraved with the upturned parachute wings awarded to someone who had done three operational drops behind enemy lines.

'Ta very much, Major,' Higgins said, taking one and adding, 'Special ops type, eh, Major?'

Again Mallory caught himself. The little bugger had his eyes everywhere. It was a point in Higgins' favour; he was razor sharp.

'Tell me what happened – why you're in here, Bombardier?' he asked, wondering what Higgins would make of the story which he already knew.

'The sad story of me life, Major, eh?' the other man grinned and breathed out a grateful stream of rich blue smoke.

Mallory waited.

Higgins let him wait, seemingly savouring the cigarette, while his cunning eyes tried to sum Mallory up all the time. Outside the 'staffs' were bellowing – 'Move it, yer 'orrible men – or I'll have the goolies off'n yer!'

'It was the girl, sir,' Higgins said finally. 'She was our contact to the cheeseheads – Dutch to you, sir – on the black market. Cor ferk a duck, didn't she have a pair of lungs on her!' His eyes lit up at the memory and Mallory

26

could imagine him gloating over the unknown Dutch girl's breasts at night in his cell and felt a twitch of pity – or was it envy? 'But that little shit of a lance-jack in the Koylis was after her – randy bugger – and that's why I did him. Of course it was self-defence. He pulled. . .'

'All right, Higgins,' Mallory cut in. He knew the story already. Higgins had murdered a fellow black marketeer on their base near the German-Dutch frontier because the other man had intended to confess to the Military Police that there was a whole gang of them stealing compo rations meant for the front and selling them to the Dutch black market. 'Higgins, you were in Berlin as an embassy guard before the war, weren't you?'

The question caught the little soldier off guard; it was obviously not one he had expected.

'That's . . . right, sir,' he said slowly, looking curiously at Mallory. 'I picked up another of my languages there – Hindu, Arabic, Frog and German – and a nice case of clap too from a big blonde I met on the Kudamm.' He grinned suddenly. 'Lovely grub.'

'Talking of your love life, they tell me you got around with the maids at the various German ministries.' Higgins shrugged with mock modesty. 'Would you know this chap?' Mallory took the first photograph out of his pocket and pushed it across the table.

'Him, natch. It's the '*Gift* Dwarf' personally. He had the prettiest maids of all. They all thought the boss would make film stars out of 'em, but all he—'

'And this one?' Mallory interrupted, showing him the other photograph. It was blurred and vague, but it was the only one that C had been able to find. For such an important member of the Party, he had kept remarkably in the background.

Higgins stared at it for a moment and then said, 'Of course, that's Martin – Martin Bormann. Inge worked for him. Big brassy piece. Of course he'd snaked her himself – he did it to all his maids – but I didn't mind sharing her

27

with a Jerry. I'm a generous sort of bloke like that.'

'I bet you are,' Mallory said ironically and put the photographs away. The little soldier had recognized Bormann immediately; it was really all he wanted to know.

'Pardon me, sir, but what's all this about? What we having this little chat for – you're not from the Sally Ann or anything, are yer?'

'Would you like to get out of here, Higgins?' Mallory asked slowly, staring carefully at the other man.

Higgins shot him a sharp look. 'Oh, no sir, I've found a home in Aldershot glasshouse. The sarnt-major brings me a cup o' char in the morning and then there's a bit o' drill to pass the time and then we have a nice comfy cell to go to at night with no randy bints to prevent us getting our beauty sleep. Of course I want to get out of this bloody place, Major! It's putting years on me!'

'I can get you out. There'll be no trial and your record will be clean. You can start all over again.'

'Why?'

'Because you're needed.'

'Where?' Higgins twisted his head to one side and looked at the other man with his cunning little eyes. 'No, don't tell me, Major, let me guess. Germany, ain't I right?'

'You'll find out soon enough,' Mallory answered coldly. 'Well, do you want to accept my offer or not, Higgins?'

'What's in it for me?'

'I've told you.'

'That's not enough. I want my rank back – Bombardier.' He grinned wickedly at Mallory. 'Stripes seem to attract them.'

Mallory nodded. 'You'll get your rank back, Higgins.'

Bombardier Higgins rose to his feet and stretched out his hand. 'Major, you're on!'

A little reluctantly, Major Mallory took it. The palm was damp, as if its owner was sweating heavily.

The match scratched harshly in the silence of the night.

Hard blue flame spurted up in the doorway of the bombed shop, illuminating his face momentarily. Kim caught a quick glimpse of the waiting man's broad Slavic face. It was him. He clicked his blackout torch on and off twice and started to cross the inky-black street whistling *There'll Always Be An England.*

Boris stepped out of the air-raid shelter, looked left and right. There was nothing to be seen save the lone searchlight poking its icy finger into the sky above London for bombers which would never come again.

They shook hands in the Continental fashion and Boris said in his heavily accented English, 'Well? Do they know?'

'I th . . . think, so, B . . . Boris,' he stuttered.

'What makes you think it?'

'Just the way C is behaving. He ordered a s . . . search of the files f . . . for the Nazi bigshots two d . . . days ago and Q branch is k . . . kitting out somebody f . . . for an op in G . . . Germany.' The Englishman cursed inwardly – his bloody stutter was awful tonight. He supposed it had something to do with the *treff*; he was always very tense when he had to meet Boris like this. 'My considered g . . . guess is that C knows.'

Boris was silent for a moment. A long way off a dog barked. Otherwise London was deathly silent, as if it were a village and not the capital of the British Empire.

'I have always trusted your guesses, Kim,' he said finally. 'I shall report accordingly to the Director in Moscow. You have done well. Thank you.'

'Anything else I c . . . can do, Boris?'

'No, we will take care of the rest. Now you go, I shall follow in one minute.'

They shook hands again and then the arch-traitor began to walk down the bombed street, softly whistling the stupidly patriotic ditty.

In the corner a fat drunken G I was singing:

> *'My father's a black market grocer.*
> *My mother makes illegal gin,*
> *My sister sells sin in the Underground.*
> *Kee-rist, how the money rolls in.'*

Bombardier Higgins grinned, 'That's the stuff to give the troops, Yank,' he said enthusiastically.

'Screw the Eighth Air Force!' the G I growled without looking up. 'They've had me buddy – that's for sure.' He started to sing again.

They passed deeper into the little London pub with its sawdust covered floor, its bar occupied by two pale-faced paratroopers in their maroon berets, morosely sipping the weak war-time beer, both of them with golden wound stripes on their sleeves. Mallory guessed they had been hit with the Sixth Airborne which had made a combat drop on the east bank of the Rhine the previous month. He nodded at the elderly publican, who was obviously surprised to see a major and another rank. 'Two pints please,' he requested.

Mallory took a sip of the beer and wished it was whisky, but the chalked-up notice on the blackboard outside had read 'beer only', so there was no hope of that.

'Gnat's piss,' Higgins commented, 'but better than nothing, eh, Major?'

Mallory nodded gloomily. 'Now where are these women you said you'd be able to find here?' he asked.

'Don't worry, sir. . .'

'I'm not. I'm not looking for it.'

'When the news gets around that Higgins 175 is on the razzle they'll be in here like bees round honey. It's me charm, you see, Major.' He grinned at the Major in the flyblown mirror behind the bar.

Mallory sniffed and concerned himself with his beer. Behind them in the corner the drunken G I was singing:

> *'I don't want to join the Air Force.*
> *I don't want to go to war.*

30

I'd rather hang around Piccadilly Underground.
Living off the earnings of a high-born – ladeee. . . .'

The publican meanwhile polished his glasses and whistled *When the Lights Go On Again in London* through a gap in his front teeth.

Two young women came in, all clattering wooden heels, dyed brown legs because of the stocking shortage, and skinny bodies beneath the too short floral frocks, bubbling, 'Gin and It, 'Arry. Our tonsils is hanging out!'

In the mirror Mallory could see Higgins' wicked little eyes light up.

The publican looked sourly at the two young women with their flashing eyes and flushed cheeks. 'Gin and it,' he intoned. 'You can't be right in the head, we ain't had gin here – even for Yanks – for nigh on five weeks. Yer'll take port and lemon like yer allus do and like it.'

'That's no way to talk to ladies, guv,' Higgins said, reaching into his battledress pocket. 'But let me send the boat out, ladies.'

They giggled in unison and the skinnier of the two made an attempt at a curtsey by way of thanks. Mallory sighed and hoped Higgins would get it over with soon so that he could take him back to C's safe house in which they were being lodged until the briefing was finished.

The girls drained their glasses swiftly and giggled again. 'Same agen, ladies?' Higgins asked, the complete gallant now.

'If I have one more,' the skinnier of the two simpered, 'I'll feel it.'

'Go on,' Higgins urged, 'have one more and I'll feel it *for* you!'

Mallory looked at his image in the mirror a little helplessly, while a grinning, happy Higgins now started to chat with the girls. But the little soldier's hopes of success in bed were not to be realized that night. Just about the time the drunken G I from the Eighth Air Force had launched into

31

There's a Lancaster leaving the Ruhr heavily laden with terrified men, shit scared and prone on the floor, the heavy blackout curtain was thrust aside and squat, broad-faced soldiers started to pour in, their shoulders made even broader by the enormous epaulettes they bore. All of them wore the silver wings and the grey berets of the Polish Parachute Brigade, which had taken such a terrible beating at Arnhem the previous autumn. And they were drunk, very drunk.

Swaying wildly their leader staggered up to the bar and before the astonished publican's eyes started to pull out white five pound notes, which he dropped in the big wet ashtray carelessly.

'Enough?' he asked finally in a thick accent.

'Enough for what?'

'Drink – good drink,' the Pole answered. 'No pissy beer. Whisky, gin – for me – comrades.'

The publican looked at the crumpled pile of white fivers. There was at least fifty pounds lying there. He swallowed hard and avoided looking at the rest of his customers, who were watching intently.

'I do just happen to have two last bottles of whisky. . .'

'Bring,' the Pole interrupted him gutturally. 'Is good, bring!'

Higgins nudged Mallory. 'Not bad profit, eh, Major. I reckon the old crook is making about eight hundred per cent mark-up on each bottle.'

Mallory shrugged.

Rapidly the Poles downed the first bottle, their broad, sallow faces flushing red, their dark eyes darting angry glances at the others at the bar. They started on the second bottle.

Suddenly their leader nudged Higgins in the ribs, nearly making him spill his beer over the skinny girl's lap, and cried, 'Airborne – British Airborne, he shit!' He glowered in the direction of the two paratroopers.

Higgins' eyes blazed. 'Shove it, Sunny Jim,' he said

32

threateningly, knuckles tightening white around the handle of his beer glass, 'shove it where the sun don't shine.'

The Pole spat in the sawdust, his dark eyes smouldering with anger and resentment. 'You insult?' he asked softly.

'Yer, you dumb Polack,' Higgins cried, 'I insult.'

There was a sudden silence in the bar. In the corner, the drunken G I stopped singing. The two paras turned their heads slowly like men who had been through a lot and were very, very tired.

'Yes, we dumb Polacks. We fight Arnhem, while you English run way.'

'Me heart bleeds for you, *Polack*,' Higgins said.

Mallory looked at his companion warningly in the mirror. Higgins ignored the look. Mallory could see he was ready to smash the beer glass into the Pole's face at any moment.

But the Pole beat him to it. He said something in his own tongue to his comrade. Next instant he splashed the contents of his glass in Higgins' face. The little bombardier went back spluttering and momentarily blinded.

'Gentlemen, please gentlemen,' the publican called desperately. An empty whisky bottle sailed through the air and shattered the big mirror. Mallory caught one last glimpse of the Poles as they rushed forward, heard the command in a language he recognized and then the light went out and the bar was a mass of grunting, struggling men. Mallory felt someone grab at him. Instinctively he side-stepped and chopped his hand down. The Pole, if he was one, sprawled among the broken glass of the bar. Someone hit Mallory a stinging blow to the side of the jaw. He reeled back, abruptly groggy, red stars exploding in front of his eyes. Thus it was that when the scream came, it seemed to come from far, far away.

Mallory shook his head. Hard. Then he felt Higgins' grip on his arm. 'You all right, Major?' the bombardier gasped.

Mallory's eyes spun into focus once more, just as someone – perhaps the publican – snapped the light back on.

33

The Poles were staggering out of the door, dragging a drunken or injured comrade with them. It was then that the skinny girl screamed and pointed a trembling hand at the bar, her mouth open stupidly but no words coming from it.

One of the paratroopers lay slumped forward, his face in a pool of spilled beer.

'*Jesus H Christ!*' the abruptly sober GI breathed in shocked awe.

From between the man's shoulders, there protruded the metal hilt of a combat knife. Dark red blood was trickling slowly, very slowly down the dead paratrooper's back.

It was only fifteen minutes later, as they walked in stunned silence through the blacked-out streets, that it came to Mallory. He stopped abruptly, the sound of his heavy nailed boots echoing down the deserted street. 'Did you hear what the Pole said before they rushed us, Higgins?' he demanded.

'No,' Higgins answered, stopping and looking at the major's face, a tense eerie silver in the reflected light of the probing searchlights. 'I was too busy trying to avoid getting the piss knocked out of Mrs Higgins' handsome son.'

'He said "*horoscho*".'

'And who's he when he's at home?'

Mallory ignored the comment, his mind racing. 'It's a Russian word. I picked it up from the Russian instructors in Albania last year. It means "good" or perhaps better "okay".'

'So?' Higgins asked without interest.

'So what would a Pole be doing speaking Russian?'

'Search me, Major,' the bombardier shrugged.

They walked the rest of the way to the safe house wreathed in a heavy silence.

2

It was 23 April. Soon the Führerbunker would be under siege, but as yet it still retained communication with the outer world in the form of a single underground cable. Although its occupants could hear the hollow boom of the Russian barrage, the bunker itself had not yet come under direct fire. Drunk or sober, most of them still believed there was a chance of their being rescued by German troops still fighting in the West.

Hitler shared that opinion. All that morning the Führer received messages from his various commanders and each one seemed to please him and give him new confidence. Thus as the morning started to draw to a close and the assembled staff officers began to shuffle their feet nervously, hoping soon to be released to food and strong drink, he announced in that new glazed-eyed, slow manner of his, *'Meine Herren,* I take time to make my decisions sometimes. But once my mind is made up nothing can change it.' He looked around their wooden, non-committal faces. 'I confirm the fact that I shall stay in Berlin. We stand on the threshold of victory. The army of the West will liberate us yet.'

There was little reaction from his officers and one of them ducked nervously as a salvo of Russian rockets landed not too far away near the Reichchancellery. S S General Fegelein, the brother-in-law of Hitler's mistress, cleared his throat and rapped, 'Of course they will, *mein Führer!'*

'Natürlich . . . natürlich,' the others murmured, taking their cue from the S S officer. It was not safe to have a

35

contrary opinion in the bunker – the S S guards had already shot two 'defeatists' in the courtyard at the back that very morning.

It was just then that Bormann came in, tugging uncomfortably at his tight collar as usual, followed by Goebbels. Both the remaining members of the Nazi Prominenten were excited.

'Forgive me, *mein Führer*,' Bormann blurted out, 'but we have just received a signal from Reichsmarschall Goering.'

'I thought someone's report was missing from this morning's briefing,' the Führer said. 'Very well, Bormann, let's hear it.'

Bormann couldn't wait. At last his opportunity had come to rid himself of his old and greatest enemy. His sausage-like fingers trembling a little with excitement as he read:

'Mein Führer, is it your wish, in view of your decision to stay in Berlin, that I take over complete control of the Reich in accordance with your decree of 29 June 1941?'

Bormann flashed the listening Hitler a quick look and then continued:

'If no answer has been received by ten p.m., I shall have to assume that you have been deprived of your freedom of action and I will consider the terms of your decree as being in force and act for the good of our people and Fatherland. God bless you and speed you here as soon as possible. Your most loyal Hermann Goering.'

Bormann slapped the signal down on the map table with a gesture of finality, trembling with artificial rage. 'There we have the salad!' he exclaimed, using the peasant phrase of his native Mecklenburg. 'The double-dyed traitor.'

For a moment Hitler didn't seem to react, his face expressionless, his eyes glazed, then he dismissed the officers with a feeble wave of his hand. Gratefully they filed out, leaving Hitler alone with Goebbels and Bormann.

Immediately the Reichsleiter cried: 'Goering is a traitor,

mein Führer! His action amounts to a *coup d'état*. Not only that but he has sent similar signals to all the members of the cabinet. At midnight, if you don't do something, he will take over the Reich!' He glared at his master's fat chest, devoid of any decoration save the 'Blood Order', heaving with anger.

'He must be shot at once,' Goebbels urged, knowing now that with Goering out of the way, he and Bormann would be the main two contenders for succession and his chances were better than those of the Party secretary's.

'I agree,' Bormann cried, not wanting to be left out. 'There is an S S unit near to his residence, I have checked. They will carry out the execution loyally.'

To both the other men's surprise, Hitler shook his head. 'No, no, gentlemen, we must not supply the outside world with more propaganda against the Reich. No, we will not kill him – we will remove him from office. Draft a cable accordingly, Bormann.'

'*Jawohl, mein Führer,*' Bormann replied, exchanging a brief look of triumph with Goebbels.

Back in Bormann's office, filled with the hum of the Enigma machines, the two of them drafted the message:

Your action represents high treason against the Führer and National Socialism. The penalty for treason is death. But in view of your earlier service to the Party the Führer will not inflict the supreme penalty if you resign all your offices. Answer 'yes' or 'no'.

'That should fix Fat Hermann for good, eh Bormann,' Goebbels said as he limped out to his own quarters.

Bormann waited till he had closed the door of the operations room, then he hastily scribbled a signal of his own:

To Commandant S S Obersalzberg: Arrest Marshal Goering for High Treason.

With a grin on his fat flushed face, knowing now that there was only Goebbels and himself, he signed it, 'Adolf Hitler'.

The Enigma hummed as the female operator hit the keys of the coding machine and, far away in the middle of the English Home Counties, the last message to be sent from the beleaguered bunker started to come in.

The big four-engined Flying Fortress hit the tarmac with a howl of protesting rubber, jumped twenty feet in the air and slapped down on the runway again with a thump that jarred every bone in the big blond army captain's body.

At the controls, the twenty-two-year-old Army Air Corps colonel, with the stump of an unlit cigar clenched between his dingy teeth, fought to bring the big bomber to a halt before it rolled off the runway. He made it with yards to spare and handed the controls to the crew-cut co-pilot straight out of stateside flying school.

'Okay, sonny,' he said, rolling the cigar stump from one corner of his mouth to the other, 'she's all yours – and watch it, don't get yer dick in a wringer!'

'Yessir,' the red-faced boy answered, who was coming over for his first tour in the UK, and took over the controls as if they were red hot.

The young colonel winked at the blond captain and his thumb and forefinger formed a circle of triumph. The long haul across the Atlantic, with the one re-fuelling stop at the Azores, was over. They had delivered the brand-new B 17 to the Eighth Air Force. Slowly the gleaming silver bomber started to roll towards Upper Heyford's control tower.

The colonel came over to the captain's seat, a rough arrangement of blankets and ammunition boxes.

'Old Jolly,' he announced, peering out of the window, 'and am I glad to see the place! It's my third tour over here, but I guess the only kind of action I'm gonna see this time is in the hay. Brother, are those English dames something! Horny ain't the word for it!'

He bent down next to the OSS captain and started to pull out what he called his 'pantie openers': a hundred pair of nylons, a small drugstore of assorted cosmetics, a crate of oranges – 'and a gross of rubbers,' he concluded his whispered inventory. 'Guess they should last me the first week, eh, Captain?' He winked again.

The captain returned his grin and began to sort out his gear.

'Old Jolly, it's only the barrage balloons which stops it from sinking into the ocean,' the colonel chattered. 'But I love it. Jeez, I don't think I've ever had my ashes hauled so much as here – it was worth fighting the Focke-Wulfes for.' He flipped open his 'little black book', as he called it and began searching through the addresses and telephone numbers of the English girls it contained. 'You wanna couple of introductions for the weekend, Captain?' he queried. 'I've got hundreds of them.'

'No, thanks,' the blond captain answered, slinging his musette bag over his shoulder as the big plane finally rolled to a stop. 'I've been here before, you know, Colonel. I've got a few addresses of my own.'

The colonel took in the silver para wings, the two purple hearts and the red, white and blue ribbon of the D S C and said, 'Yes, I guess you have. What's your plan, Captain?'

'First train out of Oxford for London, Colonel.'

'Tail?'

The captain smiled. ' 'Fraid not. A mission.'

'Mission, hell the war's over in Europe, Captain!' the young colonel exclaimed in surprise.

'You know what they say: "war's hell, but peacetime'll kill ya".' Easily the army captain jumped out of the plane and began to stride down the gangway.

There was only one cab waiting outside the guard-room at the exit to the camp and five or six young soldiers from the Army Air Corps hurrying towards it, obviously wanting a ride to Oxford. But the cabbie, as ancient as his vehicle, obviously knew that officers tipped better than privates. Without hesitation, he urged the battered old Morris through the running privates and pulled up with a squeak of rusty brakes in front of the heavily laden captain. 'Want to go to Oxford, guvnor?' he asked, wiping his dripping bulbous nose with the sleeve of his dirty fawn raincoat.

'That's right – to the station,' the captain answered, taking in the cab and the cabbie, with his walrus moustache, cloth cap and the First World War medals pinned to the lapel of his coat.

'Righty ho, sir, then hop aboard before that lot over there,' he indicated the privates with a dirty finger, 'does us a 'arm.'

The captain threw in his musette bag and settled into the creaking leather with a grin as the cabbie crashed home first gear and rolled forward with a lurch. Now he knew he was in England again.

Almost as soon as they had driven out of the Air Corps base and turned left on the road which led to the main Northampton–Oxford road, the ancient cabbie, sitting bolt upright behind the high wheel, with his cap back to front so that he looked like Bleriot flying the Channel for the first time, started to tell his 'Yankee jokes', as he called them.

'Did yer hear the one, sir, about the Yank who was standing next to the Cockney girl in Hyde Park when the wind blew up her skirt. He sez to her, " 'Airy, ain't it", and she sez to him, "What did yer expect, Yank – *feathers*!" ' The cabbie bellowed out loud at his own humour and for one frightening moment the captain thought he'd have them off the road, as his body shook with laughter.

It was just after the fork where the side road leads off to the right, running through some dank, ill-kept pine woods, when it happened. The ancient Morris coughed, spluttered, jerked convulsively, as if seized by a last paroxysm, and died. Noiselessly the cab rolled on for a few more yards, losing speed all the time, until it finally came to a stop.

'Ballocks,' the cabbie growled and jerked on the big handbrake. 'This is a ruddy turn-up fer the books.'

For five minutes he spun the starting handle time and time again until he was red in the face and leaning weakly against the bonnet, his chest heaving, the air wheezing through his lungs as if propelled by a pair of cracked leather bellows. Then he flung back the bonnet and started to tinker angrily with the engine, while an impatient American kept looking at his watch ever more frequently. He knew England's war-time trains: they were few and far between and very crowded. More than once he had been forced to travel slung in the baggage net or sitting on the seat in a smelly john. If he didn't get to Oxford soon he might well have to spend the night on some icy, uncomfortable railway station. Besides it had been all systems go in Washington; Big Bill had told him at least three times in the space of the hour's briefing that he had to get to London by the speediest means. Hence the flight hitched in the B17.

Feeling the pain in his legs a little now after the long haul across the Atlantic in the cramped provisional seat, he opened his door and limped to where the cabbie bent cursing over the engine. 'Where's the fire?' he queried.

'If I only bloody well knew, guvnor,' the man growled, not taking his head out of the bonnet. 'But yer see that sodding carb there. . .' The American captain bent to take a closer look. He hardly felt the prick of the needle in his side.

Five minutes later they were on their way again, the motor running smoothly enough in spite of the blocked carburettor, with the American captain fast asleep, mouth wide open, in the back seat.

3

It was a typical April day in the Highlands. The thin bitter Scotch drizzle chilled to the very bone; the wind which howled down the glen, in which the S I S's special advanced training agent school was situated, seemed to come straight from Siberia. Everything, or so it appeared to Mallory, was grey: the old Gothic castle which housed the 'students', the sky, the loch, even the very heather which stretched to the grey sombre foothills beyond.

The only thing that was not grey was the faces of the agents, training everywhere in small groups in the wet heather. Here the predominant colour on the sweat-lathered, strained faces was crimson, as the army instructors put the 'students' through their paces, doubling them through the glen with 60lb packs on their backs at a cruel pace.

'Now, short course,' their sergeant-instructor, with the blancoed crossed-rifles of a musketry instructor on his sleeve snapped, 'this is the drill. Hilltops – ten and two o'clock. Got 'em?' The three 'students' of the short course nodded. 'Bren guns on either one. Firing tracer. Soon as yer see a hit on opposite slope, give it burst. Need twenty hits outa twenty-five to qualify. Got it?'

Again the three of them nodded, and Major Mallory smiled. The tall sparse N C O was like all the musketry instructors he had ever known; none of them had ever seemed able to complete a full sentence.

'Blow one blast on my whistle. Off yer go. Ten minutes to complete the course. Got it?'

'Got it,' Higgins 175 mimicked his hard, broad Yorkshire accent. But the little bombardier's irony was wasted on the instructor.

'All right,' he snapped, and pointed a long forefinger at the American, 'you first.'

The American took out his magazine and slapped it into the side of the Sten. Then as an afterthought he checked it to see that the magazine was securely fixed. 'Watch your little finger,' Mallory advised. 'If you get it in the way of the ejecting cartridge cases, you could lose it.'

Captain Piludski nodded and said easily, 'Thanks, Major, but I've used the Sten before. . . . A couple of times in France.' There was none of the usual Yank boasting in his voice, Mallory told himself. The big handsome OSS man knew what he was about.

The sergeant-instructor poised his whistle at his lips. 'Now,' he snapped and blew a shrill blast.

The American was off pelting down the glen like the trained athlete he was. From the hilltop to his right, the Bren-gunner opened up. White tracer zipped flat across the valley. Tiny puffs of smoke, as the burst struck home, erupted on the other hillside. The American didn't hesitate. He stopped, swung round and, without appearing even to take aim, fired a tight controlled burst. His red tracer hit the target almost before the last of the smoke had evaporated and then Piludski was sprinting down the glen once more, as if the devil himself was after him.

'Well, bugger me,' the sergeant-instructor said finally, lowering his binoculars as the American completed the course and slumped to the wet heather five hundred yards away, his great chest heaving violently.' A perfect score. Twenty-five hits out of twenty-five!'

One moment later, Mallory was sprinting down the course, admittedly a little slower than the American, but using his energy more economically, making less of a show of crouching on both knees in the US fashion before firing, instead firing directly from the hip.

'Good grief,' the NCO breathed, 'what a turn up for the

books! Another perfect score.' He looked at the little Cockney. 'Well, Sunny Jim, and what are you going to pull out of the hat, eh?'

Higgins 175 grinned wickedly. 'You'll be surprised.' He crouched and waited, his Sten-gun still slung over his shoulder, but both his hands clutching something, hidden from the instructor's eyes.

The whistle shrilled once more. Higgins ran, but at a much more leisurely pace than the two officers. To his left, the unseen Bren-gunner on the hillside opened up. Higgins ducked. His right arm came up like that of a professional bowler. A dark object sailed through the grey sky towards the gunner's hide. An instant later it exploded and the gunner, his uniform scorched, his face black with smoke, was rolling out of his cover and down the wet hillside. Higgins ran on. The other gunner opened up. Higgins didn't hesitate. His thunderflash flew through the air, landing right on target, while behind him the sergeant-instructor, lobster-red with rage, was blowing mad blasts on his whistle.

Five minutes later, Higgins had completed the rest of the course at a leisurely stroll, his wizened cunning face set in a knowing grin. 'Sergeant-instructors,' he grinned, *'I've shat 'em!'*

Major Mallory shook his head, in mock wonder. Nobody, it seemed, was going to impress the second member of his new team.

The last stage of the short course that C had insisted they should take before returning to London was with the instructor in unarmed combat, a former inspector of the Shanghai Police. As he greeted them, he took out his false teeth and placed them on the tree stump next to the coconut-hair mat. His face was bland and seemingly innocent, but Mallory watching his small, dark eyes knew the instructor was anything else but innocent.

'Now, gentlemen, I take it you have all had some sort of training in unarmed combat before. Most of the advanced

44

students who come to this particular arsehole of the world have.' He smiled winningly at them with his bare wrinkled pink gums. 'But I fear that you might have learnt the wrong tricks. What do I mean? I'll tell you.' Again he smiled, but those dark, ever-watchful eyes of his did not light up. 'Your aim, as you might have been taught before, is not to kill Old Jerry. Oh, dearie me, no. Your aim is to put him in dock for six months to a year. Dead, Old Jerry is no burden on the state; wounded, he is. A swift kick in the appendages will do more to keep him in dock than any bullet will ever do.'

His voice hardened suddenly and Mallory could see the tightening of the jaw muscles which indicated that the instructor was preparing for action. 'You,' he barked, pointing at Higgins, who was holding the pole which doubled for a rifle, 'come at me, butt raised, as if you were gonna land me a fourpenny one on the old head.'

'You really mean that, squire?' Higgins asked, playing for time, eyeing the elderly ex-policeman, trying to work out in advance how he would act.

'Course, laddie. Open invitation. Smash open my head – if you . . .'

Higgins leapt forward before he could complete the sentence, hoping to catch the grinning instructor off guard. He failed badly. The toothless instructor's left arm flashed upwards. It blocked Higgins' blow. In the next instant his right foot came upwards. The steel-tipped boot smashed into Higgins' crotch. The bombardier went flying backwards to fall in the wet heather, his face contorted with agony, vomit on his lips, writhing back and forth, hands clutching his injured testicles.

The instructor grinned at the other two. 'Oh, I really must be more careful with my big plates o' meat, mustn't I, gents? But you see what I mean by a good swift kick in the goolies, don't yer?'

He walked over to a groaning Higgins and pulled him to his feet easily. 'Always expect the unexpected, mate,' he said. 'My pal the musketry instructor tells me you're a bit of a lad for the unexpected yourself. Now, if you'll forgive the pun, the boot's on the other foot, eh?' He grinned toothlessly at his own joke. Higgins glared at him, his face ashen.

The instructor turned to the other two. 'Remember, gents, never trust anyone in this world. Where you gents'll be going, even more so. And remember, always expect the unexpected.'

Mallory nodded his agreement. There was no room for noble concepts of morality and decency in the war in the shadows; he had learnt that to his cost in Albania.

'Now then, who's going to be next?'

Mallory opened his mouth, but Piludski, his face abruptly pale and set, his eyes no longer so easy-going, beat him to it. 'I'll have a go, Sergeant,' he said, quietly.

The instructor smiled, not hearing the underlying tone of menace in Piludski's voice.

'Ah, our American gentleman. Of course.' He picked up the padded pole which Higgins had dropped, and handed it politely to the blond giant. For a moment or two they faced each other across the mat, while Mallory watched them with interest, knowing that the instructor was watching Piludski's eyes, not his hands. Piludski lunged. The elderly instructor swung to one side with surprising speed. Piludski stumbled. The instructor's hands flashed. Piludski yelped with pain as the instructor dug his hip into his and exerted pressure. An instant later, the pole flying from his hands, Piludski was sailing through the air to land with a thud on the mat, all breath knocked out of him by the impact.

'Dearie me,' the instructor said, not breathing heavily, 'I must take it a little bit more easy. I don't know my own strength. Now this . . .'

'I want another crack at you,' Piludski gasped from the mat, glaring up at the instructor.

The instructor looked down at him mildly. 'Of course,

friend.' He bent down to pick up the padded stick, but Piludski shook his head. 'No, not the pole. Bare hands,' he said.

'All right . . .'

Piludski dived for him, straight from the mat. The instructor was quicker. His right arm shot out stiffly, palm turned outwards. Piludski ran straight into it. His head shot backwards, as the heel of the instructor's palm caught him directly under the chin. Next instant the instructor had inserted two fingers into his nostrils and pulled hard. Piludski screamed, falling backwards, thick red blood spurting out of his cruelly injured nose.

The instructor sniffed, breathing a little harder now. 'Lesson, number two, never lose your temper.'

'Now that's enough,' Mallory snapped, realizing that the training session was getting out of hand and that their instructor was a sadist.

The instructor swung round to face the major. 'I don't think you have the authority to . . .'

It was the opportunity that Piludski had been waiting for. Blood still pouring down his chin, he dived forward. With all the weight of his powerful shoulders, he crashed into the instructor. He went down in a heap, all breath knocked out of him.

'Always expect the unexpected,' Piludski gasped and smashed his clubbed fist into the instructor's face.

'And lesson two, never lose your temper!' Higgins yelled delightedly, picking up the groaning instructor's false teeth and pitching them far into the heather.

Twenty-four hours later they were speeding through the night to London and the briefing, lazing in a first-class compartment in the Edinburgh express, with pale-faced envious sailors from Scapa packed in the corridor outside, wondering what was so special about the three civilians.

While the other two dozed, their faces red and tired from their exertions on the 'short course', Mallory considered them, finally coming to the conclusion before he fell asleep himself that with this particular team he stood as good a chance as any of succeeding in the mission.

That night he did not have his usual Albanian nightmare.

4

As Miss Pettigrew ushered them into his office, C remained seated, allowing the men to stand to attention in front of his desk. Without a word, he studied the three of them with cold grey eyes.

The bombardier was well turned out and he had the red leathery face of an old soldier. A typical old sweat, he told himself, of the kind he had often had before him in the trenches in the first show when he had been the Blues' adjutant. Cunning, unscrupulous, and out for number one.

Mallory looked strangely ill at ease. But his colour had returned and he looked well and fit, save for the eyes, which were as alert as ever, but betraying a deep hurt.

It was the American – Piludski – who came as a surprise. He was not at all the type he had expected, the kind who smiled all the time inanely and probably conversed in animal grunts. Smile Piludski did and he was big too, but his lean face and swift eyes conveyed quick intelligence and determination.

'Hm,' he cleared his throat, 'please sit down.' He pushed a silver cigarette box across the big table. 'Smoke if you wish.' Nobody moved save the bombardier.

Reaching over he took one cigarette which he placed behind his left ear and another which he lit noisily, grinning at C all the while.

C's grey face remained unchanged, but he recognized the action as one of deliberate defiance – 'dumb insolence', they had once called it in the Blues. The other ranker was showing he was not impressed one bit by this strange, mysterious civilian who presided over an organization that possessed no name. The man would need watching; the type tended to be bolshie, both in attitude and politics. He'd warn Mallory.

Painfully, he rose to his feet, as if his skinny body was very weak or very fragile, and walked slowly over to the big map on the other wall, covered by a mess of red and blue pencil marks.

'As you can see,' he commenced, 'Nazi Germany is about finished. Our troops have reached the Elbe, the Russians too. Further south, General Patton's men are already deep into Bavaria. Resistance in the west is nothing much more than a mere token. To the east, however, our Intelligence maintains, the Germans are putting up a better show, especially in Berlin. There the Hun is holding out against three Soviet armies, aided by the renegades, fools and traitors from half a dozen European countries, including a few even from America.' He shot a glance at the big American.

'Back in Washington,' the American interrupted, his face as cheerful as ever, 'the general told me they've *even* got some Englishmen in the SS these days, sir. They recruit them from the POW camps.'

C glanced at Piludski with brief annoyance, but continued. 'At present, according to our Intelligence, the First White Russian Front and the First Ukranian Front have surrounded Berlin, linking up somewhere to the east between Potsdam and Nauen. However, their ring is porous. To the north and north-west, beyond the Havel bridges, the situation is considered fluid and confused. We have reason to believe that there it is possible to slip out of the trap – and, naturally,' he gave them a cold smile and added significantly, '*slip in!*'

'Now the Prominenten, as the Hun calls his bigwigs, have gone to ground – here – in a bomb- and shellproof underground bunker not far from the Berlin Reichchancellery.' He pointed to the street map insert. 'The area is the Hun equivalent of our own Whitehall. Two days ago on Hitler's birthday, all the Prominenten were there.'

'How do you know?' the bombardier asked, speaking for the first time.

Mallory looked at him out of the corner of his eyes and thought of that Victorian manor house, surrounded by Nissen huts, which contained the greatest secret of the Second World War. C would not tell him about that. Mallory was right.

'None of your business,' he replied sharply. 'Take it from me, *we know*!' He then continued his briefing. 'Since the birthday, however, the rats have begun to leave the sinking ship. Big Two has gone south and according to our information is to be put under arrest for treason. Big Three is at present discussing peace plans with the Swedish Count Bernadotte. Big Four seems to have moved north, possibly heading for Denmark. So that leaves us with Big One and Big Five and Six – all of them still in the bunker.' For the first time C seemed to become aware of his listeners' bewilderment. 'Ah, the code names!' he exclaimed and smiled at them with false warmth. 'I'm afraid that we are addicted to them in the Old Firm. Dates back to the days of the Old C in the first show – he gave everything a code name. Fanatic about it. So what do they mean, eh?'

Mallory wondered whether his question was rhetorical or whether he intended to reveal any more of the strange operation that they were soon to embark upon. But before C could speak, the little Cockney snapped, 'Well, you don't need a crystal ball to know who Big One is – it's Old Adolf himself, and if the other blokes are not in Berlin, which seems to be the only place of importance to us, who's Big Five and Six?'

C leaned forward, a slight flush tingeing those grey sunken cheeks of his, as if he might be angry and was about to make some sharp retort, but when he spoke again, it was clear that he had thought better of it.

'For the time being,' he began, 'it is better that you don't

51

concern yourselves with that particular problem, though as you rightly have said, Bombardier Higgins, we are interested only in the Hun capital. And why?' This time he did answer his own question. 'Because, gentlemen, you three are going to be sent to Berlin.'

Leaving the three men opposite him to absorb that information, C rang the bell on his desk for Miss Pettigrew, saying easily, 'I think a spot of tiffin is called for now, don't you?'

Tiffin!

The memories raced in Mallory's mind. The Albanian briefing had ended on that invitation too, he recalled, sipping C's favourite Earl Grey tea and wondering what the new mission would bring him. If he had only known the horrors that had lain before him!

The Red partisans, into whose hands he had fallen when the R A F Dakota had crashed in the black mountains of southern Albania, had beaten him for a solid week, pausing only to take deep swigs of the native *raki*, while he had watched them fearfully through puffed-up eyes, as they squatted in their baggy Turkish trousers, their leathery, hawk-nosed faces under their skull caps impassive. Then the Russian 'advisers' had taken over. They had brought their own torturer, Poitr, from Moscow with them. He had been trained, or so they said, by Beria himself. What agonies he had gone through at that man's command, with those soft eunuch's hands of his continually stroking the hard steel muzzle of that precious revolver he always carried.

On the last day, the day he, Mallory, had finally broken and told them why he had been sent to Albania, Poitr had taken over the torture himself. Stripped naked, a great colossus of a man, his woman's breasts dangling over his massive hairless paunch which had ended in the tiny organ of a three-year-old boy, he had stared a long time at the prisoner on the floor of the dirty cell, his pudgy paws stroking the hard, long metal tumescence of his revolver lovingly.

Finally he had spoken in that soft lisping voice of his: 'Regard me well, Major Mallory. What you see before you is a man in name only. What a terrible fate, you are probably thinking, eh?' He had grinned down at the wreck on the floor, spittle dribbling down his soft hairless chin. 'Me, I have never experienced a woman. I have of course never felt the desire.' He shrugged easily, his breasts shivering repulsively. 'But you have enjoyed the caresses of a beautiful woman. You know the pleasures of a female body, all that sweat and excitement.' He had laughed, sending spittle flying everywhere. Then his voice had lowered to a barely audible whisper, but there had been no mistaking the awful menace in it, as he had posed that menacing question: 'Major Mallory, would you like to be like poor old Piotr?'

He had been seized by a terrible unreasoning fear. No, no they wouldn't do *that* to him. *No!*

And then it had happened. Piotr had cried a sudden order. Before Mallory had been able to react, the Russians had spread-eagled him on the floor, ripping what was left of his dirty, blood-stained rags from his terribly beaten, emaciated body and there the naked monster had towered above him, rope now in his pudgy hands, his lips red and slack with greedy anticipation.

Mallory had screamed one last time. Suddenly his body had been swamped by that soft flabby mountain of flesh, which had stunk of cheap cologne and physical corruption, and it was happening, that awesome excruciating burning pain in his loins. . . .

They had brought him back to England that autumn a very sick man. Physically he had recovered from the torture quickly enough, but mentally his progress had been much slower. How slow he had not realized himself until that grey Saturday in December 1944 when Hitler had launched his last counter-offensive in the West. On that icy

53

snowy December day, as the Germans broke through in the far away Ardennes, Mallory, now outwardly fit and healthy again, had been invited to one of those discreet remote country houses in which C entertained his 'good boys', agents back from the field, who had 'put up a good show', as the spymaster always expressed it in his out-of-date slang.

Drink had flown freely and for every agent there had been at least two 'popsies', good-time girls down from London, selected for their beauty, discretion and availability, by no less a person than C's aristocratic mother, lady-in-waiting to the Queen herself.

Mallory had got rapidly 'sloshed', as the phrase of the time had it, and halfway through the drunken orgy, financed unknowingly by the humble British taxpayer, he had staggered up the grand Elizabethan staircase, clutching two giggling beauties, crying to the clapping, cheering, drunken throng below, 'It's been a long, long time, chaps!'

It had been a disaster. Despite the ardent caresses of his companions, his body had failed to respond and the night of love ended in shame and embarrassment before it had even begun.

The next time, the same happened. And the next. 'Nothing wrong with your outside plumbing, old boy, as far as I can make out,' the Old Firm's M O had said, washing his hands at the basin. 'Probably the grub those wogs gave you. Seen a few cases like yours of late.' He had dried his hands and looked at Mallory's haggard, depressed face in the mirror over the wash basin. 'Yes, I'll put it down to the food, Mallory. I'll give you a chitty for special rations.' He had smiled in that fake confident way of doctors the world over. 'Soon have you going at it like a fiddler's elbow again, old chap.' But the special rations had not helped.

The urologist had washed his hands more carefully than the Old Firm's M O. But then he was a specialist. 'Couldn't find a thing,' he had announced. 'No lesions or anything. All the usual bits and pieces are quite in order.' He had been oddly embarrassed. 'Think I'd better recommend you to my colleague, Mr Jacobson.'

With Jacobson came the truth. He had looked at Mallory through his big horn-rimmed glasses, blinking like a large owl, and said in that thick Viennese accent of his, 'It's not physical at all. The torture had no effect in that way.' He pursed his thick lips, as if he were going to kiss someone. 'In my considered opinion, your problem is psychological.'

'And what is that supposed to mean, Doctor?'

Jacobson had looked slightly annoyed, as if he did not like his train of thought being interrupted. 'Mean? You've had a traumatic experience. If I had a couple of months with you – er – on the couch, I could probably pin-point it more easily.'

Mallory had laughed dismissively. 'There is such a thing as a little war going on in Europe.'

'Your experiences during your imprisonment,' Jacobson had continued his lecture, 'have shocked you so much that now you are unable at present to – er –cohabit.'

'And the future, Doctor?'

'Oh,' Jacobson had answered airily, apparently indifferent, 'you'll recover in time – probably.'

It was then that Mallory had decided he did not want to live much longer – probably. . . .

'How are we going to do it?' C asked, finally finished with his 'tiffin'. 'How are we going to get to Berlin in the first place?'

'Not you. *Us,*' Higgins corrected the grey-faced spymaster, who was hunched over his empty cup, his grey claws around the thin china, as if it offered his cold body some warmth. The bombardier knew he had nothing to lose – the Old Boy would get rid of him as soon as he was no longer needed. He knew that instinctively. All the same, he was no longer in the glasshouse and while there was life, there was hope; in the days to come there would be a lot of chances to change all that.

C pretended not to have heard Higgins. Instead he said, 'The first stage will be routine. Out from Croydon to Brusssels by aeroplane.'

Mallory smiled a little to himself. C would say 'aeroplane'.

'From Brussels you will be taken by staff car to Field Marshal Montgomery's H Q in Germany. There, arrangements will be made by the Field Marshal to get you through the front. General Barker's Eighth Corps area is apparently the most suitable spot for an operation of that kind. Once you are through the German lines, you are naturally on your own. However, from the information we possess here, the only real obstacle facing you will be the River Elbe, the last natural barrier between the front and Berlin.'

Piludski spoke for the very first time since C's announcement of their objective. 'Sir, I'd like to know what kind of cover we will be using.'

C gave him the thin cold smile he reserved for Americans. 'Naturally, Captain. You all speak German to varying degrees, but in order to ensure that you won't run into trouble on the language front, my Q branch is working on an *Ostarbeiter* cover.'

'*Ostarbeiter?*' Piludski queried.

'Yes. In order to keep their war industry going, the Hun imported millions of workers from the east, promised them special heavy rations and all that sort of thing. Now there are thousands of them wandering around all over Germany, without work and food, trying to get back to their native countries in the east. Most of these chaps pass through the German capital on their way. Hence Q's selection of that particular cover for you chaps.' He let the information sink in, then continued, 'You'll be given five thousand Reichsmark each – and in a special money belt, you'll have one thousand dollars each.'

56

'The good old greenback eh,' Piludski said enthusiastically. 'Nothing it won't buy, including the Gestapo, sir'.

'Let's hope so,' C said in a voice that suggested that their interview was drawing to a close. 'Well,' he said cheerily, 'that's about all, I think.' He looked at their expressions with a benign smile on his thin face. 'Any questions, chaps?'

'The mission, sir,' Piludski asked politely, 'what are we supposed to do when we reach Berlin?'

C did not seem to hear the question. 'Well, then,' he said, 'that'll be all, what.' Before Piludski could persist, he pressed the old-fashioned bell on his desk. Miss Pettigrew came immediately, almost as if she had been listening with her ear pressed to the door.

'Show the gentlemen out, Miss Pettigrew, would you, please. Oh, Major Mallory, please stay behind for a moment.'

C waited patiently till the padded door had closed behind the other two. Now the contained look vanished from his faded grey eyes to be replaced by one of anxious concern.

'Mallory,' he began urgently, 'before you go, let me emphasize the importance of this mission for the Empire and the whole of the western world. We *must* deal with Big Six before he makes contact.' His voice faltered for a moment and leaning across the big desk, he grabbed Mallory's wrist in his own. 'At the club I explained to you what the Prime Minister thinks. He feels the situation is as grave as I do. If you fail this time' – Mallory thought of Albania and winced inwardly – 'then the Bolshies will be on the Channel coast within the year probably. Six months after that,' he hesitated for a fraction of a second, as if even he dare not express that awful thought, 'we'll know that this bloody business since 1939 has been for nothing. The tyranny we've been fighting will rise like a bloody phoenix. *It'll mean World War Three....*'

*   *   *

The large balloon sailed through the bright blue April sky like a sluggish grey snail, carried by the light warm wind. At the street corner the cloth-capped paper-boy, who was at least seventy and wore the Boer War ribbons on his shabby jacket, was shouting hoarsely, *'Yanks in Leipzig . . . Monty ready to cross the Elbe. . .Jerries ready to throw in the sponge . . .'* Further up the street, council workers were beginning to screw back the bulbs into the street lamps, ready for normal lighting again soon.

'Well, what are we supposed to make of yon little lot, Major?' Higgins asked as they entered the park, which lay behind C's headquarters.

Automatically Mallory returned the salutes of two young guardsmen. 'I thought it was pretty obvious,' he answered, feeling a trace of envy as he watched the American admire the pretty legs of a passing W A A F.

'Not for Piludski, the dumb Polack,' the American laughed, showing excellent white teeth. 'So the old boy told us we were going on a mission to Krautland to attempt to break through to Berlin. But to what purpose?'

'Yeah, that he didn't tell us,' Higgins agreed.

Mallory recalled the first op he had carried out for the Old Firm flying out from Southampton to Gib. only to be told there that he was going to enter a neutral country and destroy its most major bridge. He wouldn't have gone then, if he'd known that. All his instincts would have told him not to go. Now he was in the same position that C had been back in 1940. They *had* to go and he had to do the convincing; he had to keep his strangely assorted little team together somehow or other.

'It's really on the old "need to know" principle, chaps,' he began slowly, as they walked through the park, filled with uniformed lovers on park benches and on the grass. 'By that I mean to say what you don't know won't hurt you, as they used to tell us at prep school when I was a boy. I can only tell you at this stage of the op that our first

58

priority is to get into Berlin. What we will have to do there will be told you at the opportune moment.'

Piludski slapped the palm of his big hand against his forehead in mock indignation. 'You British!' he exclaimed. 'You're still as arrogant as if you were still running one-third of the world, instead of being the new poor second cousins.' He saw the look in Mallory's eyes and added hastily, 'Sorry Mike, I didn't mean that – honestly.'

'It's all right, Paddy.'

'It just slipped out, Mike.'

'As the actress said to the bishop,' Higgins commented sourly. 'Okay, so we'll make beautiful corpses, eh. What say you officers and gents accompany me to a well-known knocking shop?'

'A knocking shop?' the American queried.

Higgins made an explicit gesture with his stiff middle finger.

'A whorehouse?'

'Right at last. Now come, you officers and gents, we might as well enjoy our last night in the Big Smoke. God knows what tomorrer'll bring . . .'

She looked at him almost sadly with eyes that were blood-shot and dark-circled. Upstairs, bedsprings were squeaking energetically. She took the cigarette he offered her and breathed out a grateful stream of blue smoke. 'Sorry,' she whispered and ran a hesitant gentle hand over his sweat-lathered naked body as he lay there on the rumpled damp bed, pausing momentarily at the red ugly traces of the gunshot wounds. 'I did try.'

'I know you did,' he said softly, eyes not on her, but fixed on the cracked ceiling from which the whitewash drifted down in slow flakes like sad snow. He had failed yet once again. He was no longer a man.

For a while he and the whore were silent. Above them the sound of the rusty bedsprings squeaking had ceased. A water tap ran. Faintly Bing Crosby crooned, *Don't Fence Me In.* A woman laughed.

'You know,' she whispered, 'you're not the only one. There are a lot like you.'

'At thirty?' he exclaimed, raising his head slightly from the soiled pillow and staring at her worn pale face.

She nodded.

'But *not* at thirty?' he persisted.

'Oh, yes. It's the war, you see.'

'What's the war got to do with it?'

'You soldiers – all of you – you carry it around with you like . . . like an invisible kitbag. It's with you all the time. You think you can come in places like this and see a girl with her knickers off and in black stockings and that's that. You can forget it. But you can't. . . . She stopped.

The two of them stared numbly at the silver wash of moonlight coming in through the un-blacked-out skylight, softening the outline of the upright chair where his clothes were draped.

'What can't we forget?' he asked at last.

'The war and . . .'

'Go on,' he prompted.

She hesitated, her opium-like voice dead in the silver shadows, as if she did not dare even to utter the words. 'It's . . . you've all got . . . got . . . the smell of death about you.' Then she began to cry.

Two: The Way In

'He was a born survivor. If anybody got out it would be him.'

A. Speer, Hitler's Minister of War Production, 1971

1

Braunschweig 80 Kilometres, Uelzen, 20 Kilometres, the bullet-pocked yellow and black German road sign read. To the right of the typical cobbled road with the sandy verges common to that part of Northern Germany was a burnt-out Sherman. Around it lay the graves of its crew, each rough birchwood cross hung with the rimless helmet of the Armoured Corps. To the left was a straggle of infantry from the 'Desert Rats', the Seventh Armoured Division, dug in the sandy soil in narrow slit trenches, their weapons at the ready, anxiety apparent in their eyes. To a watching Mallory, these youngsters were far from celebrating victory: they knew they could still get killed this April day. Somewhere in the far distance a German 88mm cannon was pounding away with brutal regular persistence.

The handsome young American infantry captain who was one of Montgomery's 'eyes and ears', his select band of informants on what was going on at the front, eased back his helmet to reveal the red, wrinkled band around his forehead, and said, 'That's outlaw country out there, gentlemen.' He beamed at them. 'Got to be a real tough hombre to take it.'

Piludski sniggered at the captain's fake western accent, while Mallory stared at the scene.

It was a beautiful spring afternoon. Luneburg Heath was bright with wild flowers and the air was sweet with the scent of heather. At any moment Mallory expected to see a picnic party appear, enjoying North Germany's favourite holiday area as they had done before the war. Instead a group of stretcher-bearers, their boots clods of thick mud, came toiling wearily across the *Heide*, bearing with them their burden of dead and dying.

'What's the situation?' Mallory asked, while Higgins squatted, his hand cupped around a compo cigarette, and surveyed the no-man's land up ahead.

'If we only knew,' the young staff captain groaned. 'There's everything out there from veteran S S troopers, out to sell their hides for a last crack at us, to stupid young Hitler Youth kids, armed with those goddam one-shot suicide weapons – those *Panzerfäuste** of theirs. Were-wolves, too, *women* and men, just begging to die for the Führer and Fatherland. Crazy, real crazy.' He mopped his damp brow, as if it were all a bit too much for him.

'Is our journey really bloody necessary?' Higgins muttered moodily, but no one took any notice of him.

'Okay, I don't want to put the breeze up you, gentlemen,' the American continued, 'but I just want to warn you. The Krauts haven't given up by a long chalk. They pulled a real wing-dinger of a surprise counter-attack on Uelzen the day before yesterday and nearly bagged the master himself.' He meant his boss, Field Marshal Montgomery. 'The whole bunch of us, cooks and clerks, had to turn out to repel the bastards.' He focused the glasses hanging from his neck. 'If you take in that bunch of birch trees at ten o'clock, you might see them. Our guess is that they've got an m.g. post – probably a spandau – covering this road from there.'

Obediently, both Piludski and Mallory followed the direction of his gaze with their binoculars, but they could see nothing. Mallory told himself that as usual the Germans had buried themselves deep in the earth; they were past masters at digging-in.

'Their back-up is just to the right of that burnt-out Mark IV at two o'clock.'

They swung their glasses to the right. A wrecked German

---

*A primitive form of the bazooka.

tank swung into the bright circle of calibrated glass, a gleaming silver shell-hole skewered in its side, one track flopped out in front of it like a broken limb. Mallory noted the fresh brown earth beyond the track and told himself the U S captain was right. They were dug in there as well.

'That's obstacle one,' the captain continued. 'Then beyond the hill there is a small hamlet – Diedenhofen, or Diesdenheim – something like that. They've probably got that fortified too to deny us this road. That's obstacle two. But after that,' he rolled over on his back and looked up at their tense faces, 'it should be relatively plain sailing – the Kraut front is as thin as an eggshell – till you reach the Elbe.'

'Famous last words,' Higgins growled sourly, 'roses . . . roses, all the shitting way.'

'Oh, shut up, Higgins,' Mallory snapped. 'Now what's the drill, Captain?' he asked.

'Well, what we do know about the Krauts is that they're pretty short of bodies . . . .'

'They're not getting mine,' Higgins snickered.

'So their front is, as you have seen, basically a series of strongpoints, with gaps in between. Okay, my master has agreed to let you have a troop of tanks from the First Royal Tanks and two platoons of infantry from the Green Jackets, good guys although these days most of them are replacements. With the infantry we take out the strongpoints on both sides of the road – obstacle number one. In the meantime, the Royals will barrel up the road in their Shermans and attempt to rush the hamlet. I doubt if they'll make it without more infantry, but that's not important at the moment. As soon as they hit the place and start taking incoming mail, you guys bale out. From there on in, you're on your own.'

'You mean up the sodding creek without the paddle, Captain?' Higgins butted in once more.

'You could say that, Corporal,' the young U S captain said cheerfully. 'Now then, gentlemen, I suggest we get out

65

of this uncomfortable field. My master wishes to take tea with you.'

'*Tea!*' Piludski moaned and slapped his forehead. 'China tea in the middle of total war! You limeys still seem to think that this is 1850 and you've got a divine mission to rule the rest of the world, or at least your top dogs like that Field Marshal of yours just now do.'

Mallory looked at Piludski a little surprised. They were billeted in a barn, with Higgins squatting on a compo ration box morosely, sipping looted German *kognak*, while he cleaned his pistol for what might well come this night. 'And what occasioned that, Paddy?' he asked.

For once that good-humoured easy smile was absent from the big American's handsome face. 'Just the way you and Monty talked.'

'How did we talk?' Mallory asked, slipping back the slightly oiled slugs into the magazine.

'As if . . . as if, me and that other American Joe didn't really exist, as if you limeys made the important decisions in this war – that's how you talked.' Sourly Piludski took a bit of the biscuit and bully beef sandwich he had fashioned himself from the compo ration. He looked like a man who realized he had said too much already.

Mallory looked up and smiled thinly at the big American. 'Problems, Paddy?'

The other man's face lightened. 'Yeah, I'm just plain scared, that's all. It makes me sore. Remember this is my first mission since last year and the last one was a real beaut – a snafu right from the start.'

Mallory recalled C's story of Piludski shot in both legs, 'literally crawling' back to the Spanish frontier. He understood well enough.

'So I'm getting jittery, especially as we don't know really what the Sam Hill this mission is about.' Piludski looked directly at Mallory, his green eyes a mixture of challenge

66

and the need for reassurance. 'Yeah, what is our *real* mission?'

'Bloody suicide mission – that's what it is,' Higgins broke in morosely. 'If the Jerries catch us in these duds,' he indicated his worn jacket with the fading letters O S T, indicating a foreign worker from the East, on the shoulder, 'we're for the chop. No denying it.'

Mallory said nothing. He *couldn't* tell them, yet they had the right to know.

'Well?' Piludski prompted.

'Yer?' Higgins added, putting down his chipped tin mug of tea. 'Yer, what kind of a lark is this anyhow?'

Outside, the roar of tank engines starting up drowned the howl of the German mortar. Mallory breathed a sigh of relief; he wouldn't have to tell them *just yet*. Instead he rose and stowed his pistol inside his shabby three-quarter length jacket. 'Let's just call it the phoenix assault for the moment, shall we?' And with that he was gone.

Moonlight flooded the cobbled country road, bathing it a cold silver. Up ahead the pink glow of the permanent barrage tinged the horizon. On both sides the fields were filled with the high hulks of the Royal Tank Regiment's Shermans. Somewhere a German spandau was hissing hysterically. Red and white tracer zipped through the night. Behind a tense Mallory, standing next to the group of Green Jacket officers, Higgins urinated for the third time in the last ten minutes. Everyone was tense.

To their immediate front a red flare hissed into the sky, hung there for an age bathing everything below in its eerie freezing light and then dropped like a fallen angel. It was the signal.

'Fags out,' the young captain, in charge of the infantry, commanded. 'Major, you'd better get your chaps mounted up.' He indicated the nearest Sherman.

'Yes – and the best of luck,' Mallory said hoarsely, as the infantry started to toss away their cigarettes and straighten up their packs, the only sound the clink of a bayonet scabbard or the tin mug they all carried striking against a buckle.

'If only there are no sodding mines,' the captain said, as if speaking to himself. 'Follow me.' He gripped his ashplant more firmly in his right hand – it was his only weapon – and started down the centre of the road as if he were going for a midnight stroll. Behind him his men began to move forward behind the cover of the hedgerows, their bodies already bent as if they expected the hard burning slugs to hit their soft yielding flesh at any moment.

Mallory shook his head in admiration. 'The infantry,' he said half-aloud, 'the poor bloody infantry.'

'Silly sods,' Higgins sneered and, reaching up, pulled himself on to the 30-ton metal monster, dropping behind the cover of the turret at once. Hastily the two others followed.

All was silence. The only sound was their own heavy tense breathing and the faint noise of the infantry's hobnailed ammunition boots on the cobbles. Had the Germans abandoned their positions of the afternoon? Perhaps they hadn't been there in the first place? Were the infantry walking into a trap deliberately for their sakes? A hundred-and-one questions raced through Mallory's head. He would have sold his soul at that moment for a stiff drink.

The minutes ticked by leadenly. The permanent barrage, the ever-present background music of a war, rumbled on. Now he could no longer hear the infantry, but Mallory could visualize that lone captain, with his absurd Ronald Coleman moustache, grown undoubtedly to hide his youth, striding on alone down the centre of the road, swinging that stick he affected, his heart shrinking with fear at every fresh step.

'The foot-sloggers should be about level with the Jerry positions now, sir,' the sergeant in charge of their tank whispered. 'It looks like the verges is clear of mines at

68

least. Them new schuh-mines of theirs is real sods to . . .'
The rest of his sentence was drowned by a sudden burst of
m.g. fire. Mallory jumped as fiery red tracer bullets sliced
through the silver darkness.

'Here we go,' the tank commander yelled, as spandaus
opened up from both sides of the road and the first slow
Bren began to return the German fire. With a great roar,
the Sherman's 435H P engine burst into life. The air was
suddenly full of the acrid stink of petrol fumes. All around
them engine after engine roared.

'Hold tight, gents!' the tank commander yelled. 'Here
we go!'

Frantically they grabbed for a hold on the turret as the
30-ton American-made tank lurched forward, its tracks
showering mud and pebbles behind it, and burst through
the hedge. It crashed down on to the cobbles, slithered
round crazily and started up the road towards the ever
mounting crescendo of the infantry fire-fight.

The Sherman jolted over the first bodies. The young
Green Jackets lay sprawled there in the abandoned pos-
tures of those violently done to death. The tank pressed
them into the cobbles, its tracks abruptly red. Mallory swallowed hard, his face contorted with horror. Was anything
worth this? Lead pattered on the metal of the turret like
tropical rain on a tin roof. His horror was forgotten. He
ducked immediately. Crouched low, the tank commander
swung the turret m.g. round and fired a wild burst in the
direction of the German fire. A shrill scream of agony rose
even above the clatter of tank tracks. The fire stopped
abruptly.

'Got the sod!' the sergeant cried triumphantly. But he
was stopped the very next instant by a bullet in the centre
of the forehead.

'Bloody hero!' Higgins gasped, as he and Mallory
helped to lower the dead man into the green glowing in-
terior of the tank. Mallory caught a glimpse of a broken
ashplant and then they were through, leaving the snap and

crackle of the infantry fire-fight behind them beyond the rise.

The Shermans slowed down to a walking pace, spreading out now, the radios crackling instruction back and forth. The corporal-gunner, who had taken over from the dead N C O, eased the earphones back from his head and said, 'Sir, the officer said to tell you he's taking half the troop straight into the Jerry village. We're to take that little side road over yonder.' He indicated the track running to the left of the church against which the red-brick houses huddled as if seeking protection in God this terrible night. 'If we run into trouble, you're to make a bolt for it while we give you covering fire. All right, sir?'

'All right, Corporal,' Mallory answered with more confidence than he felt.

Slowly the two groups of tanks rumbled towards the silent, dark hamlet, the noise of the fire-fight almost vanished now. The place seemed abandoned. Not even a dog barked. Mallory stared up at the church steeple. Nothing. No pale blur up there which would indicate an artillery observer. If there were people in the place, military or civilian, they must have buried themselves deep in their cellars.

They came ever closer. Now the leading Sherman had begun to trundle slowly by the first shabby low houses, surrounded by unpainted white-picket, wooden fences. Up on the turret of their tank which was moving at a snail's pace, the corporal whispered, as if he were afraid someone might hear him, 'Looks as if Old Jerry has gone and done a bunk, sir, I th—' There was a savage crump. A sheet of purple flame shot into the darkness. A whirling object trailing fiery red sparks behind it hurtled towards the lone tank. Metal struck metal with a hollow boom. For a moment nothing happened. Abruptly the Sherman staggered to a halt. A sheet of bright red fire sprang into the air.

'*Panzerfäust* – hit the rear sprocket!' the corporal cried. 'There goes the sodding Ronson!'

As if to confirm his fear, the second tank exploded and suddenly terror-stricken men were reeling from its turret, their coveralls alight.

'Oh, my sweet Christ,' Piludski whispered in horror.

From all sides rifle and machine-gun fire erupted from the houses on both sides of the little village street. The fleeing crew members crumpled up and lay still and burning on the cobbles, as the other Sherman raced forward.

A bundle of stick grenades sailed down from a house and dropped neatly into the open turret of the second tank, an instant before the commander remembered to close it. They exploded with a tremendous roar. The Sherman skidded and smashed into the nearest wall, coming to a smoking rest in a pile of red bricks. No one got out.

'Bloody hell!' the corporal cried. 'Let's get out of this! Driver, see—' he began in a yell.

But the driver needed no instructions. As the three civilians hung on madly to the suddenly violently swaying turret, while the Sherman heeled like a ship at sea caught by a tremendous storm, he smashed the tank through the wooden door of the nearest barn. They clattered on, scattering wood and straw in every direction. Mallory caught a glimpse of a big brown plough horse, its eyes wild with fear, foam collected around its muzzle, break loose from its stall and clatter crazily in front of them. They emerged from the other side. A narrow lane faced them. Fifty feet ahead there was a ramshackle barricade of farm carts, old crates and furniture hurriedly dragged out from the cottages on both sides. The driver put his foot down hard. The 425H P engine roared. The three civilians held on with all their strength. A white face under a heavy coal-scuttle helmet looked out of a shattered window to their right. The corporal fired instinctively. The burst ripped the German's face away. He dropped from the window and hit the cobbles like a sack of wet cement. They charged on.

Fire stabbed the night from behind the barricade. Heart pounding, brain racing, hardly perceiving the wild cries

and angry shouts on all sides, Mallory could still admire
the bravery of the Germans manning that pathetic barricade. Did they think they could stop a Sherman with that
collection of junk? The Sherman's high glacis plate
smashed into its centre. Pieces of wood flew in every direction. A German cried out in terror, arms outflung, as if
appealing to some God on high for mercy. On this April
night there was none. Screaming, he disappeared under
the churning tracks.

They burst through. Germans were scurrying for cover
in all directions. The corporal's machine-gun chattered.
The enemy were galvanized into frenetic action, dancing
and reeling backwards like puppets in the hands of some
mad puppet-master, and then they were through: the
road ahead looked clear.

Mallory wasted no more time. 'Bale out!' he cried.

His comrades needed no urging. Pistols clutched in
sweaty hands at the ready, they dropped over the side and
disappeared into the shadows.

Mallory waited only to order, 'All right, Corporal, radio
we're through. And many thanks!' Then he, too, had
dropped from the heaving metal deck of the Sherman and
doubled into the shadows.

Thirty minutes later, all was silent again and the three of
them were hidden in a deep fragrant pine forest, suddenly
exhausted as if they had run a great race, their limbs
trembling uncontrollably. But they had done it; they were
through the German line.

The stench was almost unbearable. Marshal of the Soviet
Union Zhukov patted his nostrils with a dirty handkerchief soaked in cheap cologne and stared out of the shattered window of his Berlin command post at the ruins
which trembled and quivered as if they were alive. But
then they were. The last day's great artillery barrage had
disturbed the tremendous rat colony which lay under the
wrecked buildings opposite. Now they were everywhere

with their twitching noses, disgusting long tails, plump scurrying bodies, trying to find a way out before it was too late.

'A parallel, comrade, eh? Rats abandoning a sinking ship?' The little man with the shaven head and the mouthful of stainless steel teeth standing next to the gigantic, dimple-chinned army commander said nothing but then, Zhukov told himself, Comrade Hertz rarely said anything. He sniffed and, raising his voice above the roar of a battery of rocket-guns, continued, 'Old Leather Face, of course' – he meant the Soviet dictator Stalin – 'is screaming for action. Two years ago he would have put me in a labour camp in Siberia for so much inactivity. But this is 1945, comrade, and today I'm too big even for him.' He jerked a thumb at his bemedalled barrel-chest proudly. 'But still he screams back there in the Kremlin. Why haven't I taken Berlin yet? Why haven't I got to the Fritz? Don't I know that politically everything depends upon that? *Boshe moi!* Does he think I am a magician?'

The little civilian with the stainless steel teeth, who looked, in his shabby German suit, like anybody, or nobody, still said nothing. A long time ago Comrade Hertz had learned it was safer to remain silent in Russia.

Across in the ruins, a solitary German, a scarecrow of a figure, was venturing his way hesitantly across the rat-infested rubble. Obviously he was searching for loot, bending every now and again to turn over a piece of promising debris, kicking out violently whenever he spotted one of the rodents which were everywhere. The little Russian's eyes narrowed and he began to watch the scene with more interest; he knew rats – after all, he had dealt with human ones most of his adult life. The Fritz was heading for trouble.

'Old Leather Face naturally hasn't the faintest idea of what kind of problems we are confronted with here in Berlin. How would he back in that palace of his, with his orgies and his gala dinners?' Zhukov dabbed his sweating face again with the cologne-soaked handkerchief. 'But to cases. That treacherous dog Koniev,' he meant his greatest military rival General Koniev, Commander of the First Ukrainian Front, 'is in trouble in the south. The Fritz gave him a nasty black eye in the Spree Forest the day before yesterday.' He grinned, revealing big square false teeth. 'Just what he deserved, I must say. My own front is in good shape, of course. But we're still only moving at a snail's pace. By the Holy Black Virgin of Kazan, any pissy-arsed little Hitler Youth Fritz can hold up a whole battalion in this stone desert providing he's got enough guts – and enough ammunition. So, to make it brief, Comrade Hertz, it is not going to be as easy and as smooth as your masters back in Moscow probably told you it would be.'

'*Ya ponimayu,*' Hertz answered promptly, taking his eyes off the lone German and the ground which quivered visibly beneath his feet, clad in dirty, sole-flapping house slippers.

'*Horoscha,* I'm glad you do. Now then, Hertz, this is what I am going to do to speed up your immediate mission. I'm going to put in my 150th Rifle Division. It is an elite formation with over fifteen hundred *Komosomol* * and Party members.' He grinned suddenly. 'We must allow them the honour of dying for their beloved Leather Face while there is still time if they wish.'

Across the way, the German had nearly reached the top of the pile of brick rubble, which moved dangerously beneath his feet, but he did not seem to notice; he was too intent on his loot.

'Yes, Comrade Marshal,' Hertz said without particular interest.

'It will be their task to capture the Reichstag. It'll be a tough nut. It is held by the S S. But once they have it, it is only a matter of metres to the bunker, where Hitler is hiding out.' Zhukov paused, as if he expected a question.

* Soviet Communist Party Youth Organization.

None came. Hertz had learned that questions were dangerous and remained obstinately silent.

The big marshal frowned. Hertz irritated him. The skinny, shabby agent looked like nothing on earth, but his record, he knew, was tremendous. He had already worn the Red Banner three times over for his bravery behind the Fritzes' line. Even before the war, the little Jew had been a courier to the illegal German CP. Then from 1941 onwards he had been Moscow's illegal *rezident* with the German branch of the Red Orchestra till the Gestapo had rounded up the great spy ring early in 1943. Thereafter, he had dropped twice in West Prussia and Upper Silesia to make contact with comrades there and prepare for the advance of the Red Army. All the same, one could pass the man in the street and not give him a second glance. Momentarily Zhukov wondered what made the Jew tick; then he dismissed the thought and got on with the briefing; he had other things to do this day than waste time on a spy.

'Once the Reichstag is taken, Moscow can signal him to come. All you'll have to do, Hertz, is to be out there somewhere when the Fritz starts to run to ensure that the little traitor runs in the right direction.'

'I will take care of it, Comrade Marshal,' Hertz said in that subdued, meek Yiddish voice of his so that he sounded like a damned fifty rouble a month pen-pusher.

'Good, now . . .' his sentence remained unfinished, for from over the road there was a shrill, blood-curdling scream of absolute horror and pain. Zhukov stopped short and looked up. The German had sunk up to the hip of his right leg in the rubble; attached to his right hand was a large brown rat, its razor-sharp teeth clamped deep into his flesh. Now the terrified Fritz was swinging the thing round and round, trying desperately to cast it off, its long tail whipping the air, its fur drenched in the spray of human blood.

Zhukov swallowed hard.

More rats were coming out of the rubble now as the man

tried to free himself, his screams renting the air, the rat choking on his blood and flesh, but not prepared to let go. Suddenly a rodent darted forward. With a jump it rose in the air and planted itself on the trapped man's big nose. A second later it had sunk its teeth in his right cheek.

'God Almighty!' Zhukov swore, the sour bile rising in his throat and threatening to choke him. Hastily he fumbled for his pistol holster, unable to take his eyes off that terrible scene, as more and more of the horrible brown creatures scurried forward, nostrils twitching pleasurably as they scented blood. His hand shaking violently, he pulled out his pistol and took aim at the trapped Fritz. Just before he fired, he looked at Hertz to ascertain his reaction.

The little agent's eyes were sparkling with delight. Now he knew what made Hertz tick.

'The Elbe,' Mallory announced.

Gratefully they dropped to the cropped grass behind the cover of a glade of birch trees, which flourished everywhere in the sandy soil of the delta. They stared at their front. Like a great black raven the darkness was already beginning to sweep across the Mecklenburg plain on the other side. Within the hour it would be night, but visibility was still good enough for them to be able to take in the wrecked Tiger to the right, its long overhanging gun seeming to point right at them, and a jumble of paper and letters thrown back and forth by the wind around it, as if its crew had emptied their pockets before they had fled. To their left was a destroyed bridge, its central span collapsed into the water, but still visible above the wild white stream flooding through the shattered girders. As for the river itself it was full of the debris left by the fleeing German army: ammunition boxes, smashed boats, bodies floating face downwards. But they were the only signs of human life. To Mallory it seemed as if the whole broad plain on the eastern bank was empty. But he was taking no chances.

'Paddy,' he ordered the American, who had the keenest

eyesight of the three of them, 'can you see any kind of Jerry defence line?'

Piludski took his time, searching the opposite bank from left to right, peering at every hollow, checking every grove of birch trees.

'No, I don't think,' he began, finally, 'that there . . .' he stopped short, his handsome face abruptly hard. 'Wait a minute! See that clump of bushes at ten o'clock, to the right of the wrecked bridge?'

'Got it,' Mallory answered.

'See that slight gleam?'

'Yes.'

'It's the barrel of a small cannon, no, more than one.'

'It's a *Vierlingflak*,' Higgins announced.

They both turned to stare at him. 'How do you know?' Mallory asked.

'I was in the artillery, wasn't I? Once saw one of those bastards wipe out a whole company of the Coldcream Guards in North Africa within five minutes. Just like that!' He clicked his fingers and made Mallory start. 'Four barrels, firing 20mm shells at sixty rounds a minute. And they didn't know what hit 'em. Wiped them off the face of the map it did.'

'So the bridge is out,' Piludski expressed Mallory's own thoughts. 'I thought we could work our way across it – most of it is above water – but not with that monster guarding it. No dice.'

'Agreed,' Mallory said morosely. 'We've got to find another way.'

'These things are sent by the Good Lord to try us,' Piludski said, with a grin.

'Bugger that for a tale,' Higgins said sourly. 'I'd rather swim.'

'Okay,' Mallory made up his mind. 'We'll wait till it is completely dark, then we'll sneak down to the bank and see if we can find some sort of a boat. But remember where that cannon is. We've got to keep well away from it.'

Piludski stretched out his full length. 'I'm gonna hit the sack. It's gonna be a long night.'

It was a long boring hour, with the only sound the faint rumble of the barrage in the far distance. All of them tried to sleep, but midges descended upon them relentlessly. Instead, the three of them lay there in silence, each preoccupied with his own thoughts. Eventually, Higgins gave up. He rose to his feet and took out the last cans of self-heating soup. He pulled the tags in the centre which activated the heating element.

The rich nourishing soup, usually only handed out to special troops such as the commandos, had its effect. Conversation started up again. Piludski handed around cigarettes and they sat there in the trees, grateful for the smoke, which soothed their nerves and drove away the midges, hands cupped carefully around the tiny red firefly of light, chatting softly. Inevitably, the conversation turned from 'subject normal', mainly Higgins' amorous adventures in the various 'far-flung outposts of Empire', as he called them, to their mission.

In essence it was the same question that they had posed to Mallory thirty-six hours before in the barn outside Uelzen : What were they being sent to Berlin to do?

'He's right you know, Mike,' Piludski had supported Higgins. 'I mean that old gent of yours – C – gave us a real old snow-job back there in London.' He stubbed out his cigarette a little too energetically. 'We have a right to know.'

Mallory recalled C's cold considered words to him after Miss Pettigrew had escorted the other two out, leaving him alone in the office : 'Of course they will want to know, Mallory. The human being is incurably curious. You will have to tell them something. A little at a time. But not everything until you are in position. Remember that other ranker, Higgins, is a rogue, out for number one. Not to be trusted as far as you can throw him. As for the American,'

C had shrugged his painfully thin shoulders, 'let us assume that he will be a moralizing fool like most of his kind when confronted with the kind of truth you would have to reveal to him. Basically the two of them are *expendable*. The one you need because he is the only chap we can find who can identify your – er – victim. The other because it is politically expedient at this time to have an American involved.' There had been a sudden flicker of animation in those faded cunning eyes which had seen so many brave men go to their deaths from that remote office. 'Use them as long as you need them – no longer.'

Mallory forgot C's words. 'We are to contact a man in Berlin,' he said, slowly.

'Go on, Major,' Higgins prompted with unusual interest.

'He is a Swede, some kind of businessman established there for many years. Since 1942, however, he has been working for the Old Firm.' Mallory looked at Piludski.

The American nodded to indicate he understood. 'I suppose he thought he'd get on the gravy train before it was too late, since the Russians had whipped the Krauts at Stalingrad.'

Mallory was surprised at the sudden venom in Piludski's voice. 'Something like that, I dare say, but he's our contact.'

'But what's he got to do for us and what's all this ballocks got to do with this here Big Five and Six lark?' Higgins persisted.

'I don't know, honestly,' Mallory lied quickly. 'He'll give us our final instructions there.' Knowing the conversation had already gone too far, Mallory rose hastily to his feet. 'Keep your eyes peeled,' he ordered. 'I think I'll take a crap before we set off.'

Thunder smashed down on the delta like a mailed fist. Rain was driven into the water like spikes, bouncing upwards and exploding like miniature volcanoes. Lightning crackled across the horizon, revealing, in brief electric flashes, a world which looked as if it were melting and running in the pouring rain.

'Nice weather for ferking ducks!' Higgins yelled in Mallory's ear as they trudged towards the bank, already soaked, bodies bent against the pelting rain and wind.

Mallory grunted something.

Under his breath, Higgins muttered, 'Up you, too, mate!'

Slipping and sliding they started to descend the muddy river bank, cursing angrily every time they fell, the wind howling around their ears.

Piludski reached the bottom first and slipped, going into the water up to his ankles. Hastily he clambered out, cursing, 'God Almighty, it's colder than a witch's tit!'

'Yer get yer share of it, mate,' Higgins said, wiping the rain from his face.

'All right, spread out. Let's see if we can find a boat and get this show on the road before the Jerries spot us.'

'Heaven help a sailor on a night like this,' Piludski grumbled, but he went readily enough.

Five minutes later, they had found a tiny rowing boat, minus its oars, with an abandoned *Wehrmacht* machine pistol in a pool of water in the bottom.

'Best I could do,' Piludski said apologetically, holding the tiny craft as it bobbed up and down on the violent water.

'Prefer it to swimming,' Mallory snapped. 'Come on, let's get aboard.'

Awkwardly they scrambled into it as Mallory pushed off. At once they were seized by the current and had to paddle furiously with their cupped hands in an effort to keep the little craft in the general direction of the opposite bank, thirty yards away. In the violet glare of the lightning which ripped the sky apart in jagged electric pieces, Mallory could see the streaming red mud of the bank. There were no signs of a reception committee. In spite of his soaked, miserable condition and waterlogged boots, he started to feel better. They had nearly made it. 'Another couple of minutes, chaps,' he urged, 'and we're over!'

80

But that wasn't to be. With frightening suddenness, a searchlight clicked on from the opposite bank. 'Christ,' Higgins cursed, 'I forgot they're flak! They'd have searchlights.'

Automatically they stopped paddling and ducked low in order to present the smallest possible target. As if hypnotized, they followed the progress of that cold white finger of light, as it came ever closer. It submerged them in its blinding glare and swept over them, leaving them blinking and gasping with relief. Then silently it swung back, to catch them sitting upright and completely off their guard.

'*Da ist jemand!*' a hoarse voice cried in sudden alarm.

'*Wo denn, Eugen?*'

'*Da in dem Boot! Bist du blind? Du musst die doch sehen!*'

'*Ja, jetzt habe ich die!*'

'Over the side?' Higgins gasped, having followed the conversation as well as the other two had.

'No,' Mallory snapped. 'We'd be sitting ducks in the water. 'We . . .' The rest of his words were drowned by the tremendous chatter of the four-barrel flak cannon. A burst of shells came zipping flatly over the suddenly glowing water, dragging burning lights behind like a myriad angry hornets. Abruptly the water all around them heaved and bubbled and the boat rocked furiously. Malory could feel the heat on the back of his neck as they hissed by.

Another couple of moments and it would all be over. No one could survive another blast like that. The next time they would be dead.

Piludski got to his feet awkwardly, setting off the little boat rocking once more. 'Hold her steady for Chrissake!' he snarled and raised his pistol, completely outlined by the great white beam which held them trapped there. As if he were on some peace-time range instead of himself the target for a terrible weapon of war, he took aim. Mallory caught his breath. Piludski's outstretched arm was rocksteady. If he were afraid, he showed nothing of his fear.

At that moment, Mallory realized he was watching perhaps one of the bravest acts he had ever witnessed.

In the very instant that that fearsome cannon started to chatter its song of death, Piludski squeezed the trigger. The pistol jerked slightly in his big capable hand. There was the clatter of smashing glass, a scream of pain and abruptly they were immersed in total darkness and the stream of white and red shells had swept by them harmlessly.

One moment later, they were clambering up the mudbank and frantically running for their lives in that wild crazy night. . . .

2

'Reichstag!' Colonel Antonov of the 150th Rifle Division said to his assembled officers, who lay in the rubble just in front of Herzt, peering at the neo-classical home of the German Parliament, now being systematically pounded by a 75mm cannon at close range.

Hertz blinked his little eyes free of the smoke of war and stared at the building, its side scabbed with shellfire, flames leaping up in the upper storey. In the years since the end of the Weimar Republic he had stood in this same spot perhaps a good half-dozen times, but on each occasion he had been a hunted man. Now he was the hunter. It was a good feeling; for the desire to hurt and kill was the only pleasure left for Abraham Hertz.

Antonov started his briefing, his back pressed against the safety of a brick wall, and the S S who held the Reichstag opened fire immediately the shelling ceased. Twice the Russians had demanded their surrender and twice their sole answer had been a rapid burst of m.g. fire. The S S would fight to the bitter end; there was no doubt about that.

'I shall throw in three battalions,' Antonov said. 'You Stefan Andreyevich Noystroev,' he addressed a young broad-faced officer whose cheeks were covered in pock marks, 'you will have the centre with your battalion.'

'Yes, Comrade Colonel.'

'You will take with you the Red Banner Number Five of the Third Shock Army, and as your battalion contains the greatest number of Party members, you will have the honour of the final assault and capture. It will mean the Hero

of the Soviet Union for you, if you pull it off, naturally.'
Antonov frowned at the young captain. *'If!'*

'No "ifs",' Noystroev said with enthusiasm of youth.
'My boys'll do it. We'll take Hitler's hut for you, with one
arm tied behind our backs and our eyes blindfolded.'

There was a burst of laughter from the other officers at
such confidence and Antonov smiled.

Hertz was bored. He had seen so many heroes in his
time. Beria's secret police soon turned them into sobbing
cowards, just like the Gestapo did in Germany. He took
his gaze away from the conference and looked idly behind
him. Ruins, nothing but smoking ruins. In spite of Old
Leather Face's grandiose plans for the German capital, it
looked to him at that moment as if Berlin could never be
rebuilt; it would remain a stone desert for all time. He
stopped short. A civilian was crouched in the rubble watching the officers. No, he wasn't watching them; his attention
was concentrated on himself, Hertz knew that instinctively.

It was naturally nothing new to see civilians in the front
line. Ever since Hertz had arrived in Berlin the previous
week, he had been coming across Germans in the midst of
the fighting all the time; it was inevitable in the confused
street battles. Yet most Germans did not hang around in
the presence of the Russians: they were far too scared.
The Fritz opposite, however, was staring at him with unwinking concentration, obviously completely unafraid.
Why?

Before Hertz had time to consider that question at any
length, Colonel Antonov called, 'Comrade Hertz, Comrade Hertz, over here, please.'

For a colonel-of-infantry who had fought the Fritzes
since 1941, Antonov was exceedingly polite, but so were
all his officers; they parted out of Hertz's way immediately.
The agent knew why. Jew as he was, he carried the authority of Beria with him, an aura of fear and death.

'Yes, Colonel?' he asked in that humble manner of his.

'I am going to entrust you to Captain Noystroev here,

84

Comrade Hertz,' Antonov said. 'His men will attack at 1400 hours this afternoon after a short preliminary artillery barrage. May I request you, please –' Hertz smiled to himself. Infantry colonels in the Red Army usually never said 'please'. '– to do as the Captain says. I am making him personally responsible for your safety. We cannot afford that the 150th Rifle Division may be accused, well, you know, Comrade Hertz?'

Comrade Hertz did. If anything happened to him, Colonel Antonov would find himself in Siberia in short order, or worse. 'At your service, Colonel,' he said politely, playing the role of the humble, grateful little Yid he had adopted in 1920 when the Red mob had come for his parents in Minsk and he had told himself as a terrified sixteen-year-old fleeing for his life that the only way for a Jew to survive in Russia was to remain insignificant, unnoticed.

He let Antonov finish his orders, strolling away to where the Lend-Lease jeep was waiting to take them back to Marshal Zhukov's H Q. He would collect his kit there and return in time for the attack on the Reichstag. It would be amusing to watch a real battle.

The little German with the unwinking gaze was still lounging, apparently waiting for the scruffy, slant-eyed Siberian driver to throw away his cigarette so that he could pounce on the precious butt. But Hertz knew instinctively that that wasn't the German's real reason for being there; he had been engaged in clandestine warfare for too long not to sense such things. He stared hard at the German with his long hooked nose and dark piercing eyes.

'What?' he began.

Behind him there was the firm tread of Colonel Antonov coming back to the jeep.

'*Kak shal!*' the little German said suddenly and then, '*Jong.*' An instant later he had disappeared into the ruins, leaving Hertz staring after him in surprise. The German had spoken to him in a language he had not heard this many a year – *Yiddish!* And what was a pity?*

The skinny-ribbed horses stank in the warm April sunshine. Their sickly, throat-catching odour mingled with the pungent medical smell of the horse-drawn ambulance train which had been caught out in the open by the Red Air Force. Up ahead, the wagon bearing the multiple 20mm flak cannon which had been supposed to protect the German convoy had been hit too, its horses caught in the act of bursting into a panic-stricken gallop, bloody holes stitched along the length of their still sweat-glistening flanks, eyes wild and staring. Somehow the sight of those dead horses affected Mallory more than that of the dead men sprawled everywhere like carelessly abandoned broken dolls.

They had been marching all day now, avoiding the main roads which were packed with refugees and what was left of the Greater German *Wehrmacht*, retreating from the advancing Americans because they had been ordered to but fearful of what would happen when they bumped into the Russian ring around Berlin, taking whatever empty second-class roads they could find or making their way cross-country.

The two Englishmen, both Regulars, took the march in their stride. Both had been hardened by the day-long, prewar route marches customary in an army which had not yet been mechanized. The American was different. He was accustomed to riding everywhere. As he had confessed to them with a weary smile, 'Well, you know the Yanks, fellers. One man in the line and five to bring up the Coca-Cola!' And he had laughed. But now Mallory could see he was no longer laughing. The hot, long afternoon was having its effect and he was lagging, sore-footed, ever further behind them as they plodded along the dusty, glaring white country road.

* *Kak shal* (Russian) = 'What a pity'.

About four o'clock Mallory finally called a halt and Captain Piludski sank down gratefully, closing his eyes and groaning, 'Wake me up when the war's over. My dogs are killing me!'

Mallory nodded to Higgins. 'Have a look at Captain Piludski's feet, Bombardier,' he commanded, 'I want to check our position.'

Higgins, his face brick-red with the sweat, angrily threw away the cigarette he had just lit. 'Thought that was an officer's job – looking at his blokes' plates-o'-meat?'

'So you've been elected an honorary officer here and now,' Mallory answered without looking up from his map. 'Now move it!'

Muttering to himself, Higgins bent down and removed Piludski's boots and socks, while the American lay back, feet extended, eyes closed, as if it were all happening to someone else.

'Cor, stone the sodding crows!' Higgins gasped when he saw Piludski's feet. They were red-raw, a mess of burst and unburst blisters, swollen and bleeding a little at the heels. 'You Yanks know sod-all about soldiering. do yer? Should have had them socks rubbed with soap this morning, give 'em a bit of thickness with them thin-soled civvie shoes. Wouldn't have got them bleeding blisters if yer had have done, mate.'

'Didn't think,' Piludski groaned, as a faint breeze stirred his feet.

'Yer know what thought did, don't yer?' Higgins said without sympathy.

Mallory put away his map and frowned. After a moment he took a pin from his lapel and heated it until it went black with a match; then systematically he started to burst Piludski's blisters. The big American did not make a sound, but when Mallory was finished, his green eyes were glistening. It had hurt like hell, Mallory knew that. All the same, he forced a grin and said, 'Thanks, Mike. Now what are you gonna do for your second act?'

Mallory didn't return the grin; his face remained sombre. 'Paddy, to be honest with you, I don't think you're going to manage much further with those feet. From here they look like raw steak.'

'They feel like it too, Mike.' He hesitated. 'So?'

'So!' Surprisingly enough it was Higgins who answered the American's question for him. 'So we need wheels for you.'

'What do you mean, Higgins?'

'I mean, Major, that by the look of that up there,' he pointed to the black mushroom of smoke rising slowly to the sky a couple of miles away to their front, 'a Jerry depot is going up in the air so that the nasty Yanks won't get their greedy paws on it. And where there's a depot there's something worth nicking. It was just the same at Dunkirk in '40. For yours truly it was caviare and champagne all the way to the coast.'

'I bet it was,' Mallory said grimly. 'Well, go on, Higgins.'

'Well, whatever I can nick, I'll try to parley into wheels – a bike or something like that – for the captain.'

'My kingdom for a horse!' Piludski groaned.

Mallory wasn't listening. His brow set in a frown, he considered for a moment. Was this just an excuse for the little Cockney to do a bunk? He wouldn't put it past him. All the same, Higgins would hardly desert them in this confused mess, caught as they were between two fronts; his knowledge of German wasn't good enough for him to get through by himself. He knew, too, Piludski could not go on at the moment. He needed a day for the blisters to settle. Tomorrow probably he would be able to march again.

'All right, you rogue, off you go. I'll give you two hours. And remember, if you pull any tricks, you'll be straight on inside again, when we get back.'

'If,' Higgins said cockily and was gone.

One hour later, an ancient Opel appeared on the horizon.

'Quick – in the ditch!' Mallory snapped drawing his pistol.

His pain forgotten, Piludski moved with the speed of the professional athlete he had once been. Tensely, their pistols drawn, the two of them waited there as the old vehicle, squeaking and creaking audibly, as if it might fall apart at any moment, got ever closer. Then suddenly Piludski grinned – he had recognized the driver. 'It's Higgins! The little bastard has struck the jackpot!'

One minute later, Higgins drew up next to them with a squeal of rusty brakes and announced proudly, 'Your coach awaits you, Cinderella!'

Mallory and Piludski gazed in open-mouthed awe at the ancient Opel with its slit upholstery and glassless windows, the straw which still clung to its roof revealing that it had probably spent the fuel-less war in some farmer's barn. 'How . . . how did you get it, Bombardier?' Mallory stuttered finally.

'Charm – and seven kilos of tinned meat nicked from the depot when the Jerries' backs were turned – and another kilo as a kind of bonus.' Suddenly he looked down at his dirty nails with mock modesty. 'I could have had the farm woman's daughter as well for another tin, if I'd had the time.'

Mallory's relief gave way to exasperation. 'Let's get out of here, before you start a harem.'

Then they were trundling on their way east again, Piludski's bare feet stuck out of the rear window, a beatific smile on his face as the wind soothed his blisters.

To Mallory, walking again now that their petrol had finally run out, it seemed as if every shed, barn and garage in Brandenburg had opened its doors to spill its contents on the roads leading away from Berlin. The three agents, pushing their way eastwards against the stream of refugees, had never seen such a confusion of vehicles. Gleaming chauffeured limousines, obviously belonging to important

Party officials, 'golden pheasants', as the peasants cursed them behind their backs, mingled with ancient farm carts drawn by plodding oxen, piled high with possessions, topped with a mattress as protection against low-flying Red Army aircraft. In between were bicycles, wheelbarrows, dog-carts, even a great lumbering steam-roller moving westwards at five miles an hour, belching black smoke.

'It's the big bug-out,' Piludski said, as they paused and watched the refugees stream by, no eyes for anything but the sky from which death came at periodic intervals and the horizon which brought safety or at least hope.

'They *must* be sodding scared of the Russkis to do a bunk like that,' Higgins commented. 'Look at that old bint there, for instance, she's losing her drawers, but she ain't even got time to pull 'em up. She has got the wind up, proper.'

And so they should have,' Piludski said softly, almost as if he were speaking to himself. 'After what they did in Russia, they've got it coming to them – and it couldn't happen to a nicer bunch of guys.'

'Talking of the Russians,' Mallory interrupted, 'I think they're not too far away. Look at that.' He pointed at the horizon.

Outlined a harsh black against the blood-red of the setting sun, the three of them could make out the horsemen as they paused there, rising slightly in their stirrups as if to obtain a better view of what lay before them to the west.

'Russians?' queried Piludski, his eyes suddenly sparkling.

'Think so, probably Cossack cavalry. I don't think the Jerries have much cavalry left. They've eaten all their old nags.'

'Well, now ain't that dandy!' Piludski exclaimed, face wreathed in smiles. 'We've made it, then.'

'Not quite. I think we'd better get into that barn over there and have a look-see first.' Not heeding the American's protests, he strode swiftly across the field towards the abandoned barn just as the refugees became aware of what lay behind them and panicked, abandoning their possessions and running screaming into fields as if Satan himself had suddenly made an appearance.

It was an incredible spectacle. Squadron after squadron of cavalry, their fur-capped riders rising and sinking rhythmically, their equipment clinking, sabres at the ready, banners streaming in the breeze, as they trampled over the refugees' abandoned possessions, eyes set on the far horizon like their Cossack forefathers who had last ridden this way pursuing Napoleon nearly a century and a half before.

'Christ, you almost expect Tolstoy to appear at any moment!' Piludski breathed, eyes wide with awe.

Mallory nodded his head in silence. What had C said? If we don't stop them, they'll turn the clock back in Central Europe a thousand years or more.

'Well?' Piludski finally demanded as the cavalry disappeared at last to be followed by sweat-lathered, weary Siberian infantry, dressed in earth-coloured blouses, most of them flourishing schnaps bottles.

'Well what?' Mallory echoed tonelessly, knowing what was to come.

'They're Russians, aren't they – they're our allies. What in Sam Hill are we hiding here for then? They can help us on our way and I'm goddam sick of hoofing it.'

'Yer,' Higgins urged. 'I could just go a big drink – and look at the lungs on that girl soldier over there, the one with the moustache! Ain't got nothing like that in our A T S.' He grinned. 'I think I joined the wrong mob.'

'I agree with you, Paddy, that they are our allies,' Mallory said carefully, selecting his words with care. 'But look at them. They're combat soldiers, simple peasant boys by the looks of them. What do you think they'd do if we simply popped up here now? At the best, they'd take us for Jerries and give us a hard kick up the arse. At the worst, they'd take us for spies – they have a spy phobia, as I know all too well. They'd have us up against the nearest wall before you could say Jack Robinson.'

'Forget about Miss Tits,' Higgins said hastily. 'I've just decided I don't love her after all.'

Piludski did not smile. 'But I speak Russian,' he said. 'Hell, Mike,' he added, his face a mixture of anger and bewilderment, 'I could explain to them.'

'And if they wouldn't listen?'

'At least we could give it a whirl.'

'No,' Mallory said firmly, 'we *won't* give it a whirl as you call it. We do as I say. I have made my decision.'

Higgins put one finger under his nose to represent Hitler's moustache and raising his right hand said, 'Yes, *mein Führer.*'

Savagely Piludski struck the turf with his fist and said, 'Okay, Major, strike one – play ball.'

Five minutes later they were on their way again.

Moodily, Higgins puffed at his cigarette, staring at the black pall of smoke on the horizon. Over there was Berlin and according to the major, sleeping in the corner of the wrecked abandoned barn, they'd make their way into the German capital tomorrow morning. What then?

It was all right for people like the major. They always landed on their plates o' meat, whatever happened. That was because they were upper class. It wasn't fair, but it had always been that way in Blighty. Mallory and his lot didn't have to put themselves out; everything seemed to fall into their laps without them even sodding well trying.

If he weren't to drop into the shit, he'd always had to think ahead. He took a deep drag at his cigarette and glowered at the sombre skyline. What did it hold for him? He had a thousand Yankee dollars in his concealed money belt. Once the fighting had stopped in Berlin, that kind of money could take him a long way. Some kind of bint with a place of her own, a start on the black market, and then when he'd made his pile and everything was back to normal, he'd do a bunk. He fancied Australia. He'd met Aussie soldiers while he'd been up the blue in '42. They were easy-going types, common like himself. He grinned wrily at his own description. He'd fit in nicely there.

But what about the sodding major? Higgins stared at the skinny officer crouched in the corner on the heap of dirty straw. He was a cold fish, but tough. In spite of his old school tie and pound-notish accent, Mallory was a killer – he had no illusions about that.

What if he stayed with the major and Yank till he had completed his part in this crazy mission, whatever it might damn well be? Could he do a bunk then and get away with it, without the major screaming blue murder? Higgins considered and decided he couldn't. He knew too much already. Although he had tried not to show it, that little grey bloke back in London who had briefed them had put the wind up him. Whoever he was, he was a nob, with a lot of pull. Would a geezer like that let him, Higgins, go on the trot? No, he wouldn't. At the best they'd have him back in the Kate Karney, posted to the North West Frontier or some arsehole of the world like that; at the worst, it would be back to Aldershot's glasshouse. No, it would have to be Berlin. Once there, somewhere or other, he'd have to sling his hook.

'Penny for them, Higgins?'

The little bombardier turned, startled. It was the Yank, looking up at him curiously. 'Eh?'

'Penny for your thoughts, Higgins. You look as if you've just caught yer dong in a wringer,' Piludski said easily, a smile on his broad handsome face, though his eyes remained cold and searching.

'Just thinking.'

'About what?'

Higgins shrugged. 'Not much. Tomorrow, I suppose.'

Piludski nodded his understanding. 'Berlin, eh? Yeah, I

guess it could be a bitch. What do you think we're gonna do when we hit it, eh, Higgins?'

The bombardier shrugged again. 'Search me, mate. I thought you'd know, you being an officer and gent.' He indicated a sleeping Mallory. 'Hasn't his nibs spilled the beans to you yet?'

'No, Higgins. Major Mallory is playing this one with his cards close to his chest. I'm just as in the dark as you are. Though,' there was a sudden cunning look in Piludski's eyes which Higgins hadn't seen before. It was there only for an instant, but Higgins saw it all right, 'a smart operator like you must have figured out *something*?'

Momentarily Higgins lowered his gaze so that *his* eyes didn't give away what he was thinking at that instant. Piludski wasn't all that he was supposed to be, he told himself. It takes one to know one. Beneath that friendly, easy-going typical Yank exterior, there was something else not quite kosher. At that moment he could not quite put his finger on it, but he would eventually.

He lifted his gaze and met the American's look, now frank and open again. 'Well, I'll tell you this, Captain, for what it's worth: whatever we're gonna do in Berlin, it's gonna be nasty, bloody nasty. . . .'

Smoke lay heavy and choking over Berlin-Zehlendorf. In the air-raid defence water tank to their right there were bodies everywhere, victims of a phosphorous bomb attack who had plunged into the water to stop the burning and had drowned instead. Already the civilians looting the rubble were beginning to run, as the shrill sirens heralded the next attack with chill urgency.

The first flares started to come down, cutting through the pall of smoke with savage beauty. Drifting down like multicoloured dragons, trailing fiery sparks behind them as tails, they illuminated the terrified chaos below them.

Thump . . . thump . . . thump! the fifteen-year-old Hitler Youth anti-aircraft gunners started to pump shell after

94

shell into the sky. In an instant it was filled with drifting puff-balls of grey-brown smoke. Searchlights cut the clouds, seeking feverishly for the Russian bombers.

'There they are!' Piludski cried, as they crouched behind the fragile protection of a tall chimney, all that was left of what had once been an apartment house. 'God, don't they look good!'

A formation of *Stormavik* dive-bombers were caught in the harsh silver lights, flying defiantly onwards, not deigning, or so it seemed, to notice the flak, which was exploding all around them with furious intensity.

'Famous last . . .' Higgins began, but his words were drowned, as the first plane wiggled its wings and suddenly peeled off, appearing to fall out of the sky, its engines howling. Coming down almost vertically at 400 mph, it seemed to be heading for a tremendous crash on the city below until at the very last moment the pilot pulled it out of that horrifying dive. Tiny black eggs tumbled in crazy profusion from its blue-painted belly.

'*Down!*' Mallory yelled.

They ducked, mouths opened instinctively so that the blast would not puncture their eardrums, hands held protectively in front of them, as if the pathetic naked flesh would prevent the steel shards from penetrating their soft bodies.

In an appalling, bone-shaking crumping roar, the first bombs exploded. The earth trembled beneath them with the impact. Hot blast hit them in the face like the blow from a wet fist. Acrid explosive smoke filled their lungs, leaving them choking and coughing for air. Hardly had they recovered before the next dive-bomber had flung itself downwards in that death-defying dive.

The world went crazy. Flames, fumes, flying steel. Across the road a shelter received a direct hit. People tumbled out of it, naked and burning. A mother and her child, ablaze from head to foot, ran down the road hand in hand, mouths open in a frenzied shrieking that was

95

soundless, until they fell in the middle of the road, burning still in that bright curtain of magnesium, shrinking into charred pygmies in front of the three crouching men's horrified eyes.

Now the twin-engined *Peltyakovs* were following the dive-bombers in, dropping fire-bombs from 2000 feet, saturating the whole area with them. Everywhere the bright, glaring-white flames shot into the air, driving the civilians out of their shelters, as they ran to escape that terrible all-consuming heat.

Mallory felt the air torn out of his lungs. He started to gasp like an ancient asthmatic. Further up the street, something began to move towards them that looked like a medieval woodcut of hell. A huge rolling ball of flame and dust, perhaps twenty foot high, was driving in front of it naked screaming human beings, their flesh already burning and hanging from them in long black strips, their hair alight and writhing like purple snakes.

Higgins saw the danger first. 'The water tank!' he screamed in fear. 'Burn us alive. . . . *The water tank*!' Without waiting to see the others' reaction, he sprang to his feet and pelted crazily towards the great raised tank.

Mallory and Piludski reacted a second later. Summoning up the last of their strength, they ran for the reservoir as if the devil himself were behind them, their ears full of the flame's tremendous roar and the piteous screams of its victims. Just in time, they climbed over the high steel side and dropped into the water among the bodies. The searing flame swept over them. Mallory dived to the bottom. Above him the water bubbled and boiled. There was the stench of burning flesh. Mallory felt the water grow hotter and hotter. It was almost unbearable, and then it was past and he was lying on the surface of the water among the lobster-red, boiled dead bodies, gasping like a stranded fish.

Now it was getting dark. Everywhere that long afternoon, as they had wandered through the shattered, burning Ber-

96

lin suburb, Mallory had heard the languages of half of Europe spoken all around them. For six long years the German war industry had run on the labour of the workers, conscripted or bribed to come from the occupied countries, to work in the Reich. Now, there were no more factories left standing for them to work in, and they slouched aimlessly through Zehlendorf, looking for loot and drink, eyed suspiciously by the SS and green-uniformed *Schupos* who were everywhere. He guessed that once it was completely dark there would be some sort of curfew for foreigners, and he didn't want them to be stopped by a patrol; the papers Q Branch had supplied them with in London weren't that good.

He stopped at a corner. To their right there was a burnt-out fire engine, its crew still in position, one behind each other on either side of the heat-buckled ladder, their helmets and equipment still intact, but their bodies burnt to skeletons.

Higgins tipped his workman's cap, 'Hallo, gents,' he said cynically. 'Don't yer feel it a bit draughty without yer knickers on?'

'Shut up,' Mallory snapped irritably. He was still cold and wet from the involuntary bath in the water tank and he, like the other two, hadn't eaten for twenty-four hours. His stomach rumbled audibly.

'Just trying to bring a little smile to yer face, Major,' Higgins sneered.

Mallory ignored him. Instead he said, 'Listen, we've got to get off the streets – soon. I'd give it another half hour and then it'll be blackout time. My guess is that they'll have some sort of curfew.'

Piludski nodded sagely, watching a heavily armed patrol of Waffen SS stamp past, led by a one-armed rogue with evil eyes and a blood-stained bandage wrapped around his bare head. 'Yeah, shoot first and ask questions afterwards.'

'Something like that.'

'What do you suggest, Mike?'

Mallory took his eyes off the S S men, telling himself he had rarely seen such a desperate bunch of thugs as they were, and frowned. 'Well,' he began, 'what would you do if you were a Berliner tonight?'

'Apply for an immediate transfer to Hamburg, Sir?' Higgins sniggered.

'Wise ass,' Piludski said. 'Me, I'd get myself as deep below the earth as I could bury. You saw what happened in that raid.'

'Exactly, Paddy. Most of these civilians will soon be tucked away in the cellars. As for the soldiers, if they're off duty they'll be there too and if they aren't, they're certainly not going to pick any house which is still standing as a defensive position.'

'You're right there, Major,' Higgins agreed. 'First kind of a target you'd look for in the artillery – anything left standing above ground is gonna get the first plastering. Stands to reason, don't it? Your ordinary gunner can't do much against something buried half a dozen yards below ground.'

'So we've got to find an intact house, Mike?' Piludski concluded.

'Exactly. Come on, we haven't got much time left.'

They found what they sought nearly half an hour later: one of those once pompous, now shabby, streets, built for prosperous burghers around the end of the nineteenth century at the period of what the Germans call the *Grunderzeit'* * when money was pouring into the newly formed Reich.

Time and six years of war had taken their toll. All of their tall windows were boarded up, most of the roofs had gone, and here and there the ornate scrolled gables had disappeared, carried away by some R A F bomb or Russian shell.

'Looks just the job,' Higgins said, as they surveyed the silent street.

* Literally, 'foundation time'.

'They all look abandoned,' Piludski remarked.

Mallory nodded, studying the street, the shell-holed pavement littered with branches from the trees, which had probably once been the street's pride. He made his decision. 'All right, you see that one in the middle of the row to the left – the one with the peeling stucco?'

'Villa Irma?' Piludski said, peering through the gloom to make out the name written in ornate script across the front of the second storey together with the legend: *Erbaut 1902.**

'Yes, but I can't see the name, Paddy. O.K., that looks our best bet.'

Piludski moved forward, but Mallory caught him by the arm.

'Not so quick, Paddy. We don't go in through the front door, you know.'

Higgins sighed, as if he were bearing a great burden. 'Yanks,' he moaned, 'don't know their arse from their elbow! You'd never make a tea leaf, Captain, in a month o' Sundays.'

'*Tea leaf?*'

'Oh, forget it, Paddy,' Mallory said impatiently. It was really getting very dark now and he could almost hear the heavy tread of the Waffen SS. 'Let's go through the garden – the nearest one here, work our way down the back lane. They must have something like that for the tradesmen. We'll come up through the back garden and have a look-see from there. If there's anybody still living in this place, they'll be in the kitchen. Warmth and cooking, you see, and less danger from bomb blast with the smaller kitchen windows.'

Piludski scratched the back of his blond head. 'I see I've got a lot to learn yet, Mike.'

'It's been a long war, Paddy. . . . Come on.'

They halted behind some raspberry bushes. Ahead of them, lay the kitchen, its window unshuttered, but criss-

* Built 1902.

99

crossed with sticky paper to stop bomb blast. Mallory frowned. Why wasn't the window shuttered? An oversight, or was the villa inhabited? His gaze pierced the gloom, searching the building, checking the high ornate chimneys for smoke. But there was none.

'Well, what now?' Piludski asked.

'You were a baseball player, they tell me,' Mallory answered. 'Here,' he picked up a stone. 'Throw that against the back door. We'll see what happens then.'

Piludski took the stone and looked at it a little nervously. 'It's a long time since I pitched that kind of distance,' he said.

'Oh, you never forget. I'm still pretty good with a googlie myself,' Mallory urged him. 'Come on, time's a-passing.'

Awkwardly, but in the approved fashion, which Mallory remembered from the pre-war newsreels of American baseball games, Piludski 'wound-up' the stone, one leg stuck out in front of him, body twisted and then, with a muffled grunt, he flung it. It hissed through the air and hit the door squarely in its centre. They could hear the tremble of the glass inlet.

Tensely they waited.

Nothing happened!

'All right, Higgins,' Mallory ordered, drawing his pistol while next to him Piludski breathed out hard and mopped his abruptly damp brow, 'off you go. We'll cover you.'

'Yer,' Higgins grumbled, 'it's allus the sodding poor squaddie who gets the dirty end of the stick.'

He rose and stole softly across the overgrown lawn, littered with rusting pieces of shrapnel and the broken glass from the shattered greenhouse, body bent double. For a moment he hesitated at the door, then he tried the handle. The door was locked. But Higgins was prepared. He took a piece of Bakelite out of his jacket pocket and inserted it between the lock and jam. He heaved. Once, twice. A slight crack. Next moment the door swung open. Higgins turned and raised his thumb in silent triumph.

They clattered through the villa in their heavy shoes. The rooms were in utter confusion. There were books, papers, clothes, shoes, male and female, everywhere, with the wardrobe and cupboard doors flung wide open, as if the house's occupants had left in a hurry.

While Higgins scouted around for something to eat, Mallory searched the bedrooms, noting the stiff moustached worthies in the uniform of the pre-war Imperial Army who graced the walls in yellowing photographs and the obligatory portrait of Hitler, posed romantically in a long cloak, with a loose lock of black hair draped over his noble forehead and the legend below: *We thank thee, our Führer!*

'Nazis who bugged out when the Russians started to approach?' Piludski suggested, kicking aside a pair of green crêpe-de-Chine cami-knickers which lay on the floor next to a woman's high heel shoe.

'Could be,' Mallory agreed, staring around a little suspiciously, nostrils twitching at the heavy scent of perfume that hung over the bedroom.

'Horny ones,' Piludski said, 'that's for sure.' He picked up the packet of contraceptives that lay on the little night table next to the big bed. 'They weren't particularly interested in producing cannon-fodder for their beloved Führer.' He giggled at the name on the packet. '*Vulkan* – volcano, what a brand-name for a rubber!'

Mallory grunted and started to go down the gloomy stairs, lined with portraits of elderly gentlemen in high stiff collars and pince-nez, who looked out at the world, narrow faces full of self-righteous nineteenth-century disapproval. Piludski followed.

'What did you find, Higgins?' he asked.

The little Cockney swallowed the pickled egg he had found in the big stone jar in the cellar and held up a bottle of clear liquid. 'Not exactly what I'd call a balanced diet, but there's eggs, mouldy carrots – and gin. They must have been a boozy old bunch. There's dead soldiers everywhere down there. A right old orgy they must have had before they did a bunk.'

'But what makes you think they did do a bunk?' The voice was husky, female and held only the faintest trace of a German accent.

Higgins let the bottle drop. It shattered on the stone flags of the hall. As one they spun round.

In the dusky light stood a woman. As she descended the stairs a little drunkenly, her pure silk nightdress revealed her slim, naked body. But it was not her body, the bottle she carried in one hand, nor her beautiful face under the unruly blonde hair which caught the surprised men's attention. It was the small pistol in her right hand which she held with surprising steadiness for a drunken woman faced by three strange men.

'Christ,' Higgins said in a sinking voice, 'this time we ain't half been caught with our knickers down. . . .'

3

Now they had been in the bunker eight days. Even so, the evening tea party for the Führer's intimates took place as if this was peacetime and they were back in the Berghof in the tranquil mountains, gazing at the vast panorama of the Bavarian-Austrian alps. But now the Dresden china cups rattled and the silver spoons of the Führer's personal service, monographed '*A H*' for Adolf Hitler, trembled every time a fresh Russian salvo landed. Their talk was different too. No longer did they entertain the Leader with light-hearted chatter about the latest Maria Roekk movie to the background music of some Strauss waltz on the gramophone. Now the background music was the moans of the wounded in the hospital shelter and their chatter was of suicide.

'Let the first Ivan show his brutish face around that corner and I'd shoot,' Magda Goebbels declared, her flat but beautiful face full of determination, 'then I'd turn the gun on myself.'

Eva Braun looked at the other woman with admiration. She knew she was going to kill her own six children too soon. 'I'd never have the courage to do that, Frau Goebbels,' she said in her thick Bavarian accent. 'Never!'

Affectionately, Hitler patted his mistress's hand, '*Tschapperl!*' he whispered soothingly, using the Austrian expression. 'You know you won't have to.'

General Krebs, his broad face brick-red with drink and his eyes not focusing correctly, for he had long given up any pretence in Hitler's presence and was drinking cognac out of his delicate little cup, said thickly, 'I deem it an honour to die for the Führer. But I wouldn't want to disfigure myself by missing the target because my hand shook. When the time comes, I want to die at the head of a group of fighting men.' He looked at Hitler for his approval.

Hitler shook his head slowly. 'And what if they capture you, my dear Krebs? What if they make you collaborate, betray your personal oath to me like they must have done with Paulus after he was captured at Stalingrad. . . .'

Bormann wolfed down another *petit four*, wishing it was a lump of good strong *Mettwurst*, and listened to the absurd conversation with inner contempt. For the last twenty-four hours now, since they had all realized, even the most stupid of them, that they would not be relieved, life in the bunker had been reduced to three activities: hectic, unashamed coupling – he had no objections to that; hadn't he 'had' every one of his *'Blitzmädchen'** since they had moved into the bunker – boozing and this interminable talk of the best way to commit suicide. What fools they were, he told himself. Even the Führer, whom he had once respected, had become little better than an old woman, sitting among these affected fools, sipping his peppermint tea and eating his overly sweet cakes like a satiated bourgeois.

'And what about you, my dear Bormann?' the question penetrated his consciousness. Suddenly the Reichsleiter became aware that the rest of the *Kaffeeklatsch* were staring at him.

'How do you mean, my dear Führer?' he replied, using the same absurd phrase.

'How will you end it all?'

Bormann gave him a twisted smile. *'Mein Führer*, it is a thing I have thought a great deal about these last few terrible days.' He fought for words.

'And?'

'I waver between two methods.'

The others craned forward, teacups poised, as if what he

* Operators.

was to say was of world shattering importance; even Josef Goebbels stopped eating the biscuit he had placed in his mouth with those delicate fingers of his.

'Drowning myself in the Spree, or allowing one of our own loyal S S men to bayonet me.'

'Like Nero?' Krebs said, drunkenly.

Everyone frowned. Hitler said sternly, 'The parallel is wrong. There is nothing more I could have done. I am *not* fiddling while Berlin burns.'

'*Natürlich ... natürlich,*' everyone said hastily, including Bormann who told himself that he couldn't stand this farce much longer. If they were going to kill their fool selves, then let them get it done with – *and quick*!

Hertz crouched in what had once been an office and watched the attack through the shell-hole in the wall, The 150th Rifle Division's bombardment was over. Now the infantry, slight young men in earth-coloured smocks armed with round-barrelled tommy-guns, were beginning to slip in and out of the smoking rubble, hitting the ground fast every time a slug struck the bricks, but always getting up again and heading ever closer to the embattled Reichstag.

Hertz looked at their faces with interest. There was a seriousness about them that clashed with their youth. Did they know they were going to die? And for what they were dying? Did those boys realize that they were going to their deaths prematurely because at an air field not a hundred kilometres from Berlin, a handful of shabby Germans – Pieck, Ulbricht and all the rest of the emigres – were waiting anxiously to fly in and take over? Ironically enough they were killing one lot of Germans in order to pave the way for another group of Fritzes wanting to come to power.

A furtive noise disturbed his reveries. Hertz swung round, heart beating furiously, pistol in hand. It was the little German, the one who had watched him and Antonov so intently the day before, and this time he wasn't alone;

105

at his side, standing there on the wrecked stairs, was a woman, dressed in ill-fitting striped pyjamas of the concentration camp. But it wasn't the woman's clothes which caught his attention at that moment; it was her face – yellow and wasted away to a death's head, her black eyes burning fiercely with the dying energy of a consumptive.

Hertz jerked his pistol up. 'What are you doing here?' he asked in his fluent German.

The man replied in equally fluent German, though Hertz thought he could detect an accent, 'We mean you no harm, comrade. All we wish to do is to talk with you.'

'Are you a Communist?' Hertz asked, noting the 'comrade'.

'No, we are not Communists,' the man said. 'You are our comrade because . . .'

'Because you are a Jew,' the woman broke in a dry hoarse voice, as if she were burning within, when the man hesitated over that word 'Jew', which for twelve years now in Germany had meant torture and death.

There was a sharp burst of tommy-gun fire outside, followed a second later by the high-pitched hysterical hiss of a spandau. The three of them ducked as white glowing tracer zipped through the gap where the window had once been and ran the length of the opposite wall in a series of vivid blue sparks. Hertz waited a moment, counting the length of the burst, and then, judging correctly when the Fritz gunner had finished the belt, he scuttled hurriedly to where the strange couple crouched against the head of the stairs. He plumped himself down beside them. Just in time. The unseen gunner sent another burst of tracer hissing frighteningly into the room. Obviously he had taken Hertz for a forward artillery observer. The three of them huddled together and Hertz could smell the death odour which clung to the woman.

'Now then,' Hertz snapped, when the second burst had ended, 'what is this? Why are you watching me? Don't you know I could have you shot?'

106

The man was suitably frightened, but the black eyes of the dying woman flared up angrily, 'Shoot us – *Jews*?'

Hertz shrugged. '*Jews*, what does it matter to me? You are Germans first, just as I am a Russian first.'

'Do you really believe that? For two thousand years we have always been Jews first in the eyes of the gentiles. So this century it has been the Germans' turn to beat and kill us. Last century it was the Russians and the Poles. And before,' the consumptive woman threw up her claw-like hands in angry impatience. '*You know*! I don't have to tell you. Any Jew born in Europe inherited that knowledge with his mother's milk.'

The woman's passionate little speech had its effect on the man. Hertz could visibly see him pick up courage. Leaning forward, he said, 'Comrade Hertz.'

Outside there was a loud hoarse '*Urrah*'. The infantry were going in for the final charge on the Reichstag.

The other man began again, 'Comrade Hertz, we know why you are in Berlin. . . .'

'Escaped British prisoners-of-war,' the girl sneered.

She had lined Mallory, Piludski and Higgins against the opposite wall, their hands above their heads, while she listened to their explanations, occasionally taking a drink from the bottle of champagne, but her eyes on them all the time and the pistol unwavering in her firm hand.

Mallory let Higgins do the talking, while he studied her. The German woman was obviously upper class with her elegant features and intelligent, though somehow blurred eyes, as if she had once been hurt and was still confused as to why it had happened to her in particular. But in spite of the obvious hurt, the woman was tough. He had seen women like her all over the Continent in these last six years: women who had been forced to grow up too soon, tackle tasks which had once been the preserve of men, and who had been through so many emotional crises that the only way they could survive was grow a thick tough skin.

Mallory knew she would not hesitate to pull the trigger of that little pistol if she had to.

'Tommies who escaped from a camp, found those *Ostarbeiter* clothes and then just happened to turn up in besieged Berlin,' she summed up Higgins' pathetic story in her fluent English. '*So –*' she took a drink of her champagne, her green eyes cynical and wary, '– how clever of you!'

'Just ordinary blokes, miss,' Higgins said with mock modesty.

'The officer back in the U K before we got nabbed told us it was our duty to escape if we were ever taken prisoner.'

Mallory knew she had not swallowed the lies Higgins had thought up so quickly.

'Did he now? And did this mythical officer of yours say how you would get the clothes off the back of some miserable *Ostarbeiter*, who would be naked without them?'

Higgins opened his mouth to say something, but she stopped him with a threatening jerk of the little pistol.

'And wasn't it very clever of you not to turn west and try to reach the western allies on the other side of the Rhine. No, you British gentlemen had to walk right into the centre of a battle, somehow managing, without any knowledge of the language, to penetrate both the German and Russian lines.' She took a final drink and dropped the empty champagne bottle carelessly to the littered floor. 'I'll tell you what you are, you are spies, British spies, though God knows what you think you may achieve here *now*! No matter. We in Berlin still have enough ammunition to take care of the three of you. God knows, we have had plenty of practice these last years.' There was boundless contempt and hurt in her voice. For a moment her pistol wavered.

Piludski didn't wait for a second invitation. With a great roar that startled even Mallory he dived forward. She squeezed the trigger instinctively. Piludski yelped with pain as the little slug hit him in the shoulder. But he did not let himself be stopped. With all his weight he crashed into the girl, bowling her over to reveal white shapely naked thighs and a dark flash of hair. Her long, blood-red nails ripped open the side of his face. Piludski smashed his fist against her chin and her head clicked back. The pistol fell from senseless fingers and she lay still.

'What now?' Piludski said through gritted teeth as Mallory cleaned the ugly gash in his shoulder with the gin Higgins had found and started to tape the field dressing to the ` wound.

Higgins stared down at the unconscious girl, her body clearly outlined against the thin material of the nightdress, with undisguised lust in his eyes. 'I know what *I* could do for her. Bit o' sausage meat and then . . .' He clicked his forefinger back and forth as if he were pulling the trigger of a pistol.

Piludski looked at Mallory in alarm. 'We can't kill her in . . . in cold blood, Mike.'

Mallory did not reply; he concentrated on the shoulder.

'What the hellus are we gonna do with her?' Higgins snarled. 'We can't lug a bit of gash around with us. Christ, the first chance she gets she screams for the Jerry rozzers – then what? We're right up the creek without a sodding paddle.'

Mallory finished his task and frowned at the girl, slumped in the corner, a lock of her unruly white blonde hair fallen over her brow. With a grunt, he bent down, picked her up and deposited her on the sofa in the corner under the ageing photograph of an officer in the full uniform of the Imperial Death's Head Hussars. *'With soldierly greetings to my old comrade von Prittwitz. Field Marshal Mackensen,'* he read the inscription in the jagged *Sutterlin* script the Germans had used before Hitler's takeover.

'She is a woman,' Piludski said, obviously made uneasy

by the Englishmen's silence. Outside the Russian guns had opened up once more. A big attack was going on somewhere or other in Berlin. Little trickles of plaster fell from the ceiling on to the girl's still body like snow.

'What do you suggest, Paddy?' Mallory broke the heavy silence that reigned in the dark room.

'Well, we could tie her up here and leave her, when we move on tomorrow, Mike?'

'She'd probably starve to death. No one is going to come down this street in the near future till the Russians come. That way she'd die – but slowly.'

Piludski bit his lip. 'Then we've got to take her with us tomorrow when we meet your Swede. Perhaps he can take her off us.'

In the corner Higgins took another swig of the German *Korn* and gasped as the fiery white spirit hit the back of his throat. 'Cor stone the ferking crows,' he said in disgust. 'What a fuss about a bit of snake-meat! Croak her and have it done with.'

Mallory said nothing, while Piludski looked at him appealingly. Then he took another look at the unconscious girl. 'I'll sleep on it,' he announced drily. 'Higgins, you've got first stag till midnight. I'm on till two. Piludski you're on next. We stand to at four. We've got a busy day in front of us tomorrow.' He yawned and saw the flames dancing in crazy patterns on the wall. Berlin was burning again.

Five minutes later, he and Piludski were snoring in an exhausted sleep and there was no sound in the room, save Higgins' periodic swigs of his bottle and the girl's soft whimpers.

Ilona Graefin von Prittwitz, had been sixteen in 1939 when the war had broken out. That last hot August night she had spent in her bed, with her brother Lothar talking to her, softly but confidently, full of the bright new creed he had absorbed at the S S Cadet School at Bad Toelz. The window curtain had moved gently in the soft summer wind

110

and the pale silvery wash of the full moon had bathed Lothar so that he looked like some figure out of Germanic mythology. '*A new start for Europe . . . a chance to get rid of the old sick pack who have ruled the Continent for too long. . . . A Europe of the youth. . . .*' the bold enthusiastic phrases had poured from him, as she had clasped his hand until it hurt. Just after dawn when she had finally fallen asleep, he had slipped away to join his regiment *SS Germania*. She had never seen him again. He had been killed, leading an assault company, on 3 September: they had buried him in some obscure Polish village, whose name she had long forgotten.

Lothar had been the first. Her father had been recalled to take over an infantry division the following year. He had missed the campaign in France, but not the one in Russia. He had come home from the failed drive on Moscow at Christmas 1941, his eyes haggard with fear and grief, exhaustion etched invincibly in deep lines on his fine soldier's face. After the *Bescherung** at the Christmas tree when he had handed her the presents he had brought with him from Russia, he had muttered something about 'my poor boys', gone into his study, locked the door and shot himself. At the age of eighteen, she had been alone in Berlin.

But not for long. The local Kreisleiter had got her drunk for the first time in her life two days after her father's funeral. 'A fine soldier, a fine German, who died as he had lived, in the spirit of self-sacrifice and loyalty to our Führer Adolf Hitler,' the Kreisleiter had declaimed boldly at the open grave, and then raped her on the floor of the study, still lined with black-edged cards of condolence. The next time he did not need to rape her; she liked it, in spite of his pot-belly and mouthful of gold teeth and the way he dug his big greedy fingers into her breasts when he was aroused. After the Kreisleiter had been sent to Russia to take over some administrative job, there had been others:

* German present-giving ceremony on Christmas Eve.

young handsome officers in the *Alpenkorps*, *Afrikakorps*, *Leibstandarte* and a score of other elite formations, who were doomed to die soon.

Always there had been champagne, Johannes Heesters singing something or other from an operetta in his fine baritone voice, candlelight and the inevitable 'night of love'. Letters would follow for a short while from Mersa Matruh, Smolensk, Bucharest, Crete, those places where 'Germany's destiny is being decided in blood' (as the Party orators had it). Then she would hear that he had 'Fallen for Folk, Fatherland and Führer', and there would be another lover, as tall, blond and as handsome as his predecessor, only the uniform would be different. Death, violent death hung over all of them and she knew it. Thus it was better to drink and forget it.

'Live for the moment!' she'd cry at their parties, raising her champagne glass, draining it in one greedy gulp and shattering it with a wild throw; and the young men would laugh and do the same, carried away by the alcohol and the excitement of the moment. Later when she was really drunk and it was over and they would lie there in bed, she would whisper drunkenly, 'I knew a boy like you long ago in '40, or '41 . . .' But the face she could never recall of the boy she had known in '40 or '41 and then she would sob.

By the spring of 1945, she knew with the clarity of a vision that she would not survive the war. When Berlin fell, she would kill herself. For Ilona Graefin von Prittwitz there was no future, whatever Major Mike Mallory decided on the morrow.

Somehow Hertz did not feel afraid. Indeed as he sat there in the miserable cellar with the tea kettle hissing on the green-tiled oven in the corner, listening to the steady rumble of the guns, he felt for the first time in a long time a sense of belonging. Why he did not know. The two strangers, the dying woman in the striped pyjamas and the little man, weren't Russian; they weren't even comrades.

Yet he experienced a strange feeling of oneness with them: the same kind of feeling he had known as a child with his parents back in Minsk before the mob had come.

He sipped the black tea out of the glass they had given him and stared over the rim at them; they stared back. There was no sound save that of the hissing steam. Yet Hertz could almost hear their minds racing, while they made their decision whether they should tell him or not; for he knew instinctively they had brought him to this place to tell him something.

At last the little man broke the oppressive silence. 'Comrade Hertz,' he began – the Russian started – they knew his name – but said nothing – 'have you ever heard of an organization named Haganah?'

Hertz shook his head, not taking his lips from the glass.

'It was formed a long time ago in Palestine – a kind of secret Jewish organization.'

The little man licked his lips nervously, as if he thought he had already gone too far. He flashed a look at the woman. At her nod he continued. 'In the twenties and early thirties, our main task was to take care of our settlers against the British mandate authorities and the Arabs.'

Hertz noted the 'our'. So that was where the little man had come from; it also explained the slight accent with which he spoke. Suddenly it dawned on the Russian agent. What was a Palestinian Jew doing in Fascist Berlin when for twelve years now it had been every German Jew's sole ambition to escape from the damned country? He stared at him with new interest. Still he said nothing.

'But in the mid-thirties, we naturally became interested in the events taking place in Europe. We attempted to smuggle out some of our folk who could be useful to the movement in Palestine before it was too late.' He gestured at the woman. 'Comrade—'

'Call me Sarah,' she interrupted before he could say her real name. 'The Nazis called us all Sarah, just as they made

113

us wear this.' She touched the yellow star on her emaciated chest almost proudly.

'Well, Comrade Sarah here was one of the first of us to come to Germany to help. They caught her in '43. Fortunately they needed her services as a doctor, so she did not go up.' He stopped short and made a gesture of smoke spiralling up a chimney.

Hertz nodded; the little man meant the concentration camp gas ovens. 'Go on,' he said politely, 'please.'

'Now our task has changed. Of course we still need settlers and weapons – the day of confrontation with Arabs is not far off. Soon the British will move out of Palestine. They are finished. They have won the war, but they are exhausted. They will have to give up their Empire...'

'What is this new task?' Hertz interrupted, knowing instinctively that it had something to do with his own mission.

The woman answered. 'Revenge,' she said simply, but those fanatical angry eyes of her blazed. 'Revenge for what has happened to our people here. Revenge to show the world that we will not always be the tame little Jew, who turns the other cheek. Revenge for two thousand years of history.'

'And what has this got to do with me?'

Sarah stared at him hard, as if she were trying to see something in him, known only to herself. Hertz wriggled uneasily in his stiff chair. He was not accustomed to looks like that. All his adult life ever since he had run from that howling mob, he had tried to make himself inconspicuous; noticed only when some superior had wanted to notice him. Finally, she spoke, her hoarse voice so low that he had to strain to catch her words, 'Comrade Hertz, you have come to Berlin to rescue someone. In the name of your fellow Jews, we want you to kill that man!'

114

Three: Berlin

'What is still to be decided, will be decided here
– in Berlin!'

Adolf Hitler, April, 1945

1

Eva Braun burst out of her lover's room in the bunker, her oval face contorted, sobbing hysterically. Pushing her way through the drunken mob, some openly copulating in the darker places of the corridor, she ran to Frau Goebbels' room. Flinging open the door, she rushed by a surprised Magda Goebbels who was playing with her smallest daughter, the one she had decided she would kill first, and dropped on the rumpled, unmade bed, shrieking: 'They've betrayed him again. . . . How can he stand it? Yet another betrayal. . . .' Her voice cracked and her slim shoulders heaved as she sobbed like a heartbroken little child.

Back in the Führer's private room, Hitler, his gaunt face now flushed a hectic red, tiny patches of foam in the corners of his mouth, was already telling Bormann and Goebbels: '. . . and he called himself my "loyal Heinrich". What villainy,' he screamed, 'when I made him!' He held up his hands, palms turned inwards as if he were moulding a clay figure. 'From an obscure chicken farmer in some damned Bavarian backwood to be the head of the greatest police *apparat* the world has ever seen – and now this! I expected it of Goering. Even Ribbentrop. But never *him*! Why?' He calmed himself a little and stared at the other two as if attempting to find the answer there, but their faces remained blank. Both of them were thinking privately that if they had been in Heinrich Himmler's place, they too would have attempted to negotiate with the enemy.

'It is good that we know the truth now,' Bormann said. 'Now all the traitors are unmasked. Now we know upon whom we can rely, at last.'

Hitler looked at Bormann almost sadly. 'The traitors, my dear Bormann, are everywhere. The whole German nation is a treacherous whore. It is not worthy of me.' He half raised his hands and then let them drop in a symbol of resignation. 'My affairs are in order. For many years I have always thought that I could not undertake the responsibility of marriage. Now, when the end is near I must reward Fräulein Braun with marriage. She has stuck by me more loyally than many who have received such great rewards from me. Bormann, please find someone to wed us. Thereafter I can die in peace.'

Bormann breathed an inner sigh of relief. Hitler was an Austrian bourgeois at heart. The Braun woman was going to be rewarded with the long-delayed sanctity of marriage and then the two of them would let themselves be killed, presumably happy in the thought that they had 'done the right thing'. Now at last he knew when he would be free. Abruptly he was sorely tempted to cry out with joy, but the years of suppressing his own emotions and desires in the presence of the broken man facing him had their effect. He caught himself in time. Instead of shouting, he said quietly, *'Zu Befehl, mein Führer.'*

Turning, he strode out and immediately set the machinery in motion to find a civil servant somewhere in the crowded stinking bunker who could officiate at the wedding.

Bormann had drunk a toast in champagne with the rest, while the Führer had sipped his peppermint tea and discoursed on, of all things, English culture, or the lack of it. Finally, he had been able to escape when the Führer had left to dictate his will to his second secretary, Fräulein Junge. Later, Bormann knew he would be expected to sign it as a witness, but for a short while he was free.

So now he lay on his bunk, clad in the uniform of an SS general, bottle of *Korn* in one hand and salami sausage in

118

his other, perfectly happy. All the little private feast lacked was a woman. But that would come soon too.

Martin Bormann looked at his image in the mirror that ran the length of his clothes closet. For forty-five he wasn't a bad figure of a man in spite of the thinning hair and paunch. Once he was back in the real world, he would ensure that he got some colour in his cheeks and get that paunch down. What did they say in the country? A good cock never gets fat. Well, he had been a good cock all his life, that was certain. There hadn't been a woman yet who had complained about his performance in the hay. He smiled knowingly at himself and took another powerful bite of the garlic sausage, reflecting that he owed his whole career indirectly to women. First, it had been the wife of the landowner where he had trained as an apprentice. The fine aristocratic lady had taken a fancy to him – he had been a good-looking boy. She had been no different than the rest, once he'd had the drawers off her behind the barn. Of course her husband had found out and had driven him from the estate. How depressed he had been then! Unemployed with a criminal record in 1927 when jobs had been so hard to find. But it had really been 'luck in unluck' as the peasants said. One year later in Munich, already a member of the Party, he had met Party Judge Buch's daughter, Gerda. He had seduced her within the week. The Old Man hadn't liked it, but it was better to let him marry his precious Gerda than have her run around with a fat belly and no husband to take the responsibility.

Thereafter, Buch's son-in-law, for that was how he had been regarded in the Party, had mounted slowly but steadily up the ladder; after his fool of a boss, Hess, had flown to England on his crazy mission of peace, he had become the man next to Hitler. Then it took less than two years for him to assume the most powerful position in Germany after the Führer himself.

It had been hard, damned hard. He'd had enemies enough, who would have taken him apart if he had not

119

enjoyed the Führer's protection! And by God, how he had worked to ensure he kept that protection. Morning, noon and night, he had been at 'A H's' side, always trying to sense the Führer's mood before the latter knew it himself, taking note of his slightest whim, playing the dictator's foolish vegetarian game when he dearly loved meat, forced to hide his sausages and schnaps, repressing his powerful sexual urge when he had always known that no woman could resist him. Now at last it was all over. He could be his own man again. He raised the bottle of schnaps and toasted himself silently in the mirror, some of the liquid running down his pugnacious boxer's jaw.

Soon he would have to make a break. Of course he didn't trust them. Who would? He had fought them all his adult life. He had gone to prison for helping to murder one of them a long time before. Yet they needed him. Soon he would be the only one left who could help them achieve their political aims. Afterwards they would get rid of him; he realized that already. But there would be compensations: the money, the drink, the food, the women – and the new life on another continent.

While the bunker shook under fresh Russian artillery fire, as if the whole world was going to end soon, Bormann rose and replaced what was left of the sausage in its hiding place in the cupboard. He buttoned up his jacket. The time had come to witness Hitler's Last Will and Testament. It was nearly all over. Soon he would be free of that madman at last.

The railway bridge was blocked with dead bodies. On the cobbled, shell-holed road, there were pools of fresh blood everywhere. The girl gulped and hesitated. Higgins pushed her. She staggered forward, stepping over a child's decapitated body.

They started to skirt the zoo. A lone elephant paced up and down in the elephant house. Mallory could count its ribs. As they passed, it raised his trunk hopefully, but when

120

no food was profferred, the beast let it drop in resignation. A dead hippopotamus floated on its back in its pool, its stomach ripped open so that its enormous intestines protruded disgustingly. Hastily, Ilona Graefin von Prittwitz turned her blonde head.

In front of the monkey house two dead SS men lay sprawled in the dirt next to a shattered machine-gun, but their comrades did not seem to notice. Children that they were, they were completely taken up with the remaining chimps. Swiftly the three men and their prisoner went by them.

Another cage. A dead SS man and a dead gorilla locked together in an embrace of death as if they were lovers. 'My Christ,' Higgins whispered in awe, 'this place'd put the sodding years on yer!'

Mallory stepped over a dead zebra and said, 'Not much longer. If our people are correct, the Swede lives in that street over there.'

'What street?' Piludski asked with an attempt at humour, staring at the ruins, in which it seemed that it would be impossible to live.

At the top of the wrecked street an ancient nag, pulling an equally ancient cart with wooden wheels, had collapsed and in spite of the weak protests of its owner, women had appeared as if from nowhere and were already tearing huge chunks from the piteously whinnying horse while it still lived.

'Pigs!' the girl said and looked away once again.

Mallory flashed her a look. She wasn't so hard after all, he told himself. Then he concentrated on finding their contact.

The Swede was big, old and very nervous. 'Why the woman?' he demanded in heavily accented English. 'Nobody said anything about the woman. They said there would be only three of you.' He ran a shaking old hand, covered with liver spots, around his mouth.

'Well, you can see there are four of us now,' Mallory snapped, angry with the old man for being such an obvious coward. 'Let us in.'

Higgins sneered. 'Let us in what?' He looked at the sole remaining wall of the bomb-shattered building, which bore the bullet-pocked legend: *Wennerstroem K. G. Swed. Prazisionsgeraete.*

'The cellar is all right,' the Swede said.

They filed after him through the hole in the wall of his one-time factory and clattered down the steps into the dark cellar.

'Safest place in Berlin these days,' the Swede panted and clicked on the light switch.

The place was bare, save for a wooden chair, an iron cot and a tin bath filled with water. 'These days you never know when the water supply is going to give out,' the Swede continued. Then he caught the girl's look as she gazed at the photos of nude women in black stockings and high heels which decorated the walls. 'My wife died two years ago,' he explained. 'And since the bombing I've been afraid to go out to the ladies of the street.' He giggled nervously, showing a mouthful of gold teeth. 'At my age, the pictures are better.'

They arranged themselves on the bed and one chair before Mallory asked: 'Well, what is the situation?'

By way of an answer, the Swede rose and pulled back the curtain in the corner to reveal a short-wave transmitter. 'London tells me he has sent one more message from the bunker by means of the Enigma.'

Piludski looked from the old Swede to Mallory and said: 'Enigma, bunker, what gives? Hell, Mike, how can London know what's going on before the people on the spot do?'

Mallory ignored the American's questions. The Swede had shown that he was not only a coward and careless; he was a damned fool, too, spilling the beans like that. 'And what did he say?' he snapped icily.

'He asked for directions.'

'And?'

'He has to wait till they've captured the Reichstag.'

'Then?'

'He is to make his way out of the bunker – they're leaving the choice of street to him. It could be the Hermann Goering Strasse or the Wilhelmstrasse. At all events, he'll pass across the place where the Charlottenburger Chaussee meets the Unter den Linden and go up the continuation of the Hermann Goering Strasse.'

Mallory listened carefully, memorizing the details, knowing that it would be too dangerous to visit the old Swede again.

'Did London have any further orders for me?' he asked finally.

'Only something like "good hunting". Could that be correct?' He looked at Mallory.

The Englishman nodded. '*Good hunting*', he cursed to himself. How typical of C! Did he think this was his beloved Gloucestershire and the damned Duke of Beaufort's hunt with their fancy blue riding coats?

The Swede sat down abruptly, hands hanging between his knees. 'My God,' he moaned, 'I'll be glad when this whole business is over. If I hadn't have believed so much in the allied cause I would never have got into it in the first place. It wasn't the money, believe me. . . .'

'Now Mike,' Piludski said firmly, ignoring the old man, 'what the hell is this all about? We've been risking our necks behind the Kraut lines for over a week now. We've got a right to know why.'

'Yer sir,' Higgins joined in, his face hard. 'Fair's fair. What was that old boy in London woffling on about? Who the sodding hell is Big Six and what has he got to do with our being here?'

Mallory looked at the girl, knowing that she would have to die now – she would know too much. He drew a deep breath. 'Big Six –' A tremendous roar drowned his words.

123

The cellar trembled violently like a ship at sea caught by a sudden tempest. The girl caught hold of Higgins to prevent herself from being thrown to the floor. The old Swede's face went pale.

'What is it?' Mallory rapped.

'We've got to get out of here,' the Swede quavered. 'That's the Reds attacking the Reichstag. The S S won't be able to hold them this time and they'll start pulling back this way. There'll be house-to-house fighting.' He looked desperately at Mallory. 'We must leave now. I don't want to die. Please, sir, let us not wait any longer. *Let us go!*' He held up his clasped hands in the classic gesture of supplication. *'Please!'*

Hastily Mallory considered. He had come to the Swede to get rid of the woman; now it seemed he was going to be burdened not only with her, but the terrified Swede as well. But where were they to go?

The girl seemed to read his mind. Flashing a contemptuous look at the now weeping Swede, she said, 'Well my dear English spy, there is nothing for it, is there, but to go back.'

'Go back where?'

'To the Villa Irma.'

Captain Noystroev called Sergeants Egorov and Kantariya across to him. They ducked low to escape the lead flying everywhere and doubled over to where he crouched next to Hertz. 'All right, you two heroes,' he cried above the snap-and-crackle of small arms, 'take it.' He thrust the red banner in Egorov's dirty hands. 'We're going up now.'

'On to the roof?'

Captain Noystroev nodded. At his side the little field telephone buzzed. Hurriedly he picked it up. It was Antonov. He wanted to know what the situation in the Reichstag was; it was shrouded with smoke from the blaze which the S S had started in the yard so that from outside no one could make out what was happening.

124

'I haven't got any water left, Comrade Colonel', Noystroev informed him, 'and not much ammo.'

'Hold on, whatever happens. I'll send you men with all you need.'

'We will, Comrade Colonel. We're going to have a go at planting the flag on the roof now.'

'Excellent – and look after Comrade Hertz. Your head depends upon it.'

Noystroev laughed grimly. 'At the present moment, my head isn't worth very much. The Fritzes have been trying to knock it off all morning.' He put the phone down and looked at Hertz. Somehow the little Yid seemed to have changed since the first time he had met him; there was a new thoughtful look in his dark eyes. Then he dismissed the mysterious Comrade Hertz and concentrated on the task in hand. 'You, you and you,' he cried across to the three N C Os crouched in the smoking rubble of the huge room, which looked as if it might have once been an antechamber, 'get your squads ready. We're going up. You're to protect the flag-bearers.'

'Yes, Comrade Captain.' Hurriedly the soldiers started shedding their packs, slipping fresh grenades into their belts, and draping belts of extra ammunition across their shoulders.

Noystroev pulled out his pistol. 'Comrade Hertz,' he said, not looking at the Jew, being too occupied with checking his magazine, 'just stay with the rest here. Keep your turnip down and you won't get hurt. Now you're on your own. When you see me again, I'll either be dead or I'll be on the roof of this damned place with the flag.' He clicked the safety off and rose to his feet. 'Follow me, comrades!' he roared and started forward, firing as he went, followed by the soldiers, stumbling and falling on the debris-littered floor as the S S, barricaded in at the far end of the great echoing room, turned their machine-gun on them.

Hertz kept his turnip down, but in spite of his fear, his mind was still concerned with that overwhelming question:

125

would he or wouldn't he? Soon, very soon now, he must make his decision.

His lips moving as he read the text, Bormann scanned Hitler's Last Will and Testament, while behind him Hitler's surgeon, Dr Stumpfegger, prepared to kill Hitler's dogs; even they should not fall into Russian hands.

More than thirty years have passed since I made my modest contribution as a volunteer in the First World War which the Reich was then forced to fight. In these three decades, love and loyalty to my people alone have guided me in all my thoughts, my actions and life.

Behind him, Blondi, Hitler's alsatian bitch, growled threateningly as Stumpfegger tried to force open her jaws to insert the phial of cyanide.

Bormann read on,

They gave me power to make the most difficult decisions which have ever confronted mortal man. ... It is untrue that I or anyone else in Germany wanted war in 1939. It was wanted and provoked exclusively by those international statesmen who were either of Jewish origin or worked for Jewish interests.

Bormann told himself that the statement was absurd – who cared now anyway – but the Führer was right about the Jews; they were behind everything. He had always known that.

Behind him the dog yelped and flopped to the ground. Stumpfegger nodded to the S S man with him. He drew his pistol and shot first one and then the other of Blondi's new puppies.

Bormann read on:

My reasonable proposition for the solution of the German-Polish problem was rejected only because the mob who were in power in England insisted on war, partly for commercial reasons, partly because they were influenced by the propaganda organized by international Jewry. After six years of war, which in spite of its reverses, will one day go down

126

in history as the most glorious and heroic manifestation of a nation's struggle for existence, I cannot forsake the city which is the capital of this state.

Bormann's eyes flew over the last few sentences, which were the most important for him.

But I shall not fall into the hands of the enemy who needs a new spectacle exhibited by the Jews to divert the hysterical masses. . . . I have decided to choose death voluntarily at the moment when I consider my position as Führer and Chancellor itself can no longer be maintained.

Bormann smiled softly. It was all he needed to know. He took out his fountain pen and signed his name as witness with a flourish. 'Here,' he said to Fräulein Junge, 'I've signed.'

He walked out past the dead dogs, lying stiffly in the corner. Hitler was wandering down the dark corridor like a ghost from the past, unnoticed by the drunken S S men, who were fondling the breasts of the *Blitzmädchen* and secretaries unashamedly.

Bormann watched him go. 'A shadow from an epoch that is dying' he told himself, then turning he went to his room to begin making his own preparations.

Hitler had said his last good-byes. Now, together with his new wife, Eva, he walked into their bedroom. She slumped down on the bed, her face ashen and stained with tears. Hitler didn't look at her. Instead he took out two Walther pistols from the drawer and then the poison phials which Stumpfegger had distributed to everyone in the bunker who felt they might need them.

Eva Hitler looked at her new husband. He answered her unspoken question with a shake of his head. 'No good, *Tschapperl*. They are already in the Reichstag, I know. For all I know, they might be outside the door to the bunker at this very moment. There is no other way out.'

'No hope?'

'No hope at all.' He handed her a phial of poison. 'Between the teeth – crunch it between the teeth.'

Still she hesitated.

'Now,' Hitler commanded with a trace of his old authority.

She closed her eyes and bit hard. Suddenly the room was flooded with the bitter aroma of almonds. Eva Hitler screamed as the pain exploded in her stomach. She tried to rise, but fell back, groaning piteously, one arm thrown out over the side of the couch.

Hitler turned away, and listened to her dying. Finally she was silent. Still he didn't look at his dead wife. Instead he sat at the little table, pistol in his hand. In front of him on the console there was a faded picture of his mother as an eighteeen-year-old. He looked at it without interest. He put the Walther in his mouth and pulled the trigger. He pitched forward dead, sending a flower vase flying. It hit Eva's dead body and soaked her dress with stale water.

Bormann heard the single shot. For a moment his nerve failed him. He had waited so long for this moment, but now that it was here, he didn't want to have to set the wheels in motion; for a brief instant he was frightened of what was to come. Then Hitler's adjutant, Guensche, grabbed him by the arm. 'It's the Führer!' he exclaimed.

Together they broke into Hitler's room.

Guensche staggered out again and was accosted by Hitler's chauffeur, Kempka, who was dirty and angry. 'For God's sake, Otto,' he cried to Guensche, 'what's going on? You must be crazy to send men to certain death just for two hundred litres of petrol. We haven't got any vehicles anyway.'

Guensche slammed the outer door closed so that no one in the bunker could hear. 'The Chief's dead,' he said in a hushed voice.

'Heart attack?'

Guensche couldn't speak for a moment. He pointed a

forefinger like the barrel of a pistol and put it in his mouth.

'My God! And where's Eva?' Kempka cried.

'She's with him,' Guensche managed to stammer.

A little while later Dr Stumpfegger appeared carrying Hitler's body wrapped in a brown army blanket. Hitler's face was half covered, his left arm hung down limply. Behind Stumpfegger, Bormann carried out Eva Hitler.

The sight of the dead woman in Bormann's arms was too much for Kempka. The chauffeur knew just how much she had hated Bormann on account of his brutal womanizing.

'Not a step further!' he cried warningly, dropping his hand to his pistol holster. 'I'll carry Eva.'

Bormann shrugged. 'As you wish, Kempka.' He transferred his burden to the other man. Kempka felt the wetness of the dress and thought poor Eva was bleeding. He grimaced and started to mount the four flights of stairs that led to the garden above. Once he nearly dropped her.

'Watch it, you clumsy fool,' Bormann snarled.

Kempka bit his lip to prevent himself retorting angrily. He knew Bormann and Goebbels were the two most powerful men in Germany now.

'The Ivans are giving us another pasting!' one of the tense young SS men crouched at the entrance to the bunker cried and ducked as a salvo of Russian shells slammed down, making the earth quiver under their feet.

The funeral party said nothing. Ducking, Kempka followed the others to deposit Eva next to the Führer in a shallow depression next to a large cement mixer.

Hastily Kempka and some of the SS men began to pour petrol over the two bodies, while the shells continued to rain down. Fist-sized red-hot pieces of shrapnel hissed everywhere. Once the blast turned Hitler's head and for one awful moment, Kempka thought his old chief might still be alive.

Finally the bodies were well soaked with fuel. From the

cover of the bunker's entrance, Bormann cried, 'Enough ... enough! Set them alight now!'

'Shall we use a grenade?' Guensche cried above the noise of the barrage.

'My God, not that! Here!' he picked up a rag that was lying on the ground, and swiftly doused it with petrol. 'Have you got matches?'

Guensche shook his head. 'I don't smoke.'

'Matches!' Kempka called to Bormann.

Crouched low, Bormann ran over, handed the chauffeur the matches and bolted for safety once more.

The chauffeur set light to the rag. Once it was burning well, he gave it to Guensche; he just couldn't carry out the awful task himself.

The adjutant ran to the petrol-soaked depression with it and dropped it on the bodies. The petrol exploded instantly, and a boiling ball of angry red fire mushroomed above the bodies. Against the background of the dying city, it was but a small fire. Yet to the men watching, who had served the dead dictator, it was the most horrifying. Hypnotized they watched as the flames began to consume the bodies, making them writhe and twist, as if they were resisting this final sacrifice. Thus engrossed, the watchers did not notice that Bormann was gone. He was free at last.

2

'All right, Mike,' Piludski said firmly, 'now you tell us.'

'Yer, own up Major,' Higgins chimed in, taking a drink from another bottle of schnaps he had found in the cellars of Villa Irma.

Mallory frowned. Upstairs the Swede was guarding the girl, if one could call it that; she was out of the way, but she already knew too much about their mission. Now, it was his two companions. 'All right,' he said grimly. 'Be it on your own heads. I would have had to tell you tomorrow anyway.' He licked his lips and Higgins handed him the bottle. Wordlessly he accepted it and took a deep drink.

Outside the roar of the Russian guns had died away. It looked as if the Reichstag had been captured by the Red Army.

'It's a long story,' he began.

'We've got plenty of time, Mike,' Piludski said and settled back on the overstuffed red plush sofa, while Mallory handed the bottle to Higgins.

Mallory remembered the day C had told him what their mission was to be. Fictional spymasters are supposed to reveal the ultimate secret in the confines of a panelled study with the fire casting weird shadows on the walls, a glass of brandy in hand. But it hadn't been like that at all. C had explained his task to him at the bar of his club, White's, with some chinless wonder of an upper-class aide coming up and asking every now and again: 'I say, sir, are you all right for whisky?' and hearty middle-aged men in and out of uniform brushing by and exchanging remarks about 'nags' and 'gallopers' with the grey-faced spymaster.

131

C had begun in that Old Etonian manner of his without any kind of drama, not even attempting to lower his voice. 'Of course, we had agreed right from the start that the Bolshies are out to dominate Europe now.'

Mallory had said nothing, though the information was startling enough.

'Yes, the P M and most of the people at the top have known that since late '43 when Tito began to get uppity in Jugland. Last year, Winnie's fears were confirmed when he saw what a – er – tough time de Gaulle had with the Frog C P. And of course, last November we had to take an armoured division out of the line and send it back to Brussels when the Belgie Bolshies refused to be disarmed.'

Mallory had taken a sip of his drink, realizing that although he had been engaged in the secret war for six years now he had no concept of the real battle being fought in the shadows on the Continent.

'Italy and Greece are still an awuful mess, of course,' C droned on. 'The Bolshies are making an all-out effort to take over power there, but I think our people will be able to cope.' C had paused and nodded to a red-faced cavalry brigadier. 'Hello, Jumbo. How's the hunter?' he had asked, as if the information was of great importance to him, before continuing. 'But naturally those countries are insignificant compared with Germany. That country dominates Central Europe. Privately I've always maintained that this is the German century, but I wouldn't say that to the chaps at the F O.'

An elderly waiter in a frock-coat dropped a water jug, which shattered on the floor. There was a burst of cheering from the middle-aged men at the bar and suddenly Mallory had realized just how infantile the men who ruled England were. Did not people maintain that even Churchill played with rubber boats in his bath?

'Germany – what is going to happen there, once the present show is over, Mallory, that is the big problem at the top now. I'll let you into a secret.' He leaned forward.

132

'Churchill wants a summary execution of all the German leaders who fall into our hands. Put 'em against the wall and shoot 'em. And that's that.' C had shaken his grey head. 'Not on, of course. The great British public wouldn't buy it and naturally our holier-than-thou American cousins would be scandalized. They want a big show trial. Fair and democratic and all that piffle, although everyone knows the Nazi bosses are as guilty as hell. So a trial there will be – and with what result?' He had answered his own question. 'I'll tell you, Mallory. We'll alienate a large number of Jerries. They'll reason quite correctly that the victors are paying off old scores at the expense of the vanquished. Their mood – and remember there must be at least ten million Nazi Party members by now – will be anti-western allies.'

'You say the western allies, sir?' Mallory had interjected, completely confused by now, wondering what the purpose of the little lecture really was.

'Yes, because although the Bolshies'll go along with the trial, the Americans will make the running and ourselves too. The Bolshies will keep – what do the Yanks say? – a low profile. No, the Bolshies are not going to be as foolish as we and the Americans.' He lowered his voice for the first time since he had entered the club and Mallory had had the feeling that now finally he was coming to the reason for the proposed mission. 'Indeed we have completely reliable information that as soon as the fighting's over, the Bolshies are going to offer the Old Hun an olive branch. We know they've got a tame Hun government ready and waiting in the wings in Russia – made up of Communist exiles, who are completely in Stalin's power. We know, too, that in spite of twelve years of Nazi rule, there are flourishing Bolshie cells all over Germany. Our people in the Intelligence Corps have spotted them all over the Rhineland, Aachen, Cologne, Mainz. After all, there were six million Hun Communists in 1933.'

'But sir,' Mallory had protested, 'the Germans have been

133

fighting the Russians since 1941. I can hardly see the Germans easily subscribing to the Communist cause.'

'Don't you believe it, Mallory. Not much difference between the Nazis and the Bolshies to my way of thinking – just a differently coloured flag. Only the other day the P M said to me about the Huns, "They're either at your throat or at your feet." *Ach, es wohnen zwei Seelen wohnen in meiner Brust* * and all that rot,' C had misquoted Goethe in an atrocious German accent and then surprisingly had blushed, as if he were a little ashamed of his own audacity at displaying any intellectual knowledge. 'The Old Hun wavers a lot. Hot one day, cold the other, and they do as they are told.'

'I see what you mean, sir.'

'Thought you would. Now what if the Bolshies had a real trump card up their sleeve? What if, when they set up this puppet government of theirs in their zone of occupation, they include in it a leading Nazi?' He had caught the look of surprise on Mallory's face. 'Yes, I caught you out there, didn't I?'

'But who could they find who is not hopelessly compromised, one they would not be forced to put on trial with the other leading Nazis?'

'A chap who has had nothing to do with those dreadful concentration camps of theirs, nothing to do with the prosecution of the war or all that nasty business with the Hebrews. But one who is known to every Party member throughout Germany, because he was the man who ran the Party machine. What effect do you think, Mallory, that would have, eh?'

'It would probably rally all those Nazis to them.'

'Exactly. Then, in a year or so when we introduce free elections into our zones of occupation, which we are committed to do on account of this absurd democracy thing, which way do you think the whole of Germany will vote? I'll tell you. *Bolshie!* Then the Bolshies won't be indulging

* Two souls dwell in my breast.

134

in all that moralizing American nonsense. You know: non-fraternization with the Huns, denazification and all the rest? They'll show themselves as the Hun's chum, prepared to kiss and make up.' C had looked suddenly very grim, as if he had become aware for the very first time of the full impact of his own words. 'If Germany goes Red, Mallory, it won't be long before France follows and probably Belgium too. And then what? It will be summer 1940 all over again with the Bolshies on the Channel coast instead of the Huns, and we will have fought this whole damned show for nothing.' He had drained his whisky in one gulp and holding up his hand, immediately ordered another one from his chinless aide.

'And we can't fight the Bolshies this time. The country's worn out. We are broke, over-extended, our people war-weary. And we can't rely upon the Americans. They'll be back home, making their usual post-war isolationist noises. Anyway, that innocent rogue Roosevelt – thank God he's passed away – wanted to get rid of the British Empire, and there are a lot in power in Washington who think the same way as he did.' C had pulled himself together visibly, but his hand had shaken a little as he had accepted the fresh glass of whisky. 'No, we can't allow it to happen. We must nip the Bolshie plot in the bud.'

Mallory had waited expectantly.

'So what are we going to do, Mallory? We're going to do what we did in '41. Then, I made a decision to have a man killed in this very club. You know to whom I'm referring?'

'You mean Heydrich, the German Protector in Czechoslovakia?'

'Exactly. I had nothing personal against the chap.' C's grey face had taken on something slightly resembling a smile for a moment. 'They tell me that he ran the German S D * rather like I do my own organization. Green ink, the light outside the office door and all the rest of my – · er – little peculiarities. But the man was too good an ad-

* The secret service of the S S.

ministrator and I needed a real Czech resistance movement, which would only result from the reprisals the Huns
would carry out after Heydrich's death. Of course, I didn't
realize that there would be the Lidice Massacre.'

C had frowned at his glass and the thought suddenly
flashed through Mallory's head that if the Nazis had won
the war, C would probably have stood trial as a war
criminal.

'Well, that's all water under the bridge. Now, Mallory,
I'm prepared to do the same thing once again.'

'And who is the Nazi in question, sir?' Mallory had
heard himself asking.

'The one we code name Big Six.'

That conversation had taken place only two weeks before, yet it seemed to have been in another age: the difference between the shabby upper-class London club and
bomb-shattered Berlin was too great.

'But who is Big Six?' both Piludski and Higgins asked.

Mallory frowned.

'Well, come on, Mike!' Piludski asked harshly. 'Don't
play so goddam hard to get!'

Wearily Mallory gave away the last secret. 'Big Six is . . .
is Martin Bormann. . . .'

3

The S S came just after midnight.

Like the rapacious grey wolves they were, they came slinking through gardens, checking the houses, moving on by hand signals from their N C Os. Occasionally one of them would whisper something and then the language he spoke was French. For these desperate men in the uniform of the feared German S S were the hard-bitten veterans of the Charlemagne, the French Volunteer S S Division.

Lured from their native France by the promise of adventure, loot, or the call of the 'great crusade against the Bolshevik Beast', they had rallied to the German flag to fight for three long years in Russia. Now, when Nazi Germany's fate was sealed and their comrades of the Germanic S S had already begun to fling away their weapons and surrender to the victorious Ivans, they still fought on. There was no alternative for these renegade Frenchmen. There was no way back for them; no easy way out. A return to France meant the firing squad for them. Bitter, brutalized, without hope, motivated only by a burning hatred, the Frenchmen of S S Division Charlemagne would fight to the end here in Berlin.

Skilfully they worked their way up the street like the veterans they were, already aware that the Ivans had started infiltrating the abandoned suburb; they were taking no chances. One lived longer that way.

Their leader, Monseigneur Comte Mayel de Lupe, pointed his machine pistol towards the Villa Irma, finger on the trigger, ready to fire instantly. The 'spiritual adviser'

137

of the Charlemagne Division had long been more accustomed to bullets than the Bible.

A handful of his young fanatics stole from the shadows and started working their way along the garden wall towards the silent, seemingly abandoned house, whatever noise their heavy jackboots made on the broken glass of the greenhouse drowned by the Russian guns.

Slowly, very slowly, the leading S S man tried the door handle, while his comrades tensed at his side, grenades and rifles at the ready.

The door was locked. By means of a dumb show, the soldier made it clear to the watching priest that they couldn't get in. De Lupe nodded his understanding and with the iron butt of his Schmeisser indicated that they should break it down. It was the sound of rifle butts beating on the door panels which aroused Mallory. Swiftly, his heart pounding painfully, pulling on his boots as he did so, he raced to the upstairs window and looked out.

Down below, clearly outlined in the moonlight, he saw the garden was full of soldiers, and he didn't need to be told twice what the silver skull and crossbones on their peaked caps indicated. 'S S,' he whispered urgently, grabbing Piludski's shoulder and shaking it roughly. 'For Chrissake, Paddy, get up! The place is lousy with S S outside!'

'*What!*' Piludski sprang out of bed, his hand already on his pistol.

Later Mallory remembered that his brawny muscular legs bore no gunshot scars, but that was later. 'Watch 'em, I'll get the others up.'

'Beat it, Mike.' Piludski said grimly, clicking off his safety catch and staring at the grey figures below, lips moving silently as he counted them.

Hurriedly Mallory collected the group together, the Swede trembling at every limb, as if he were afflicted by a severe fever. He looked at the girl, fully dressed save for her shoes. 'Cellars?' he demanded.

138

'Of course. Every German house has one. But you're out of luck, Englishman.'

'What do you mean?' Mallory rapped, listening to the blows of the rifle butts below. A couple more minutes and the S S would be inside.

'Full of rubble. Land mine went off next door and broke down the inner wall. You couldn't escape that way.'

'Blast and damn!' Mallory cursed.

'Oh, what are we going to do, what are we going to do?' the Swede wailed, tears streaming down his lined face.

'Shut up, you silly old fart,' Higgins snapped. 'Listen, sir, what about the roof? With a bit of luck we can cross to the house next door and be off before they notice we've gone. After all, they don't know we're here – yet.'

Mallory seized upon the suggestion. 'Good man, Higgins,' he cried.

'Not just a pretty face, sir,' Higgins began, but Mallory was no longer listening.

'All right,' he ordered, 'Higgins, you go first with the girl. I'll take the old man. Paddy, you bring up the rear.'

'Roger, Mike.'

Swiftly they ran to the front of the house, away from the S S below. Mallory thrust open the boarded-up window. The street below was deserted. He nodded his approval and stepped on to the little balcony, littered with the droppings of many generations of pigeons. The holed roof was about twelve foot above his head. He frowned. Although there were handholds enough in the peeling stucco front, they wouldn't be sufficient for the Swede. Then he spotted the iron-framed radio aerial cable. The clasps holding it to the wall as it ran up to the tiles looked rusty, but there. was no time to worry about that. Already the S S were inside the house. He could hear the noise of their jackboots on the tiled floor. 'All right, Higgins and you, Fräulein, up that aerial cable. And Fräulein, one word out of you –'

'And you're a very dead bint,' Higgins completed the threat for him. 'Now move yer arse.' Roughly he pushed the reluctant girl forward and then when she had seized a hold, placed his hands on her buttocks, digging his fingers deep into the soft flesh, and heaved her upwards.

Below, the first cautious S S man, weapon at the ready, was beginning to mount the stairs which led to the bedrooms. Hastily, Mallory pushed the Swede towards the aerial. The old man's teeth were chattering audibly and he kept muttering something about 'no head for heights'.

Mallory had no time for the Swede's fears. 'Get going or I'll kill you myself,' he hissed in German. 'Now get climbing, old man!'

Then, it was his own turn and a moment later that of the American. Directly below them they could hear the S S men stamping through the bedrooms and Mallory was under no illusion that it would take them very long to discover that the house had been vacated only a few moments before: the still warm fire in the oven below and the cigarette ends in the ashtrays would tell them that. The next question they would ask themselves would be: why should loyal Germans flee from their own troops? 'Come on,' he whispered urgently. 'And for God's sake make as little noise as possible.'

In spite of the steep slope of the roof, it proved quite easy to cross. There were fire-hooks running the whole length, and the gaps in the tiles, caused by the bombing, made useful handholds. Hardly daring to breathe, realizing that it only took someone in the garden to look up and they would be discovered, they edged their way forward. Down below, someone was shouting orders in what sounded like French to Mallory. But he ignored the fact, concentrating on keeping the shaking Swede moving. In front of him, Higgins kept touching the girl's buttocks, whether to keep her moving or because he enjoyed this opportunity of feeling her, Mallory didn't know.

They came to a brick wall and stopped. On the other side, Mallory guessed the roof was much lower. It was a turn-of-the-century decorative feature which the long-dead

140

architect could well have dispensed with. 'Move it, Higgins,' he hissed. 'Let me go first.'

'With pleasure, sir,' the other man answered, his hand pressing the girl's shapely knee, his eyes gleaming excitedly in spite of the danger.

With a soft grunt, Mallory hauled himself to the top of the wall and lay there full length, making the lowest possible silhouette. He peered down. He had been right. There was a drop of eight or nine feet. There would be no trouble about Piludski and Higgins making it. But could the Swede and the girl do it without making a hell of a noise and alerting the S S?

Mallory decided what he had to do. 'Listen,' he whispered. 'Get the old man up here and then the girl. They are to crawl down over my body.'

Without waiting to see if the other two were complying with his orders, Mallory swung himself over the edge and hanging there thus, felt the surface of the top to find the best hold. He found it and hissed, 'Okay, now – the Swede.'

Mallory gritted his teeth and took the strain. The Swede looked frail, but at that particular moment he seemed to weigh a ton. Mallory tensed his muscles, his fingers biting deep into the holds. He groaned with pain, as the Swede clambered down his outstretched body, taking what appeared to be an interminable time. And then the weight was gone and he was gulping in great gasps of air. He gave himself one moment only. It wouldn't be long now before the S S started to investigate the roof. 'The girl,' he gasped. 'Now!'

The two of them lowered the girl on to his shoulders. His nostrils caught a faint whiff of her perfume. As quickly as she could she lowered herself further down. He could feel her heart beating like a trip-hammer against his back. A nail broke. A searing almost unbearable pain shot through his hand. He bit his teeth into his clenched lips in order to prevent himself from screaming out loud. Somehow she must have sensed what had happened for, as she prepared herself to drop into the Swede's outstretched arms, she whispered, 'sorry', and even in that tear-blurred pain, he knew that she meant it genuinely. A moment later, she had dropped and that burning pain was removed from his hands. He dropped to the roof, his muscles trembling uncontrollably, to be joined by Higgins and Piludski, pistols at the ready.

Piludski took charge. 'You bring up the rear, Mike,' he hissed.

Mallory did not trust himself to speak. Nursing his injured hand, he nodded.

Piludski led them to the edge of the roof. The gap between the roof of Villa Irma and the next house was less than a yard. They crossed it without difficulty, though Piludski had to order the trembling Swede sternly not to look down. Cautiously they crawled the length of the next roof. In the Villa Irma, the S S were already rummaging around in the upper floor; the fugitives could hear them quite clearly. 'All right,' Piludski commanded as they came to the edge of the roof, 'stop here.'

Bracing his foot against the steel fire-hook at the edge of the slates, he leaned over. It was just as he had suspected. There was a balcony directly beneath him and it was only a drop of six feet or more. Swiftly he surveyed the balcony. No flower pots or boxes which they might upset and alarm the S S. A nice neat jump right into the centre of the balcony and then the two Englishmen could hand the girl and the Swede down. Thereafter, they could repeat the operation with the next balcony and the next, which overlooked the front garden.

They negotiated the first balcony without difficulty, although again the Swede had to be threatened to make him edge fearfully over the roof. It was the same with the second one. But as they started to lower themselves from the last balcony into the littered front garden, Higgins froze abruptly; hanging from the rail, he whispered urgently up to Piludski, *'Jerries – there!'*

142

Piludski craned his head round the wall. Two dark shapes stood a matter of twenty yards away, hands cupped around the glowing red tips of their cigarettes, their coal-scuttle helmets clearly identifying them as German. Their escape route was barred!

'*Shit!*' Piludski cursed angrily. 'Mike, you watch the girl – see that she doesn't shout out.'

'Right,' Mallory answered, though somehow he had a strange feeling that the German girl was no longer their – or perhaps better – *his* enemy. 'What are you going to do?'

'Get ready to make a bolt for it with the others. I'm going to tackle the Krauts.'

Before Mallory could stop him, he had swung himself over the railing with the practised ease of the trained athlete he had once been. Dropping almost noiselessly to the ground, he stole forward in the direction of the unsuspecting Germans. Mallory wasted no further time. Swiftly he lowered the girl to the waiting Higgins and then the Swede.

Sticking to the shadows, grateful for the faint rumble of the ever-present barrage which drowned any slight noise he might make, Piludski advanced to his target, aware that he must knock the Krauts out with his bare hands, if he didn't want all hell let loose.

Piludski was almost within striking distance when the smaller of the two S S heard him. He started to turn round, fumbling with the strap of his machine pistol. Piludski dived forward. He grabbed the smaller German's helmet and pulled hard. The man's chinstrap slipped under his adam's apple. His cry of alarm died instantly in a great gasp. Holding on grimly, while the smaller German's hands clawed at his throat in an attempt to remove that terrible noose, Piludski lashed out with his right boot.

The boot caught the other German between the legs. He went down, howling in agony, writhing back and forth on the cobbles, hands clutched to his ruined crotch. Piludski knew he had messed it up. The writhing German was

143

making one hell of a racket. He gave one final savage heave, and the German went limp in his arms. He let him drop to the ground with a clatter. There was no use trying to hide their presence now. Already cries of alarm were coming from the Villa Irma and someone was shouting in French, '*Sale con, allez-allez vite!*'

'Come on,' he yelled to the others in the garden. 'Let's beat it! Move it fellers, for Chrissake!'

A wild salvo of m.p. fire cut the air. It lent speed to their feet. Pushing the Swede in front of him, Piludski brought up the rear, turning twice to pump a shot at the S S men running out of the villa. A soldier screamed, dropped his rifle and stood there, bent-kneed, for what seemed a long time before he slammed down to the cobbles.

Suddenly, the Swede yelped with pain and dropped to one knee, almost causing Piludski to fall over him. 'I've been hit!' he cried fearfully, as if something like this midnight chase could never be happening to him, the respectable importer of Swedish precision tools. 'In the knee!'

'Dump him!' Higgins called over his shoulder.

'He knows too much,' Piludski yelled, firing again at the S S and halting them in the doorway.

With his free hand, he hauled the moaning Swede to his feet. 'He can still walk,' he cried, ducking automatically as a burst of machine pistol bullets sawed the air inches away from his head. 'You fellers go on. Rendezvous at the zoo. . . . *Now fuck off!*' Piludski screamed at them in sudden fury.

And then the rest of them were running frantically for the cover of the smoke-shrouded rabbit-warren of ruins up ahead. Behind them as they disappeared into the darkness, they could hear the steady bark of Piludski's pistol. After that there was nothing but a loud echoing silence. . . .

It was not until about seven in the evening that an exhausted Kempka and Guensche had staggered back into the bunker, the long task of cremation finally completed.

In the conference room there was bedlam. Krebs and an S S general were openly weeping. A *Wehrmacht* colonel was drinking cognac straight from the bottle and occasionally fondling, almost absent-mindedly, the naked right breast of one of Bormann's *Blitzmädchen*.

All of them, it seemed to Bormann, leaning against the wall, at last able to eat his beloved sausage without fear, were lost without Hitler. But he made no comment. They could play their absurd little games a while longer.

In the end, Goebbels had pulled himself together, although outside in the corridor his wife Magda was sobbing hysterically once more and telling everyone that she didn't want to poison her children, but there was no other way out to save them from the 'Russian sub-humans'. He had called the conference to order and they had begun to set the seal on the '1000 Year Reich', which had lasted exactly twelve years, four months and twenty-two days.

A message was dispatched, which Bormann and Goebbels formulated jointly, to great Admiral Doenitz, the ice-cold sailor who was running what was left of unoccupied Germany in the West. It read:

Führer deceased yesterday at 3.30 p.m. Testament of April 29th appoints you Reichpresident. Minister Goebbels Chancellor. Reichsleiter Bormann Party Minister. . . . Reichsminister Bormann will try to get to you today to orient you on the situation. The form and time of announcement to the troops and public are left to you.
Confirm receipt.

Goebbels, Bormann.

Bormann was pleased with the formulation. It would provide him with the necessary cover until the Reds decided to announce where he really was. In the chaotic conditions presently pertaining in Berlin, everyone in Germany would think he had been killed attempting to break to Doenitz, located in the North German town of Flensburg.

He looked at Goebbels and the rest. Drunk or tearful

like the new 'Chancellor of the Greater German Reich', they appeared to him like figures from another world. Completely calm, now that his own future was settled, he listened in silence to Goebbels' arguments on what should be done next. They had played their role; now it was the turn of the new men.

Some of the younger officers had urged him to make an attempt at break-out. They had their escape route worked out completely. 'Along the Tiergarten, past the zoo, Kurfurstendamm – Adolf Hitler Platz, Stadium, the Pichelsdorf bridges – one of them at least must still be standing and then across the lake by paddle-boat through the Russian lines at Wannsee.' They even knew of electrically powered boats which were completely silent.

For a while a bored Bormann had thought that Goebbels might be convinced to make an attempt, but in the end Goebbels held up his hand for silence. 'I have pledged myself to die with Hitler, gentlemen,' he said solemnly, 'yet my duty to my family is stronger than my pledge. We must make an attempt to negotiate with the Russians.' He looked at the drunken, red-faced General Krebs. 'General, you know the Ivans, you were our military attaché in Moscow before the war and speak their damned lingo. I want you to go to them under the cover of a white flag and ask their commander what their terms are.'

Inwardly Bormann had grinned. He knew what the Russians' terms would be. There would be no mercy for the *'Gift* Dwarf'; he was hated by the Russians.

Krebs had nodded grumpily. Obviously he wasn't keen on the mission.

Goebbels had turned to the others once again: 'In case the negotiations turn out negative, my decision has already been made. I shall remain in the bunker because I do not choose to play the role of a perpetual refugee in this world.' He had hesitated, for once in his career as Minister of Propaganda at a loss for words; Magda, the wife he had betrayed so often with film starlets, was standing at the door, tears streaming down her broad cheeks like a broken-hearted child. 'Naturally, escape for my wife and my children is left open to them.'

'If my husband stays,' Magda Goebbels said hastily, swallowing her tears, 'I'll stay too and share his fate.'

It was then that Bormann turned and walked out. It was like being at one of those boring Bayreuth performances of Wagner's *Götterdämmerung*, which he had been always forced to attend with the Führer before the war, full of tears, absurd gestures and even more absurd words. He needed a stiff drink. Slamming the door behind him, he had told himself, *'Gott sei Dank, nur ein Tag noch und dann zu Ende.'* *

General Krukenberg, Commander of the Eleventh S S Division, and the defender of Sector Z, or the citadel, frowned. He had problems enough with his 'citadel', which was in no way a fortress as the name suggested, but the heart of the capital, complete with banks, department stores, publishing houses, albeit most of them in ruins or flames; now apparently he was confronted by a spy.

'Well, my dear Abbé?' he asked of Monseigneur Comte Mayel de Lupe, who was the strangest clergyman the S S general had ever seen, in his dirty habit, with stick grenades tucked in the belt, jackboots, and steel helmet, a Schmeisser machine pistol held in his bloody right hand. 'What do you make of it?'

De Lupe was too much of a southern Frenchman to pretend to play the Prussian officer as some of his comrades of the Charlemagne attempted to do. He shrugged in a very gallic manner, lips curving downwards in that cynical French way. 'Tried to escape from a house we were searching. There were others with him, who spoke English. We found this on him.' He hitched up his cassock to reveal a stick grenade stuck down the side of his jackboot and took the paper out of his pocket. He flung it carelessly on

* One day more and then it's over.

147

the littered desk in front of the big, broad shouldered S S general. 'One-time pad,' he explained, 'used by agents. My guess is that the *sale con* is an Anglo-American spy.' The priest lit a cigarette and stuck it in the corner of his mouth, staring at the trembling Swede with angry dark eyes.

The general did not know whether to smile or blush. The priest's choice of language was very ripe for a man of the cloth. 'Hm,' he cleared his throat and studied the prisoner with interest. 'I assume from the papers found on you that you speak German?'

It seemed to take the Swede a devil of a long time to speak. His protruding adam's apple travelled up and down his skinny neck several times like a lift. Finally he managed to croak, 'I'm innocent, Herr General. They forced me to do it.'

In spite of the fact that two Soviet T-34s had rolled up below and were beginning to pump 75mm shells across the *Hermannsplatz*, he took his time with the frightened foreigner, telling himself that of he had been faced by the fanatical French abbé and his villains, he would have been scared too. '*Who* forced you to do *what*?' he asked patiently.

The Swede hesitated. Monseigneur Comte Mayel de Lupe didn't. His hand lashed out and caught the Swede a stinging blow across the face. '*Cochon!*' he bellowed, his dark face flushed angrily. 'Speak out!'

'*Mon cher Abbé!*' Krukenberg remonstrated with him. 'Remember you are a man of the cloth.'

The abbé looked at the German, his eyes ablaze with fury. 'We are fighting a holy crusade, General, against the Godless Red beast. We apply every means at our disposal to beat him.' He raised his hand threateningly again and the Swede, a thin trickle of blood flowing from the side of his mouth, cringed. 'Talk!'

The Swede talked, the words pouring from his bloody lips. How he had been recruited by the British while on leave in his native country; how they had smuggled the

148

decoding machine and short-wave radio to him with the precision machinery imported from Sweden for the German war industry; and how they had set him as his main task these last few weeks: the supervision of the bunker's inhabitants.

'Who in particular?' Krukenberg asked, fascinated by the spy's story despite the fact that down below a rabble of Volkssturm men and Hitler Youths were being decimated by the two T-34s. In a minute he'd have to send out a tank-destroyer team and deal with the Ivan tanks. 'The Führer?'

Miserably the Swede shook his head. 'No, Herr General.'

'Who then?'

'Reichsleiter Martin Bormann, sir.'

'And why?'

Again the Swede hesitated. He knew that the British would finish him off if he revealed what he knew – he had no illusions about the men of the British Secret Service; they would not hesitate to liquidate him as a traitor. But they were not here; the S S were. Again the abbé raised his hand. The Swede told his listeners what he knew.

'You mean,' Krukenberg stuttered, 'that Party Secretary Bormann is preparing to go over to the Russians at the first favourable opportunity?'

Numbly the Swede nodded his head, eyes on the flashing-eyed priest, who had opened the window, which was devoid of its glass anyway, and was preparing to drop two stick grenades into the open turret hatch of the leading T-34 as it came level with the building in which Krukenberg had his C P.

Swiftly Krukenberg got the details of the two men who had escaped and the girl; then he nodded to the one-legged Spanish scharführer, who stood behind the trembling Swede.

The Spaniard made the gesture of drawing a sharp knife across his throat, an evil grin all over his swarthy, unshaven face.

Krukenberg frowned. These were desperate times, he

told himself, and after all the man was a spy. He nodded once again.

The Spaniard grabbed the Swede and thrust him outside into the body-littered courtyard. In the same instant as the first T-34 exploded, the Spaniard pushed the Swede to his knees, thrust the muzzle of his machine pistol against the base of his skull, cried, *'Vaya con Dios'* quite cheerfully, and blew the back of his long Swedish head off.

At his desk, General Krukenberg did not even seem to notice. He was buried in thought. Bormann a traitor. *What was he going to do?*

It was roughly the same question that a morose Higgins asked, as the three of them crouched in the Swede's cellar, still fortunately intact and unoccupied in spite of the chatter of machine-guns and crackle of rifle fire only a couple of hundred yards away.

'What now?' Mallory echoed, equally despondently, staring at the girl, who had found a bottle of the missing Swede's schnaps and was drinking the fiery white liquid straight from the bottle. Whether she was drunk again, he didn't know: her eyes were glazed and vacant, as if she were day-dreaming.

Higgins took a drink from his own bottle. 'Yer can bet even money that that old Swede has spilled his guts by now. The Jerries won't have wasted any time with him.'

'Probably,' Mallory agreed. He had no illusions about what the enemy would do to make a prisoner talk; the defenders of Berlin were desperate men, who had nothing to lose. They knew they were going to die anyway. 'But he didn't know our exact plan and where we are going to position ourselves.'

'But the Yank did.'

Mallory bit his bottom lip, still not able to overcome the shock of having lost Piludski. He had got to like the big blond American in the few days they had worked together. More importantly, however, Piludski knew everything, as

150

Higgins had just pointed out: the plan, the target, *everything*!

'Somehow I have the feeling that they didn't take Captain Piludski,' Mallory said slowly, sounding more confident than he felt. If they had taken him and he had talked, wouldn't that mean that Bormann would be warned? Would he then venture out alone to meet his Russian contacts? But could he afford *not* to make that fateful rendezvous? A myriad questions raced through Mallory's brain, as he said, 'And even if they had captured him, I have a feeling that Piludski wouldn't talk.'

'Come off it, Major,' Higgins sneered, staring at Mallory with his red-rimmed eyes challenging, trying to conceal that overwhelming fear that the capture of the Swede and Piludski could well mean an end to his own hopes of ducking out in Berlin with the 1000 precious dollars. 'Pull the other leg, it's got bells on it. You know the Yanks by this time. All wind and piss. Full of big talk. But when the shit starts to fly they'd beat Jesse Owens – running the other sodding way! I saw 'em do a bunk in Tunisia in '43 and then again last December in the Ardennes. If the Jerries have got him, he'll spill his guts, believe you me.'

'I'm still putting my money on Captain Piludski,' Mallory said with quiet authority. Suddenly he had a moment of total recall: that terrible instant in the cell in Albania when, the tears of fear and pain streaming down his tortured face, he had been only too eager to tell Piotr what he wanted to know. 'Of course, everybody breaks under torture sooner or later, Higgins, I know that. I'm not a fool. But I think I know Captain Piludski well enough to state that he'll give us a sporting chance before he tells 'em. Twenty-four hours at least, I'd venture. By then we'll be on our way and putting into practice my alternative plan.'

Higgins' sneer vanished and he looked at Mallory's tense face curiously. 'You think the sun shines out that Yank's arse, don't yer, Major?'

'Watch yer tongue, Higgins,' Mallory replied sharply.

151

'But you do, don't yer? You think he's just like you yersen, 'cept that he speaks with a Yankee accent?'

'What you getting at?' Mallory demanded.

'Not much. I haven't had much time to think about it mesen the way we've been belting around these last couple of days. But for my money, Major, that Yank isn't – *wasn't* – the kind of bloke you took him to be.' Higgins' brow furrowed into a puzzled frown. 'It's hard to put it into words, but I'm a bit of an old lag and I can always recognize my own kind.'

Now it was Mallory's turn to look puzzled. In spite of his shock at Piludski's disappearance, Higgins' statements, malicious as they were, intrigued him. 'What do you mean – "own kind"?'

'Well, Major, a couple of times he tried to pump me about what our mission is. Now I can't see you trying to pump another ranker for info. An officer and a gent doesn't do that, even if he is a Yank.'

'Is that all?'

'Just one more thing. A couple of nights ago, just after we'd crossed the Elbe. Remember?'

Mallory nodded.

'We were all beat, but I had first stag. Anyhow the Yank talked in his sleep.'

'So?'

'Not much 'cept that he spoke in some sort of lingo that I couldn't make out. It wasn't German or Arabic or anything like that. And he tossed and turned, sweat all over his mug, as if he was having a nightmare.'

'Perhaps he was speaking Polish,' Mallory said hesitantly, wondering where all this was leading. 'I believe his parents came from Poland. He'd probably speak the language.'

Higgins shrugged carelessly, suddenly getting bored with the whole subject of the missing American. 'All I know is that that Yank ain't all he's cracked up to be, mark my words. . . .'

152

'I'm going to sleep,' the girl announced suddenly, as if it were important, slurring her words as she rose to her feet, her eyes completely out of focus.

Mallory nodded and pulled in his feet as she swayed past, bottle still clutched in her hand, to drop on the pile of blankets in the far corner of the cellar.

'Nice arse on her,' Higgins commented. 'Well,' he demanded, as her breathing indicated she had already fallen into a deep sleep, 'you made yer decision, Major?' When Mallory didn't reply, he added: 'After all, that's what you officers and gents is paid for, ain't it– to make decisions?'

'You know you are being insolent, Bombardier, Mallory said without rancour.

'Put me on a sodding fizzer then – here in Berlin, Major,' Higgins chuckled throatily at his own humour and took a deep swig of the schnaps.

'We'll do it. Like this.' He looked at the Berlin street map he had found in the Villa Irma. 'Now that the Russians have taken the Reichstag building, Big Six must be getting ready to make a break for it. What routes are open to him?' He pushed the map under Higgins' nose. The other man stared down at it without interest. 'The two main routes leading north to the Reichstag are the Hermann Goering and the Wilhelmstrasse. Both enter the Unter den Linden – here, some two hundred yards short of the Reichstag. That's where we will wait for him.'

'So you *are* going ahead with it, Major? With both the Russkis and the Jerries out for our blood and in the middle of the sodding frontline!'

'Yes,' Mallory answered, noting how peacefully the German girl slept now and suddenly feeling very protective towards her for some reason.

Higgins snorted angrily. 'Major, you really do want yer noddle seeing to! We ain't got a whisper of a chance – and you know it.'

'It's our duty, Higgins.'

153

'*Duty!*' Higgins exploded. 'How much corned beef do yer think duty'd buy in the corner shop?'

'But you're a soldier, a Regular soldier, Higgins, like I am. You must understand the word?'

'Grow up, Major. Why do yer think the likes of me ever sodding well joined the Kate Karney? For a bob a day, a bit o' hard cheese and dog biscuits for tea? Ner,' he sneered and took an angry gulp of schnaps. 'We had the choice in them days. Join up for King and Country, so the beak said, or go inside for spell. Or we'd been on the dole for so long that there was nothing else left but the Forces. We – that's my kind of bloke – took the King's shilling because we was in trouble and we was broke. It had nothing to do with patriotism or duty – oh, fuck it!' Higgins ended in sudden disgust and fear of what the morrow might bring. 'What's the sodding use? Okay, Major, you get some kip. I'll do the first stag. But believe you me, I'm not gonna stay sober very long, so don't kip the whole ruddy night.'

It took Mallory a long time to fall asleep, although he was exhausted. The knowledge that Piludski's possible capture jeopardized the whole grand plan would not allow him to sleep and when he finally dropped off, it was to dream of a naked Piludski being tortured by Piotr in that dirty Albanian cell, screaming with passionate ecstasy: '*Nyet . . . nyet!*'

Mallory awoke from a deep sleep with a start. It was Higgins. He was very drunk and completely naked save for his shoes and his pistol hanging from the belt tied loosely around his muscular thighs. 'You're on,' he said slurring his words.

Mallory looked up at him. Higgins' face was beetroot and his little eyes were glittering with drunken excitement. 'What the devil's going on, Higgins?' Mallory demanded angrily, knowing already from that hot sheen in the other man's eyes what had happened.

'I had her,' Higgins answered. 'Easy as falling off a log.

154

And didn't she just love it!' He swayed alarmingly and dropped the now empty bottle. It smashed on the floor. Higgins didn't seem to notice. 'Now I'm buggering off for some shut-eye. And let me tell yer one thing, Mr High-and-Mighty Major, I'm doing a bunk tomorrer. From now onwards yer on yer sodding own. . . . Bombardier Higgins is resigning his commission.' Swaying wildly, he staggered off to the pile of blankets in the corner from where the girl stared at Mallory, her beautiful face contorted with grief.

The runtish cross-eyed German seemed to appear from nowhere. Suddenly he was there in the middle of the smoking ruins, through which the first dirty white light of the false dawn was having a hard job to penetrate, sidling up to the booted, helmeted priest, his dirty hand raised to stop the patrol. 'You looking for some foreigners, Father?' he asked in a thick working-class Berlin accent. 'I hear they're traitors, wanted men.'

Monseigneur Comte Mayel de Lupe glared at the civilian. '*Merde,*' he cursed savagely, 'can't understand a word the *con* is saying. Doepgen,' he barked at the Alsatian corporal who spoke German, 'what did the Boche say?'

The big lumbering ex-Alsatian farm boy told the priest.

'How did he know we were looking for these men – ask him that, you peasant oaf!' de Lupe commanded.

The civilian gave an evil grimace showing a mouthful of bad teeth. 'Don't matter, does it, Father. I'm a patriotic German, ain't I? Besides you might be able to give me a packet of fags by way of a reward.'

A battery of 'Stalin organs' opened up close behind. The dawn air was suddenly full of their obscene howl. Rockets started to smash down in red, fiery fury. De Lupe knew there was no time to be wasted. He had to get his patrol under cover soon. He took out a crumpled packet of black *marhoka* tobacco and a neatly folded page of the *Volkischer Beobachter* which could be used to roll the cigarettes.

'Here,' he said in his hesitant German. 'All I can do in the way of fags.'

The little man's eyes lit up. 'God bless yer, Father,' he said. 'Even if I have to desecrate the Führer's own paper to roll them.'

'Get on with it. Where are these men?'

'Two hundred metres from here, Father – about one hundred metres from the Ivan's position. Up that street – or what's left of it – to the left. In a cellar. You'll see the smoke coming from the old stove pipe.'

'Come on,' De Lupe commanded urgently as shrapnel hissed through the air.

The Berliner said something fast which the priest didn't understand and clutched at the torn sleeve of his habit.

'What did he say, Doepgen?'

The ex-farm boy flushed a deep red.

'He said he's a Catholic and he'd like your blessing, sir.'

De Lupe tugged his arm free with a savage pull. 'Tell him he can stick my blessing up his dirty *Boche* arse, we've got no time to waste.'

The cross-eyed civilian waited till they had disappeared into the smoke, then he crumpled the packet of tobacco and threw it into the rubble in disgust. *He* had better things to smoke than that rubbish. Carefully he began to work his way back from where he had started his little infiltration mission – the Russian lines.

The German girl handed Mallory a cracked cup of lukewarm *ersatz* coffee hesitantly. She avoided the Englishman's gaze as she did so.

In the corner, Higgins snored drunkenly. Abruptly, she turned and, seizing a dirty towel, draped it across his naked loins. Higgins continued to snore on.

Mallory sipped the terrible coffee, morosely. He tried to catch her eye as she went about her tasks, but she avoided his glances. Outside, the guns were pounding the centre of

Berlin in full force. But Mallory did not hear them. He was preoccupied with the girl and the events of the night.

Why had she let Higgins have her? Had it been drunkenness? Sexual desire? And what had it to do with him? Wasn't he impotent? The doctors had said so. What could he offer a woman, especially such a woman as the German?

Slowly the girl raised her head. She had dark circles under her eyes and she looked as if she might burst into tears at any moment; the corners of her lips trembled continually. 'It was despair,' she said slowly, as if she could read his mind. 'Just despair, that's all. Mallory,' it was the first time she had called him anything save 'Englishman', 'we're all damned, so I thought. . . .' Abruptly her voice cracked and she was sobbing and he was holding her, feeling the warm wet tears running down the side of his haggard unshaven face.

It was thus that the S S found them as they smashed the lock on the cellar door with a savage burst of m.p. fire.

4

De Lupe nodded.

The Gestapo Kommissar turned slowly from the barred window. He was a big fat man with a bad squint and smelled to Mallory of sweat and cheap pomade. His green leather coat which reached to the ankles of his jackboots creaked as he moved. He looked like a caricature of all the German secret policemen that Mallory had ever seen.

'Speak German?' he asked, hardly opening his lips, the stump of unlit cigar glued to his bottom lip moving from side to side in his mouth.

'Yes,' Mallory grunted, trying to assess his situation through his puffed-up eyes.

'*Gut!*' Routinely he lashed out with a fist like a pink ham and slapped the man sitting on the little three-legged stool across the face. Mallory would have fallen, if it had not have been for the two S S men standing on each side of him. 'Nice to make your acquaintance, Englishman,' the Gestapo Kommissar said easily. 'Thought I'd introduce myself.'

Mallory blinked back the tears of pain which had filled his eyes.

'Better tell you something right from the start, Englishman. No use lying. Always get my prisoners to talk. Did it under the Old Kaiser, then Hindenburg, now the Führer. Probably do it under Joe Stalin if he comes next.' He chuckled throatily at his own humour, the cigar sliding across his mouth again. 'Say in Prinz Albrechtstrasse,

Kommissar Todt could even make a mummy talk.'* He coughed. 'Understand, Englishman?'

Mallory said nothing.

Todt kicked Mallory viciously on the right shin. He howled with pain and Todt smiled. 'Just so you don't think I'm an amateur, Englishman. Old Todt's not been an amateur for years now.'

At the door, de Lupe snarled in French, 'I shit on the Englishman, Doepgen! Tell the Boche to hurry up. The Ivans are expected to attack at ten hundred hours.'

Doepgen translated the priest's words. Todt remained unmoved. 'Tell the Father, I'll have him singing like a sweet little yeller canary within thirty minutes. Old Todt's never failed yet.' He looked down at the bedraggled bloody prisoner, eyes full of sadistic cunning. Abruptly, with startling speed for such a big fat man, he grabbed Mallory's hair, pulled his face down and rammed his right knee up at the same time. Mallory yelped with agony as his nose burst and thick rich gobs of red blood started to spurt from it. 'Probably a nice looking young feller once, eh?' Todt said conversationally, then his voice hardened. 'All right, you heard the Father? What are you English here for? What have you got to do with this Bormann business?'

In spite of the pain in his smashed nose, Mallory tensed. They hadn't been picked up during a routine search. If his interrogators knew about Bormann, then someone had told them. The Swede perhaps?

A bang across his right ear, which deafened him momentarily and sent his head reeling from side to side, reminded Mallory that he had been asked a question. 'I know . . . know nothing,' he gasped. 'I warn you as soon as we have won this war . . . you'll pay . . . for this.'

'Win it first,' Todt sneered and hit him again. Mallory doubled up with pain.

For a while Todt let him squat there, arms clasped

* Prinz Albrechtstrasse, Berlin H Q of the Gestapo.

around his stomach, rocking back and forth with the sheer agony of the blow, studying him as if he were some particularly interesting form of animal. Then he said: 'Old Todt can see you're not going to co-operate, Englishman.' He shook his head like an elderly nurse who had reached the end of her patience with her charges' foolish antics. 'Tut, tut, 'fraid we'll have to try some drastic medicine.'

'Hurry up,' de Lupe urged, feeding new 9mm cartridges into the long magazine of his machine pistol. 'When those Red heathens come, we've got to be out there to meet them. God dammit, why did I let Krukenberg involve me in this damnfool business? I've got better things to do than this.' One of the slugs jammed and, taking the large silver Celtic cross which hung from his neck, he used the badge of his holy office to lever it free. '*Allez, Monsieur le Commissaire!*'

Frowning a little now, Todt looked around the former *Wehrmacht* detention cell until he found what he was searching for: a large chipped enamel bucket, its side carved with initials and obscene drawings by the countless number of military prisoners who had used it these last years. 'Hey you, Corporal,' he addressed Doepgen, 'gimme that piss-bucket there. Go on, get yer paws on it. Yer pinkies aren't delicate or anything, are they?' He guffawed loudly, his big belly under the coat trembling so much that the stiff leather creaked.

Blushing, the big ex-farm boy picked up the evil-smelling bucket and stood holding it opposite the Gestapo man. 'Sir?'

'Over his turnip. . . . Come on, *dalli, dalli*, over his head!'

Mallory cried out loud as the nauseating container was dropped over his head, blotting out the cell, powerless to do anything, gripped now by the S S men standing on each side of him.

Tensely he waited, wondering what was to come, fighting off the desire to be sick, which threatened to overcome him at any moment.

160

Then a tremendous blow hit the side of the bucket, and the metal sang loudly. Mallory gasped with the pain of the blow. Red stars exploded in front of his eyes. His ears were filled with a deafening sound. Hot, salty blood filled his mouth.

The bucket was removed. The cell trembled violently. The walls seemed to rise and fall in waves; then his vision cleared and everything came into focus once more.

Todt was standing there, his chest heaving, a rifle held by the muzzle clasped in his great hands. Instinctively, Mallory knew he had swung the butt against the bucket with all his brutal strength. 'Now then, my little Tommy,' Todt gasped, 'gonna spill the beans?'

'Beans?' Mallory managed to croak, pretending not to understand, playing for time.

'Don't pull my pisser, man,' Todt roared suddenly, face livid. 'You know what I mean.'

Mallory said nothing.

Todt cursed loudly. 'Now the clock's struck thirteen! All right, put the piss-bucket on his head again. Now I'm going to show him. I'll take the Tommy bastard apart. . . .'

Major Mike Mallory's calvary had commenced.

Smoke lay in thick brown clouds over the shattered capital. *Katuska* rockets crashed down with frightening regularity on the citadel. Here and there a lone German 88mm gun cracked in reply, its shells tearing the burning sky apart with the sound of a huge piece of stiff canvas being ripped apart. But in the main, Krukenberg's handful of S S men from half a dozen European nations, who were still defending the couple of square miles of brick rubble which was all that was left of Nazi Berlin, had only their rifles and machine-guns to fight back against the tremendous weight of two Soviet armies.

With a dirty white bed sheet in one hand and a field cable drum in the other, the middle-aged, frightened German colonel made his way back to his own lines in a series of terrified leaps and jumps. His broad face was as grey as his breeches, adorned with the purple stripe of the General Staff. The Russian major with him shouted something urgently. Abruptly machine-gun fire scythed the air. The Russian bellowed with pain. Bright red blood jetted from his right thigh. He dropped to the brick rubble, writhing and groaning.

Colonel von Dufving dropped beside him and leant his back against a shattered wall. He was beat. In spite of the cold early morning air, he was lathered with sweat at the unusual exertion. At that moment he would have dearly liked to lie down in the rubble and sleep – sleep forever, never wake up again from this nightmare.

But he knew he must get back to the *Führerbunker* with the details of the Russian surrender terms. He licked his parched, caked lips and looked at the Russian. He had served long enough in the trenches in the First World War to know that the Russian major was too badly wounded to be moved. The Russian knew it too. Through teeth gritted in agony, he hissed, '*Davoi – nymets. Davoi.* . . . Go on, German.'

'Will you be all right, Major?'

The major nodded, not daring to speak. Von Dufving took a deep breath and started to move forward again, slugs howling off the bricks all around as he entered what the SS defenders of the citadel called the 'death zone'. Suddenly he cursed and jerked to a stop. The cable with which he had hoped to link the bunker and the nearest Russian Command Post had run out. '*Ach*, thou holy strawsack! What does it matter now?' He dropped the useless cable drum and moved on. Everywhere there were bodies, German and Russian, sprawled out in the extravagant fashion of those killed in battle, some still and undisturbed as if they were sleeping, others terribly mutilated, minus arms, legs, heads. Suddenly the middle-aged colonel stopped. An SS officer was watching him through a pair of binoculars at about fifty yards' distance.

Von Dufving felt fresh sweat break out all over his well-built body. He knew the S S; they were a law unto themselves. He had crossed over to the Russian positions on highest orders. That wouldn't worry the S S, however. Many of them were foreigners anyway, who hardly understood German. One false move and they'd shoot him, although he was a staff colonel. What did they care? They were doomed as soon as they fell into Russian hands. Carefully, he started to wave the white flag above his head, gasping with shock every time a slug tore through the material.

At last the German fire stopped. Probably the officer with the binoculars had recognized his German uniform. Cautiously, very cautiously, he rose from the shell-hole and made his way to the waiting S S, waving his bullet-holed flag all the time.

'You're under arrest, Colonel,' snapped the hatchet-faced S S officer, a Knight's Cross hanging carelessly from his neck.

'What lunacy is this?' von Dufving cried. 'Have all you people gone mad? I have been across to the Russian lines on the highest orders.'

'You mean you tried to save your miserable skin by deserting to the Ivans while the going was good, but you couldn't get across. So you had to make up this stupid story.'

'Sturmbannführer,' von Dufving said, trying to control himself. 'I am a colonel. I outrank you. Take me to your senior officer or let me through at once.'

'Only the shitting S S give orders here,' another S S man snapped, his sunk, dark-ringed eyes bitter, his mouth like a rat-trap.

'Then get me Mohnke,' von Dufving cried desperately, remembering the name of the general who had formerly commanded the S S Division Leibstandarte.

The name had its effect. General Mohnke was called to

163

the telephone from his C P. He recognized von Dufving's voice and ordered he should be let through.

Breathing a heartfelt sigh of relief, although he knew the respite was only temporary, Colonel von Dufving pushed on. The last act in the tremendous drama of the end of the Third Reich was about to commence.

Now it was almost over.

Hertz lowered his glasses and rubbed his tired, dark eyes.

'They got through?' his companion on the roof of the Reichstag asked eagerly.

Hertz did not answer immediately. Down below, a drunken soldier was telling some German in a mixture of Russian and German, '*Voina kaputt! . . . Gitler kaputt!*' Idly, Hertz wondered if the unknown German would understand that 'Gitler' was 'Hitler'. Now the Russian soldier had passed on to more mundane things, '*Du uri, Deutscher? . . .* Have you got a watch, German?'

'I said, did they get through?' his companion demanded, his Russian perfect in spite of the many years that he had been a 'sleeper agent' in the New World.

Hertz did not turn. 'Yes,' he said, speaking quietly, as if he were occupied by other things. 'At least, one of them did. One fell. Perhaps it was the German.'

'It would be better if it were the Russian major,' his companion said in that soulless objective manner of his, the sign of a perfect agent which, to Hertz, was also very frightening. 'The German colonel would probably be able to convince them better.'

'Possibly.'

'You don't seem particularly interested, Comrade Hertz, eh?'

The little Jew realized his mistake at once. The sleeper was nobody's fool. If anybody could sense what was going on in his mind at this moment, it would be him. After all the sleeper had lived the same kind of life as his own for many years too; he knew what it meant to live one half of

164

your life in a world to which you didn't belong, yet exist on a completely different level in the other half.

'No, I'm interested all right, comrade,' he said hastily. 'I was just weighing up the various possibilities in my mind, that is all.'

'And to what conclusion did you come, Comrade Hertz?' the sleeper asked. His voice was as smooth and calm as ever, but was there a hint of cynicism about it?

A chill of fear ran through Hertz. 'I think the Fritzes won't agree to our terms,' he commenced, speaking very deliberately, trying to control his heartbeat. 'I think, too, they'll react as we hoped they would when we drew up our terms of surrender. Some of the Fritzes will stay behind and commit suicide. Some of them will remain and drink themselves into oblivion – the ones who think they won't be punished. But there will be the bold spirits who will try to make a break for it while there is still a chance. Bormann will have the cover he needs.'

'Hopefully. He needs that cover.' The sleeper ran his hand through his cropped blond hair a little nervously. 'Then it would be hardly likely that one of the Reich's remaining two big noises would attempt to make a break-out by himself.'

'Exactly, comrade.'

Down below the firing was slowly dying away. From the street, Hertz could hear the sound of two Red Army men fighting over the German woman they had dragged out of the smoking ruins somewhere or other. Finally, the bigger one staggered away drunkenly and the other stumbled with his prize into the nearest cellar, already undoing the flies of his baggy breeches. 'The spoils of victory, eh?' Hertz said and smiled warily.

The sleeper grunted something or other and lapsed into a gloomy silence, while below the shooting petered out altogether.

Colonel von Dufving clattered down the dirty wet concrete

steps of the bunker. He squeezed his way through the tight low corridors packed with frightened or drunken officials and officers. Once they had been the mighty in the Third Reich. Now, they crouched or lay among empty bottles and cans like the meanest beggar.

Finally, the middle-aged colonel managed to push his way into Goebbels' room. The '*Gift* Dwarf' was calm in comparison with everyone else around him. He stumped across the room with his clubfoot, shook the weary officer's hand warmly, and asked him to tell the assembled group the state of Krebs' negotiations with the Russians.

Von Dufving did not pull his punches. He had been through too much in the last twelve hours. In quick, excited phrases, emphasizing his points with nervous gestures of his hands, he explained that General Krebs had failed. The Russians were interested in only one term – *unconditional surrender*!

Goebbels' sallow face flushed angrily. 'I shall never surrender, *never*!'

Bormann spoke for the first time. 'How long do you think we can hold out still, Colonel?'

Somehow or other von Dufving had the impression that the Reichsleiter was not really interested; his mind was on other things. 'Two days at the most, Reichsleiter. After that we'll be reduced to isolated pockets.'

'I—'

The rest of Bormann's words were drowned by a salvo of enemy shells which landed right on the top of the bunker. The whole shelter rocked violently under the impact. Tiny pieces of mortar and cement rained down upon the crouching men. Catching his breath and noting that his hands were trembling slightly, von Dufving surmised that General Krebs' disclosure of the bunker's exact position to the Russians was the cause of the sudden bombardment; perhaps the Ivans wanted to hurry them up into surrendering?

The shelling stopped as suddenly as it had started.

Goebbels regained his calm. Standing there in the middle of the sparsely furnished room lit by a single naked bulb, which might well have reminded him of his days as a pupil in a Rhenish Jesuit school, he asked von Dufving if he thought that Krebs might obtain better terms if he spoke to the overall Russian commander.

Von Dufving shook his head. 'I don't think so, Herr Minister. The Russians kept insisting on immediate surrender all the time I was there with them.'

Goebbels bit his thin bottom lip and considered what to do next. While he did so, von Dufving stared through the open door into the corridor. It was clear to the regular soldier, who had been in many a tight situation in his time, that a panic was about to break out soon in the bunker. He could read the helplessness of the situation in the wide, blank-staring eyes of the civilians who were pushing their way through the throng on completely purposeless missions. One of Goebbels' six children was carried past and someone next to the colonel in the packed room whispered, 'They'll be getting their injections soon.' Von Dufving looked away hurriedly.

Opposite him, General Burgdorf, his face red, his speech slurred with drink, announced loudly to no one in particular, 'Of course, as the Führer's chief adjutant, I have no other alternative – I shall shoot myself.'

Desperately von Dufving wondered if he would ever get out of this damned bunker alive.

Finally, Goebbels made up his mind, while Bormann watched him anxiously. 'Go and bring Krebs back, Colonel,' he commanded von Dufving wearily. 'I want to hear what he himself has to say.'

Von Dufving waited for further orders. But there were none. The little Party fanatic, who reputedly had once tossed a coin as a young man to decide whether he would join the Communists or the Nazis, had lost the final toss. His negotiations with the Russians had failed. Now on this first day of May 1945, he knew he must pay his last tribute

167

to the dead master he had served loyally for twenty years – in blood. Soon, he and his family must join those charred horrors still smouldering in the scorched blackened Chancellery garden up above.

Wordlessly Colonel von Dufving left the silent room.

On the roof the two agents waited still, while below an ominous silence hung over the ruins. Obviously the talks in the bunker had not yet ended. Out of the corner of his eye, Hertz stole a furtive glance at the tall, handsome sleeper who looked every bit the part he had played for so long. What might be going on in his mind? The sleeper's face revealed nothing. Those sincere eyes were blank; the man was occupied with his own inner voices.

Sincerity, that was it, Hertz concluded; that had been the virtue which had been the sleeper's making. He, Hertz, had always been the 'invisible man' like the one he had read about in a book by an Englishman a long time before, who had been able to go through barbed wire unnoticed. No one had ever paid much attention to a little Jew like himself, unless he had wanted attention drawn to his person. But sleeper had obviously covered his treachery in a different manner; he had been vocal, even outspoken, free, happy. Because of it he had appeared to have been one of them and in this manner had become an 'invisible man' himself.

'If everything works out as planned, comrade,' Hertz broke the heavy tense silence hesitantly, 'will you come along to the *treff*?'

For a long moment, the other man didn't answer. For a while, Hertz thought he hadn't heard the question. He bit his bottom lip nervously. If the sleeper didn't come, it would make his own decision easier, much easier. He had a sudden mental picture of that dying woman with her black eyes burning into him as she had repeated that overwhelming question in the cellar, 'Well, Jew, *will you*?' He shuddered involuntarily at the memory.

168

'You cold, comrade?' the other man asked, suddenly ending his silence. Without waiting for an answer, he continued: 'Of course, I want to be in at the end. I think I deserve it.'

'Of course, comrade, of course,' Hertz said hastily.

But the sleeper wasn't listening. His gaze was set on some private horizon and when he spoke again it was as if he were speaking to himself. 'If only you knew the years I've spent in places you'll never visit, preparing for this mission, though in those days I didn't know that it would be this particular job. Speaking another tongue, eating other foods, sleeping with other women,' he chuckled softly at the memory, 'living a lie, so far away from my own people. Ten years and never once myself, always on guard that the slightest mistake might give me away, cringing with fear when someone spoke to me in my native tongue during my courses at the university, in case it was a secret police trap, wondering – and I confess it freely to you, comrade – whether or not *they* were right and *we* were wrong. Never once in a whole decade able to look someone directly in the eye, never once able to get really drunk, in case I blabbed, never once able to have a real relationship with women, for fear I would speak my own native tongue in my sleep. . . .' He broke off for breath and Hertz thought of his own fears when he had been 'underground' in the Third Reich, when such a simple thing as urinating in a public urinal might have betrayed the fact that he was circumcized and, therefore, a Jew and an enemy of the state. *He* knew. For a moment, his heart went out to the big handsome man next to him, but only for a moment. When, no, *if* he did it, the sleeper could well be his greatest danger.

'Yes, Comrade Hertz,' the sleeper said, his voice normal, his eyes full of their usual sincerity once more, their despair and sorrow vanished, as if they had never even been there, 'I want to be present – *at the kill!*'

Hertz shuddered at the casual phrase. He flashed an anxious glance at the other man. But it had meant nothing. He breathed out a sigh of relief.

They fell silent once more and gazed numbly at the stark, sobering tableau of the wrecked capital. The once magnificent trees, stripped of their foliage by the shellfire, now looked like gaunt outsized toothpicks. Where once fine city houses had stood there were now jagged chunks of smoking brickwork and grotesquely twisted steel girders. To their right an S S half-track had struck a mine and slumped there, tracks flopped out in front of it like a once live thing which had crawled there to die. To their left a deserter, a placard tied round his neck, dangled barefoot from a twisted lamp post, swaying slightly back and forth in the breeze. And everywhere lay the debris of war, gas masks, rifles, ripped overcoats, boxes of shells, shattered machine-guns, abandoned ration cans – and bodies. Bodies everywhere.

Abruptly the two observers on the roof of the Reichstag were jerked out of their reverie by a ragged volley of fire from below, followed a moment later by the stomach-churning howl of a German multiple mortar. Hertz controlled his pounding heart and looked at his companion.

The sleeper's face lit up. 'The Fritzes are going to fight on!' he cried enthusiastically and in that moment Hertz told himself that his enthusiasm was so un-Russian. The years across the ocean had rubbed off. 'You know what that means, Comrade Hertz?'

Hertz nodded sombrely. 'Yes, comrade. He'll be coming out tonight. . . .'

Four: The Showdown

'He who eats with the devil needs a long spoon.'
Old German Proverb

1

In the cell, the wall shuddered violently under the impact of the Russian bombardment. Mallory came out of his exhausted sleep with a groan and stared at the girl, the flickering yellow candle which lit the place throwing grotesque, dancing shadows across her pale face.

Even in his own muddled state of body and mind he could see that she had about reached the end of her tether. Her green eyes shone nervously, her body shaking with every fresh explosion.

He twisted his head painfully, feeling knives of sheer agony slice into his body where he was hurt. Higgins was slumped in the corner, his dirty broken hands held over his head, muttering incoherently to himself. Obviously he had taken a tremendous beating too.

It all flooded back to him. The Gestapo man and the big lumbering S S man had beaten him up with routine thoroughness like two pugs in some shabby back street gym working over a punching bag. Back and forth, back and forth, the only sound his cries, their heavy breathing and the thud of their clenched fists on his naked flesh.

Now and again they had stopped and asked him the same old questions, but even if he had wanted to answer, he could not have: his mouth had been too full of thick blood welling up from the gaps where they had knocked out his teeth. In the end they had become sick of beating him. They had let him slump to the floor and he had lain there in blessed oblivion until the sound of rushing water had awakened him once more. Grabbing him by his bloody, greasy hair, they had dragged him into a bare bathroom. Before he had time to realize what they were going to do with him, Todt had grabbed him by the scruff of the neck and thrust him face downwards into the cold water that filled the dirty bath.

He had forgotten his pain. Frantically he tried to breathe. Water poured into his mouth. Like a madman he squirmed and struggled. But Todt had held him in a vice-like grip. A roaring blackness had begun to swamp him. Just as he had thought he must drown, Todt had released him and he had flopped down on the floor, retching agonizingly and vomiting blood and water.

'Now will you answer, Englishman?' Todt had cried.

'*Nom de Dieu!*' he had heard the strange priest cry from a long way off. 'Will he never speak?'

Todt's big booted foot had smashed into his ribs. '*Speak!*' he had roared.

But he hadn't spoken. Let them kill me, he had told himself. Nothing matters now. I've failed. Let them finish me off and get it over with.

A moment later, they had grabbed his feet and flung him bodily into the bath, showering water everywhere. His head struck the bottom. Crimson stars had exploded in front of his eyes. The air escaped from his lungs in a series of rapid belches. He had known that he was going to drown and he had accepted that knowledge. But that wasn't to be.

Suddenly there had been a tremendous explosion. The water had poured from the holed bath, leaving him there gasping frantically for air like a stranded fish. For a minute he had managed to keep his eyes open. A huge steaming hole had appeared, as if by magic, in the far wall of the cell, Todt lay groaning on the floor, cigar still held somehow on his bottom lip, staring at his foot which had been neatly severed at the ankle and now lay parallel with his face, while the priest and his men had dashed for the door, weapons at the ready. Thereafter he had passed out.

'What . . .' he began.

174

'Ssh!' the girl said soothingly, trying to make herself smile in spite of her almost overwhelming fear. She rose to her feet and reaching under her dress, pulled hard. There was a ripping sound. A piece of silk underslip appeared. Drily she spat on the end of it, like Mallory remembered seeing working-class women do before the war when they were about to clean their babies' running nose or dirty mouth, and gently started to wipe his nostrils and cheeks free of caked blood.

Despite his pain and fatigue, Mallory could feel her warm affection, perhaps even love. 'Thank you,' he whispered softly. 'Thank you very much.'

'Why . . . why do men do these things?' she asked.

Mallory shrugged helplessly. 'The war . . .' his voice trailed away to nothing.

'They're dying everywhere in the cellars now,' she said, finishing her task, her voice hardly audible. 'Not just soldiers, but old men and women, children – babies.' Her eyes filled with tears. 'Dying everywhere.'

Forgetting his own pain, Mallory clasped her to him gently. 'Don't worry, Ilona. The dying will stop soon. . . .'

For a long time they clung to each other like lost children, while she sobbed, her thin beautiful body racked painfully by the heartbroken sobs, until finally he pushed her gently away. 'It's all right, Ilona. I'll see it's all right. For you and me,' he found himself saying the words without even knowing why, yet at the same time, he experienced a surge of new hope. He had someone who meant more than physical love; he wasn't alone any longer. He pressed her thin hand firmly. 'It's all right, I promise you. . . . All right.'

She smiled through her tears. 'I don't even know your first name,' she said huskily. '*Englishman.*'

Then they both laughed.

Carefully, accepting the supporting hand that Ilona offered him, Mallory rose to his feet and limped across to

175

where Higgins crouched, muttering to himself. 'What did they do to you?' he asked.

Higgins continued to mutter.

Mallory took his shoulder and shook him. The bombardier turned round. His face was a livid red with patches of black on both cheeks. Under the eyes were charred circles of red-raw flesh where someone had pressed out a cigar or a cigarette. 'You told them,' he said wearily. 'You told them about Bormann?'

'Ah, let me alone. I've had it,' Higgins said, his voice broken. 'I'm out . . . out. . . .' The rest of his mutterings were meaningless to Mallory.

He gave up. Slowly he trudged back to Ilona, while behind him Higgins chattered on, twisting his hands incessantly in the intricate pattern of the mad.

'They beat him terribly,' Ilona said as he slumped down beside her on the dirty straw. 'I could hear the screams. Terrible!' Her hand fluttered to the side of her face and she started to cry.

Mallory grabbed her hand swiftly. 'Don't,' he commanded. 'We have no time for tears now.'

She bent her lips to his bruised knuckles and kissed them softly. 'Sorry, I won't cry.'

'Now,' he said, making his voice firm and confident, as if they still had a chance, taking in the cell with its barred window and heavy door by the light of the flickering candle, 'I want you to answer some questions.'

'Anything,' she sighed, pressing his hand.

'Where are they?'

'Out there. When the shell struck the other place and the Russians attacked, most of them left, but while you were unconscious, I heard someone moving in the next place. They've left guards there.'

'How many?'

She waited till the rattle of heavy machine-gun fire close by stopped. 'I think only two. At least I could only make

176

out two voices speaking. Of course there might be more of them.'

'Two,' Mallory mused. That might give them a chance. Painfully he rose once again and crossed to the door. It was solid wood and locked from outside. There was no chance there. He turned and tried the window. One of the boards came away quite easily. His heart leapt. But hope died almost the next second. By the grey light that flooded into the cell where the first board had gone, he could see that the window was covered with iron bars, too; the boards had been put up there in place of missing glass. 'Blast,' he cursed and caught himself almost at once. He must never frighten Ilona again. She had to believe that there was hope.

He crossed to Higgins and in spite of his protests hauled him to his feet, trying to avoid looking at that terrible face. 'Listen,' he said slowly and carefully, 'I want you to say this when I give the signal . . .'

'Let me alone, I've had it,' Higgins quavered.

Without hesitation Mallory hit him across his bruised cheeks, his rage at his torturers and Higgins lending strength to his arm.

Higgins yelped with pain and cowered back, hands raised to protect his face like an animal cringing from any further blows. 'You've got no right to hit me, guv,' he snivelled. 'I ain't never done nothing to you.'

'Shut up! Just listen. All I want you to do is to sit in the middle of the floor there and yell in German that you want to urinate. You want the bucket or whatever they use.'

'But I don't—'

'Just do as I tell you.' Firmly, Mallory took a hold of him, led him to the centre of the cell, exactly opposite the door and thrust him down. 'Now, *"ich will pissen."* That's what you have to say. Got it?'

'Ich will pissen,' Higgins said meekly, his spirit completely gone.

Hurriedly Mallory positioned himself behind the door

177

and then raised his finger to his lips in warning before commanding, *'Now!'*

'Ich will pissen!' Higgins called.

Nothing happened.

'Again,' Mallory urged.

Nothing.

'Louder. Kick up a racket as if you can't hold out any longer. Come on, Higgins, everything depends upon you. *Ich will pissen!'*

'Ich will pissen . . . ich will pissen . . . ich will pissen,' Higgins screamed the words out over and over again with the frantic persistence of a crazed man.

In the end, the guards outside reacted, but not in the way Mallory had hoped for. A rifle butt thudded against the door, making it tremble and a harsh, bored voice bellowed, *'Vor mir aus! Piss auf den Boden!'*

Mallory let his shoulder slump in defeat. They weren't going to open the door.

It was midday.

This would be the last day for all of them in the bunker. Discipline had already begun to break down before Hitler had committed suicide. Now it collapsed completely. For years the members of Hitler's entourage had carefully hidden their appetites from their puritanical master: no alcohol, no meat, no sex. Now they broke into the bunker's great reserves of food and drink.

Everywhere the drunken men and women stuffed themselves with the finest caviare smeared carelessly on white bread, washing down the sandwiches with choice French champagne, singing and laughing, as if this were a party of celebration and not the end of their particular world. An erotic fever seemed to have possessed them too. Men and women were locked together in lascivious embraces on all sides; there was even a couple making love violently in Dr Blaschke's dental chair, where once the dentist had treated what had remained of the Führer's decaying teeth.

178

But not all of the several hundred people trapped in the bunker that May Day were content to indulge in one last gigantic erotic fling before their world fell apart. Several score of them, civilians as well as soldiers, were determined to break out before it was too late. Once it was dark, they would escape. The problem was *how* and *where*. Clustered in little groups, seemingly oblivious to the screaming drunken mob all around them, thoughtful worried men discussed those questions.

Wandering from group to group, using his shoulder to push his way through whenever necessary, once pulling a copulating maid from the household from her soldier lover so he could pass, Bormann paused and listened. Now he was dressed in the uniform of a general in the Waffen S S and he carried a steel helmet hung by the strap across his arm to make it quite clear that he, too, wanted to escape. In reality, he was simply in search of the group which would enable him to carry out his own private plans.

The exit to the bunker lay in the garden at the corner of the famous 'Street of the Ministries', the Wilhelmstrasse, and the somewhat narrower Vossstrasse, opposite the New Chancellery. Opposite this corner lay the burned-out Hotel Kaiserhof, which had served as the H Q of Goebbels' Reichspropagandaministerium since 1933.

Now the would-be escapers discussed in excited whispers what direction they should take once they had left that exit. Did a break-out to the south along the Wilhelmstrasse offer any possibility of success, they asked each other. Most of the groups that Bormann listened to came to the conclusion that it didn't. There, to the south, the Ivans were dug in in force. What about to the west, then, via the burning Tiergarten? Again the answer seemed to be negative. To the east? Again, no.

In general, all groups appeared to agree that the only possible escape route open was to the north. The escapers believed that if they could work their way up the Wilhelmstrasse, using the cover of the wrecked buildings on both sides of the street, then following the Unter den Linden eastwards, then turning north along a right angle running down the Friedrichstrasse, they might reach the River Spree and break through the Russian lines there.

Standing quietly in the background, trying not to look at a drunken secretary, who was attempting to dance a naked cancan, Bormann nodded his approval. North would suit him fine. Things were going to work out just as he had planned.

Not far away from where Bormann lounged, Goebbels summoned his adjutant Guenther Schwaegermann and briefed him on what had happened over the last hours. 'Everything is lost,' he said gloomily. 'I shall die, together with my wife and children. You will burn my body.'

Schwaegermann nodded, oppressed by the doomsday atmosphere of Goebbels' room.

Goebbels handed him a silver-framed photograph of the Führer and shook his hand. 'I would like to thank you—' he began, when the phone rang.

Frowning, he limped across the room and picked it up and listened in silence. Finally, he nodded and said, 'I'll see the matter is taken care of, General, though I hardly think that—' he broke off suddenly and holding the receiver a little way from his eyes, he stared at it, as if he had been cut off abruptly. Finally he placed it back in its cradle and said, 'That was a General Krukenberg of the S S.' He paused and frowned. 'The connection was very bad, but he said something about wanting to see to Bormann. . . . I thought I heard him say that he was sending a party of S S men to escort him to his command post. There is some talk of treachery. . . . Oh, what does it matter. Schwaegermann, tell Bormann that some S S are looking for him. My time is too precious. I must devote it to my children and my wife. Good-bye, good luck and *Heil Hitler!*'

Instinctively, Schwaegermann clicked to attention and

bellowed, *'Heil Hitler!'* saluting a man who had been dead these many hours. He went out in search of Bormann.

Bormann and Schwaegermann, crouched anxiously in the exit, surrounded by the heavily armed SS guard, and peered at the burning ruins. To their immediate front a half-crazed mongrel was gnawing at something white sprawled in the brick rubble, its snout a blood-red, its teeth also dripping blood. Bormann swallowed in horror. Was it a dead human body the hound was eating? He took his eyes off the horrible sight and searched the ruins for Krukenberg's SS men.

The message transmitted by Schwaegermann was garbled enough, but frightening, very frightening. He had drunk half a bottle of *Korn* in one go immediately Schwaegermann had given him it before he had dared to come up here two hours before and prepare to meet them. A 75mm shell slammed into the rubble thirty metres away. Steel slivers, red-hot and as big as a fist, hissed through the air. Bormann ducked, his fat body trembling visibly. He would dearly love to turn and flee to the cover of the bunker below, but he knew he dare not. Once the mysterious SS men entered the shelter and were heard by the others, many of whom hated him, he would be finished. He must stay on the surface, deadly dangerous as it was, and deal with them here.

'Naturally, we must anticipate that the Ivans could be trying to pull some sort of trick on us, Sturmbannführer,' he heard himself saying to the hatchet-faced officer from the Nordland Division, who was in charge of the exit-guard.

'How, Obergruppenführer?' the SS man snapped, eyes to his front.

'They've done it before,' Bormann answered quickly, 'dressed up in our uniforms and speaking German. Done it a lot. Suicide squads, ready to sacrifice their own lives in

181

order to assassinate an important person or achieve an important objective.'

'Suicide squad, eh!' the other man grunted. 'I'll give 'em a right old Ascension Day commando with that,' he indicated the squat muzzle of the stationary flame-thrower mounted to the right of the exit. 'That'll tickle the eggs off 'em all right.'

Bormann forced a weak smile. 'I agree, Sturm. We can't take any chances.'

Schwaegermann, who had been forced to come to the surface by the other man for some reason he could not fathom, glanced at the Reichsleiter curiously. But Bormann's fat face showed no other emotion save fear, overwhelming fear.

Time passed.

As the de Lupe Hunting Commando fought their way through the smoke and rubble, dropping every now and again when a salvo of Russian shells landed close by, the priest told himself that if anyone believed in hell – which *he* didn't – it must appear like Berlin this day.

Whole blocks had been replaced by wastelands of rubble, pock-marked by hundreds, perhaps thousands of shell and bomb craters, and laced by grotesquely twisted, intertwined, reddened girders. On all sides there was an intricate chaos of gutted, windowless, roofless houses and offices with the streets vanished below mountains of rubble.

He shook his head. Once, he had set all his fanatical hopes on this city. It was to have been the new Rome for him: the renewer of Europe, rescuing it from its decadence, giving it a new creed: destruction of the Bolshevik sub-human. Now that wasn't to be. As it died, he would die – and die gladly because there was nothing else to live for. But before he disappeared from the face of this crazy world, he would take the arch-traitor with him. Bormann.

'*Attention!*' one of the men, threading their way through the smoking rubble behind him, called.

182

The low roar that had begun to the west became a scream, an angry baleful scream, its fury elemental, yet man-made and precise. De Lupe and his men didn't need to be told what the sound meant. '*Stalin organs!*'

They dropped as one. Up ahead of them the looters, civilians and soldiers alike, scattered frantically, pelting for cover. With a mighty antiphonal crash, the first salvo of rocket shells burst. Dismembered bodies flew everywhere. In an instant dying looters lay writhing on all sides. The gutters gurgled with crimson blood. Weakened buildings collapsed in a great slithering roar. Vicious tongues of flame shot up. Huge chunks of masonry crashed down on the survivors. A huge cart horse clattered through a path between the burning buildings, mane and tail afire, eyes wide and wild with unspeakable terror. Naked civilians followed, bursting out of the inferno, wading through the mire and the jellied, bloody flesh of the recently dead.

As surprisingly as it had started, the bombardment ceased, leaving behind a loud echoing silence. Awed, white-faced, wide-eyed, shaking their heads to clear away the ringing noise, the survivors staggered back to their task of looting like sleep-walkers.

De Lupe rose too. Wordlessly, he indicated that the Hunting Commando should close on him by placing his out-stretched fingers on the top of his dust-covered helmet, the old infantry signal for 'rally on me'.

'Comrades,' he began, staring around at the circle of tired, dirty faces with the eyes gleaming unnaturally bright and large from sunken sockets, 'you know we will die soon. . . .' He paused and let the words sink in, gazing at them intently. But his veterans of the Charlemagne showed no fear. 'But if we die, we die for a good cause. We die, not for Germany, but for France, for Europe. *Camarades, vive la France!*'

'*Vive la France!*' the hoarse cry from a dozen throats in a strange language startled the looters out of their daze. They stared in awe as the SS men filed by them, heavily armed, their hard young faces set in a look of fanatical devotion to death, as if they were creatures from another planet.

'Perhaps they won't manage to get through, Reichsleiter,' Schwaegermann suggested nervously, as the shelling commenced once more, interspersed with the obscene plops and belches of mortar bombs. Now, he was bleeding from his nose and ears with the shock of the detonations. He had only one remaining desire before he died – to escape into the bunker below and bury himself in the darkest, deepest room he could find.

Bormann controlled his own fear. Schwaegermann was the only witness of the conversation with Goebbels. The '*Gift* Dwarf' would kill himself soon; Schwaegermann must suffer the same fate. 'Give them a few more minutes. If they are our own S S men – genuine Germans – then they'll get through. We must get to the end of this business.' Not giving Schwaegermann a chance to protest, he turned swiftly to the hatchet-faced Sturmbannführer. 'What do you estimate their chance of getting through out there, Sturm?'

The S S officer pushed his peaked badge to the back of his cropped head with a jerk of his thumb and forefinger, spitting drily into the rubble as he did so. 'The air out there is pretty heavy with iron, Reichsleiter. I doubt if the ordinary stubble-hopper could make it. But shit, if they're S S, they could go to hell and back!'

'Then we stay,' Bormann said with more confidence than he felt.

'Till dark if necessary. Then we go.'

'Yes, Reichsleiter, it does look as if it's going to be the last chance to piss off,' the S S officer agreed. 'The S S have got a task force together, mainly from my own division, Battle Group Baerenfaenger, and a few spaghetti-eaters from the Spanish Blue Division. We've got three Mark IV tanks, and half a dozen half-tracks and armoured cars.

We'll cover the break-out.' His hatchet-face relaxed momentarily into a bitter smile. 'The S S always gets the shitty ones.'

'Buy combs, lousy times ahead, what, Sturm?' the one-armed boy manning the flame-thrower said.

'That's about it, Bubi,' the officer agreed. 'Now gentlemen, what about the Reichsleiter ordering a round of schnaps for my boys while we wait? My tonsils are floating!'

The Hunting Commando fought its way through a mass of screaming, almost hysterical housewives, looting a wrecked *Wehrmacht* supply convoy, scattering the elderly military policemen who were trying to stop them, crunching over shattered glass and debris, trampling over the dead drivers sprawled in the road in their eagerness to get their hands on the precious tins of food the wrecked trucks contained. Slowly, while de Lupe's men struggled on, the street was covered by an inch-thick carpet of flour, jam, black syrup, condensed milk, dropped or thrown away by the screaming, clawing mob. Twice the priest fell to his knees and had to be dragged to his feet out of the sticky, slippery mess by his men. In the end he had had enough of the women. 'Five rounds – *fire!*' he commanded.

His men responded to his order immediately. They raised their machine pistols and pressed the triggers. The high-pitched hysterical hiss of the Schmeisser had its effect. The women fell back, eyes wide with fear, letting their loot fall from their suddenly nerveless fingers, whispering, '*S S ... S S ... The headhunters are here!*'

Silently de Lupe and his men passed through a corridor of frightened women. They marched on, the only sound, for a while at least, the harsh tread of their steel-shod boots on the glass debris everywhere. They swung round a corner into another street. It was filled with shattered German vehicles, some of them still glowing a dull red with heat. Corpses of German soldiers lay sprawled everywhere

185

among the wrecks. De Lupe had no eyes for them. His gaze was fixed on the bullet-pocked, bent, blue-and-white street sign above his head. How it had survived the barrage which had destroyed the convoy he didn't know. But it had, although the lamp post to which it was attached had been twisted into a tortured 'S' shape by the blast. *'Vossstrasse,'* he read the name out loud, making the street sound strange with his French intonation.

He turned to the others. 'It cannot be far now, comrades,' he announced. 'General Krukenberg said it would be close to the *Vossstrasse. Allez marchez ou crevez!'*

'March or bust!' almost joyfully his veterans echoed the battle cry of the Charlemagne, and began the last stage of their long march through the shattered capital.

'Sturm!' It was the one-armed boy at the flame-thrower. 'Something moved over there – at two o'clock, right of that burned-out Opel.'

The hatchet-faced officer sat up immediately. Next to him Bormann and Schwaegermann tensed. Together the three of them stared at the rubble next to the red-glowing Opel Wanderer. All around them, the S S men hidden in the debris levelled their weapons.

For a moment, Bormann, his heart racing, thought the S S man they called Bubi had been mistaken; his ears had played him tricks, but then he, too, heard the sound. 'It could be . . . them,' he whispered to the S S officer thickly, hardly recognizing his own voice.

'You don't know, Reichsleiter,' the officer replied cynically, 'it might be Father Christmas, come to bring us an early present, eh?'

Bormann said nothing.

'White flag,' Bubi announced, his one hand curled carefully around the trigger of his terrible weapon.

They stared through the pall of smoke. A lone figure, clad in a German steel helmet, but wearing some sort of long gown that reached down to his ankles, was waving a

186

dirty white rag attached to the end of a machine pistol. Behind him cautious heads, also clad in German helmets, had appeared from both sides of a mass of rubble.

'They look German,' Schwaegermann said, hesitantly.

'But why is the fellow with the flag wearing that long thing?' Bormann interjected. 'Could be a damned Bible-thumper or something to me. Certainly not S S.'

'We'll see,' the hatchet-faced officer said easily. He cupped his hands around his mouth and bellowed. 'Advance and be recognized. Stop when I order you to. And by yourself, hands up in the air. Understood?'

'*Entendu*,' de Lupe said, wishing he had not left Doepgen, his interpreter, behind to guard the prisoners. At times like these, the average soldier shot first and asked questions later. Feeling a little foolish, for it was four years since he had last raised his hands in the air when he had surrendered to the Boche outside Verdun, he staggered across the wasteland towards the German positions. The Nordland soldiers watched the lone man carefully, eyes narrowed, fingers tensed on their triggers.

Bormann swallowed hard. 'Never seen an S S man looking like that before,' he attempted, hoping he could influence the hatchet-faced officer.

The other man said nothing, but he held his machine pistol at the ready.

The strange S S officer was now about fifty metres away. Despite the heavy pall of smoke, they could see him quite clearly as he stumbled across the ruins. Out of the corner of his eye, Bormann watched the officer's face anxiously. It revealed nothing. Could he convince him, if these were the S S men come to fetch him to General Krukenberg's H Q, that they should be liquidated?

'*Stop there!*' the officer shouted suddenly, startling Bormann. It took the man with his hands above his head a couple of moments to take in the command. He stopped awkwardly.

'What unit are you?'

'S S Division Charlemagne,' the accent was recognizably French.

'Good mob,' the hatchet-faced officer said in an aside. 'We were with them in Russia. For frogs they were good fighters.' He raised his voice. 'And why are you here?' he called.

'To speak to. . .' de Lupe struggled with the German construction, 'to Bormann. . . . On orders of General Krukenberg.'

The S S officer frowned, but Bormann watched him anxiously, knowing that he would not obey an order to shoot the stranger. He cast around frantically for some way out. In a moment the S S officer would order the man out there to come to the bunker and then, he, Bormann, would be finished. His eyes fell on Bubi, his one hand pressed tight on the trigger of the flame-thrower. He had it.

'*Ach Scheisse!*' he cried abruptly, as if he might have been hurt by something, and lurched forward directly against Bubi. The one-armed boy didn't have time to withdraw his hand. Automatically he pressed the trigger.

A hush. An angry roar. Suddenly the air was searingly hot. A greedy tongue of blue-red flame spurted out, curled around the standing man and consumed him immediately. Monseigneur Comte Mayel de Lupe fell writhing to the ground, his habit alive with flames, screaming with horror as they rose and tore at his eyes. The sour choking stench of charred flesh and the copper odour of boiling blood assailed the nostrils of the horrified men watching at the exit to the bunker; and then the enraged veterans of the Charlemagne were rushing forward, firing as they came, crying their war cry of death, attempting to reach the burning man. They never made it. The Nordland defenders opened up at once. The flame-thrower hissed again. The survivors of the first crazed charge flung themselves among the ruins and, gasping like ancient asthmatics, watched as the bricks glowed eerily and the flame reached out for them, eager to take them to its greedy maws.

188

It wreathed them. Their lungs burst. The searing flame tore at their flesh. Here and there a man screaming in panic sprang to his feet, trailing flame behind him, only to run straight into the massed machine-guns of the SS. Then it was all over. Scattered among the blackened smoking ruins there were what appeared to be a handful of naked pygmies, crouched rigidly, hands clawing the air in the permanence of death.

Bormann breathed a sigh of relief, as the machine-gun petered away to a few final bursts and then stopped altogether. 'I was right after all,' he heard himself saying, though he wondered where he got the strength to speak. 'They were some sort of suicide commando. Perhaps out to get me, eh, Sturmbannführer?'

The hatchet-faced officer pushed his cap to the back of his head and shrugged carelessly. 'Well, now we got them, Reichsleiter.' He took a cigarette from behind his right ear and lit it. What did it matter if a few more poor sods were killed or not? he asked himself cynically. Before this day was out, they'd probably all be dead anyway.

2

'In them days before the war out in India, your ordinary squaddie could live like a prince on a couple of annas a day,' Higgins was droning on, vanished completely in some crazy world of his own, as he lay crouched in the foetal position in the dirty straw. 'The niggers treated yer like a bloomin' lord. Shave yer in yer charpoy, and yer wouldn't even know they was doing it, then the char wallah'd bring yer cuppa, and if yer wanted and the orderly sergeant had done his rounds, they'd bring up a little bint for yer as well. Not one of them over thirteen, dirty randy little buggers. Them was the days.' Slowly great tears started to roll down his tortured face.

Mallory took his hand off Higgins's shoulder thoughtfully, almost sadly. There was nothing he could do for the bombardier now. He was finished; his mind was gone completely. Ilona looked at him enquiringly.

He shook his head. Outside it was beginning to grow dark again. The S S had taken his watch so he did not know the exact time, but he guessed it might be about six o'clock. The firing was beginning to die away, indicating that night was on its way; there was too much danger of killing one's own troops by shellfire in the darkness.

He sat down and automatically she slipped her arm around his shoulders affectionately. 'What do you think, Mike?' she asked, no longer any fear in her voice.

'Well, Ilona, it's not so good. We're between the devil and the deep blue sea. If the S S doesn't get us, the Russians will.' He pulled a face. 'I'm afraid it's that kind of situation.'

190

'You don't think they'll simply disappear and leave us here just before the Russians come?'

'You saw them, Ilona, when they brought in that lump of congealed sawdust masquerading as bread for us to eat a while back. Both of them, the big oaf who speaks German and the skinny one with the bandage around his head, are French. There's no way for them to go back to their country. They'll stay here to the bitter end, I'm afraid.' He pressed her hand reassuringly. 'But don't worry, I'll think of something yet.'

She squeezed his sore shoulders and her other hand dropped to his lap. There was no purpose behind the movement, just a simple accidental gesture, but it sent an electric shock surging through Mallory's loins of a kind he had not experienced since the Albanian mission. For a moment he forgot everything in the realization that at last he must have found the solution to his problem.

Ilona looked at him curiously. 'Is there anything the matter, Mike?'

He felt himself flushing furiously like a schoolboy who was about to peck his first girlfriend on the cheek. 'No, no,' he answered hastily, exploring this new feeling of confidence and hope, 'nothing, Ilona.' Carefully he took her hand and placed it on her own shapely knee, praying that what had happened to him at that moment was not too obvious. 'Now listen, Ilona, you know approximately why we are here?'

She nodded.

'Tits they had on them in them days like melons – and you could have all yer wanted for a few annas,' Higgins mumbled in the corner.

'But so far you don't know why we have to kill Bormann?'

'I met him once at a party,' she said slowly, thinking of that other Golden Pheasant, the Kreisleiter, who had made her drunk and then tossed her on the couch in her father's study and raped her so brutally, leaving her to sob and

191

bleed, while he drank the general's best cognac. Bormann had been like the Kreisleiter, all greedy piggish eyes, wandering sausage fingers, full of sexual menace. 'I didn't like him.'

'You mean you could recognize him?' Mallory interjected quickly, knowing that Higgins was useless now.

'Of course. You don't forget a face like that – like that of a bruiser who's taken to drink and too much food. At the party, he took his snout out of the trough only when he thought he could get his paws on some woman.'

Excitedly, feeling more and more confident all the time, Mallory told Ilona the reason for Higgins's presence in the team before explaining the reason why C had sent him to kill the Reichsleiter.

'You mean the Russians are going to use that Nazi swine?' she asked horrified.

He nodded. 'Not only that, we feel in London that if the Russians succeed in forming a national German government with his help then in, say, a year's time, there'll be no stopping them in Europe. In the end, it will mean another war.'

'War again! Can't the politicians get enough killing?'

'Where there is a vacuum, it must be filled by someone or other. It's an old political rule of thumb.'

She stared at him, her green eyes flashing angrily, while opposite them the crazy bombardier mumbled, 'Then yer really felt like a man. All the gash yer wanted, beer dirt cheap and fags thrown at yer. The wogs knew how to treat the squaddie in them days. . . .'

'But he must be stopped. He and the rest of the brown swine that got Germany into this mess. Now he's going to walk out, wipe his hands and say "it's nothing to do with me". No,' she said firmly, her eyes gleaming, 'he can't be allowed to get away with it!'

'You'll help me?'

'Of course, Mike.' She pressed his shoulders tenderly, the angry light replaced in her eyes by one of affection and

192

love. 'I'd kill him *personally* if necessary. There must be no more war just so that swine like that can feather their own nests. Not for England, you understand, but Germany ... for the decent German people, who fought and died,' her voice broke momentarily as she remembered her brother Lothar, long buried in that remote Polish village whose very name she had forgotten, 'because they felt they were fighting for a just cause, and not for a bunch of unscrupulous politicians, whose only loyalty was to themselves.

'Good, good, Ilona,' he said, smiling at her enthusiasm, then becoming serious again. 'But remember we've got to get out of this mess – and time is running out damned quickly.'

Ilona bit her bottom lip thoughtfully, one long curl of blonde hair hanging down over her high forehead. 'Listen, Mike, what do you think is man's most powerful motivating force?'

Mallory smiled briefly. She was very German, concerned with philosophy even at moments like this. 'Well, I seem to remember one German poet writing, *'Erst kommt das Gressen, dann die Moral'*.*

'Brecht ... Bert Brecht.'

'Yes.'

'I agree, but with one proviso. After a man fills his belly, there is one other thing that comes before morals.'

'And that is sex?'

He frowned, wondering where the discussion was leading. 'Okay, I'll buy that. But what has it got to do with us?'

She smiled at him boldly, a sudden wanton abandon in those beautiful green eyes of her, her mouth open, her pink tongue running the length of her lips provocatively. 'Just this, Mr Englishman. Sex is going to be the key which will open that cell door there. . . .'

It was now dark. In the Goebbels' room, Magda roused her children from their sleep. They blinked up at her and

* First grub, then morals.

rubbed their sleepy eyes with the backs of their tiny hands. 'Don't be afraid,' she soothed their sudden fears. 'The doctor is going to give you an injection, a kind that is being given,' her voice broke and tears flooded her eyes, but she controlled herself quickly, 'being given to all children and soldiers.'

She nodded to the pale-faced dentist, Dr Kunz, who she had convinced to do the job she couldn't bring herself to do. He stepped forward and lifted the morphine syringe, his hand shaking violently.

Magda smiled winningly at her children and one by one they bared their skinny arms to receive the final injection, which would make them sleepy. When they were all stretched out, their breath coming in the short hectic fashion of those drugged with morphine, she stepped from child to child, placing a crushed ampoule of potassium cyanide in their mouths. They were dead within five minutes.

Hitler's former chauffeur, Kempka, who was going to lead one group of would-be escapers, came to say good-bye just before nine o'clock. He hardly dare look at the six blond children stretched out so still on the rumpled beds. But Magda seemed completely calm. She asked the S S man to say good-bye to her son Harald who was in a British P O W camp, if he, Kempka, survived the break-out. Kempka promised he would.

Five minutes later, the Goebbels left the room arm in arm, the smaller man limping at the side of his blonde wife. At the door another escape group leader, Dr Naumann, dark and intelligent-looking, kissed Magda's hand as they passed. Wryly Goebbels said, 'We're going to have a little stroll up the steps to the garden. Then our friends won't have so far to carry us.' He smiled at Kempka who had struggled to carry Eva's body to the surface. They disappeared up the wet steep concrete stairway which led to the garden. A few moments passed. There was a single shot, then a second. Schwaegermann and Goebbels' chauffeur Rach ran up the stairs. They almost stumbled over Goeb-

194

bels' body. An S S soldier, smoking pistol still held in his clenched fist, was staring at the cripple, eyes wide with shock, as if he was realizing for the very first time whom he had just shot on orders. Two paces further on lay Magda, her skirt thrown up to reveal a stretch of pretty white leg and expensive silken panties, embroidered with her monogram 'M G'.

Hurriedly, the three men prepared the dead bodies, ducking low as a burst of tracer stitched the darkness in a zig-zag of lethal white bullets. Together they poured four jerricans of petrol over the Goebbels and ignited it. Without waiting to see the effect of the blaze – there was too much lead flying around – they fled back the way they had come.

It was now exactly nine o'clock. Within the next hour, the first group under General Mohnke of the Waffen S S, some thirty strong, would leave the bunker. They would be followed twenty minutes later by the Kempka group, mostly women and a few civilians, though Hitler's former chauffeur hoped that he would have the protection of the Nordland Battle Group and their armoured vehicles, already forming up somewhere above on the surface. Dr Naumann's party would come third. Still Bormann, worried now and shaky at the thought of what lay before him, had not made up his mind to which group he should attach himself.

Mohnke's people, being the first out, might have the element of surprise on their side, but there were too many men among them. If they hit trouble, Bormann knew they would fight back, and he didn't want that. Kempka couldn't help but run into the Russians. The noise of the Nordland tanks would give them away. With the Ivans blocking every exit road out of the bunker area, sooner or later the tanks would run into some sort of anti-tank barrier. That left Naumann, the sleek, cunning, former secretary-of-state in Goebbels' Ministry.

Bormann didn't like Naumann one bit. The man was a

lawyer and like all lawyers he was a shyster in Bormann's opinion; too clever by half. Besides, if the Russians did intercept either of the previous two parties, they might well be expecting Naumann's group, and he didn't fancy dying at the hands of some ignorant, slant-eyed, Siberian peasant boy. But he had to make up his mind. In the end, Bormann picked Naumann's group.

Sidling across to where its members were discussing the chances of successfully breaking through in hushed tones as if they were involved in some great secret or other, he tapped Naumann on the shoulder. 'Herr Staatssekretar.'

Naumann turned. When he saw Bormann, his face darkened still further. 'Yes, Reichsleiter?' he asked coldly.

'Can I tag along with your group, Herr Doktor?'

For one anxious moment Bormann thought that Naumann was going to refuse, but obviously he was still scared of the Reichsleiter, although Bormann had no power left now. He nodded. 'All right, you can come along with my group, Reichsleiter.' He looked down at the other man's belly, which swelled up under the grey S S general's greatcoat, with obvious disgust. 'But you're in poor physical shape. You'd better keep close to me – with the women.'

Bormann contained his temper just in time; let the swine insult him. One day, one day soon, he would be in the position to punish pigs like Naumann. For the time being he would keep his mouth shut; he needed the smooth ex-lawyer to get him started on his way. Once they were in the Wilhelmstrasse, Naumann and the rest would see him no more.

Naumann directed him to his position and Bormann, keeping his gaze lowered to the ground, joined the nervous, chattering women. In one hour they would commence their break-out.

'But Ilona, is there no other way?' Mallory said urgently.

'No,' she answered, completely absorbed in her task.

'Of course, we were good on the square,' Higgins was

muttering, still reliving those days in India so long ago. 'Out we'd get just after five before it got too hot. By Christ, we was smart in them days, all white blanco and gleaming brasses. You could have shaved yersen on the crease in our shorts. . . .'

Ilona Graefin von Prittwitz was virtually naked now, save for a skimpy pair of pink lace panties, and matching bra. In spite of his concern and the danger of their situation, Mallory couldn't take his gaze off her slim white body with the high firm small breasts. He felt the old familiar stirring of his loins and controlled himself with difficulty.

She finished her undressing and sat down graciously on the dirty straw opposite the door. 'The Judas Hole looks right down on me,' she indicated the little glass bull's eye set high in the door, at present obscured by the metal disc on the other side. 'Once they get a look,' she parted her legs deliberately and Mallory swallowed hard. He knew what she meant, 'they'll come in. Men are all the same,' she smiled at the look of concern and desire on his face. 'Thank God!'

'We was a sight to see, with the band playing and the lads swinging their arms. Bags o' swank we had, by God, *we had*! There wasn't a smarter battalion in the whole of British India. You couldn't beat the old British squaddie then. . . .'

Ilona nodded to Mallory and indicated that he should take up his position behind the door. 'All right,' she mouthed the words soundlessly. 'Now!'

'Please, please, let me out,' she cried piteously. *'Bitte, ich will nicht sterben. . . . Ich mache alles, alles was Sie wollen, aber lassen Sie mich nur heraus. . . .* Let me out. . . .' Her voice died away in sobs, her white blonde hair falling prettily over her breasts as she bent her head, her shoulders heaving, almost as if she had broken down completely.

It was a consummate performance, Mallory couldn't help thinking. If he hadn't have known that her eyes, hidden by her hands, were completely dry, he would have sworn he

197

was watching the total collapse of a demented woman who had been driven too far. He flashed a quick glance at the Judas Hole. It still remained blank. As yet the S S guards had not reacted.

Ilona seemed to sense the lack of reaction, too. She redoubled her efforts, her body weaving from side to side, racked by false emotion. 'Anything,' she screamed, 'you can have anything you want from me! But please let me out before it's too late. *Please!*'

There was a slight click. Mallory's heart missed a beat. There was a circle of yellow light coming from the Judas Hole! Next instant it was blocked out again as one of the guards peered in at the cell.

Mallory could imagine just what the reaction of the S S man was: a mixture of caution and sexual desire. Whoever was standing there would now be running his delighted gaze at that beautiful body, already feeling the stirring of desire, but wondering if it were a trick after all, or a genuine offer: a desperate woman ready to sell her body to escape death. The S S men were veterans of Russia, Mallory knew. Perhaps this would not be the first time that they had had an offer of this kind, made by some Russian woman partisan prisoner or a Jewess, trying to avoid being sent to a death camp after being picked up in a raid.

He waited tensely, the leg wrenched from the little three-legged stool, the cell's only furniture, clasped in a sweating hand. In the centre of the room, the girl continued to wail heart-brokenly, while Higgins kept up his insane dirge. The seconds ticked away. Mallory imagined that a whispered conversation was taking place on the other side of the door. Were the two guards discussing who should have Ilona first? Or were they deciding anxiously not to go in after all? Had they realized it was a trick?

The sound of a rusty bolt being drawn back made Mallory jump. *They were opening the door!*

Cautiously, the big S S man who spoke German poked his head round the door, machine pistol at the ready.

Mallory licked his parched lips and raised his improvised club.

The big SS man hesitated, his greedy peasant eyes taking in every detail of the naked body before him. Ilona clasped her breasts and offered them lasciviously to the dumbfounded man.

'Please, take me,' she whispered in a hoarse voice, running the pink tip of her tongue around her wet lips, 'but let me go. You can do what you like to me.' She lowered her eyes. 'Anything.'

Mallory's every nerve tingled electrically. He strained his ears to catch the sound of the second guard moving closer to have a look over the bigger man's shoulder. 'Now, no tricks, wench,' he heard the big one gasp thickly, 'or you'll get more than a bit of my hard salami.'

The big man moved into the cell, already fumbling with his flies. In the corner, Higgins was moaning, 'But what did I do wrong, sarge. . . . What did I do wrong . . . ?'

At that instant, Mallory sprang forward. His club descended upon the bandaged skull of the second man. He went down yelping with pain. Desperately the big one fumbled for the safety catch on his machine pistol. Seeing Mallory coming for him, he changed his mind. Swiftly he brought up the Schmeisser's metal butt. It connected with Mallory's fingers where they held the stool leg. *'Ouch!'* he gasped and let it tumble to the floor. The big SS man snapped off the safety. At the same moment that Ilona launched her body at him, he pulled the trigger. Mallory felt the searing heat as the slugs hissed by his head. In the corner Higgins screamed. Next moment the SS man was on the floor next to his unconscious companion with Ilona on top of him, a confused mess of flailing arms and legs, the girl's long nails ripping furiously at his face.

With a curse, the SS man flung Ilona to one side and grabbed for the Schmeisser on the floor beside him. Mallory beat him to it. His steel-shod boot slammed down on the SS man's fingers who screamed in agony. Mallory

199

didn't hesitate. He drew his boot back again, just as the S S man started to raise himself. With all his strength and the skill he had acquired as a centre-half at Sandhurst, he smashed the toe of his boot directly against the tip of the S S man's raised chin. There was the audible click of the man's spine breaking. He skidded across the cell floor and landed rammed against the wall, head slumped down on his chest, dead.

For a long moment Mallory leaned weakly against the wall, his chest heaving, his breath coming in short hectic gasps. At his feet, Ilona lay sprawled also unable to move. In the corner Higgins groaned piteously and repeated that strange dirge, his voice now faint and very weak, 'But what did I do wrong, sarge . . . What did I do wrong. . . .?'

With an effort Mallory pulled himself together. He hauled the girl to her feet and glanced at the smaller S S man. He was out cold. Mallory picked up his machine pistol and slung it over his own shoulder. 'Get dressed, Ilona,' he ordered her, his voice not quite steady.

'Higgins?'

'I'll have a look, Ilona.'

The burst had stitched a line of bloody holes across the bombardier's chest, through which Mallory could see the lungs, a dull grey against the bloody mess, pulsating obscenely. He shook his head. Higgins was dying.

Suddenly Higgins opened his eyes and looked directly at Mallory with that old cunning Cockney grin on his face that it had borne the first time he had met him at Aldershot military prison in what seemed another age. 'Higgins 175, sir, one of the old sweats. Bin everywhere, seen everything, snaked everything, brown, white, black and yeller.' He winked. 'Don't make 'em like me any. . .' His head fell to one side and he was dead.

For a moment, Mallory stared down at the dead soldier. Crook, lecher, murderer that he had been, he had been a good soldier, 'one of the old sweats'. Instinctively Mallory knew that, for better or worse, England no longer produced men like Higgins. Bending down he closed Higgins' eyes, wondering if he shouldn't say something over the dead man, but was unable to find the words.

He turned and found Ilona, already dressed, the other Schmeisser slung over her shoulder, also staring at the dead man. 'He died better than he lived,' she said softly.

'Perhaps,' he answered his voice neutral. Then he remembered the task ahead of them this night. Urgently he grabbed her arm. 'Come on, Ilona, if you're with me –'

'I am,' she said, quiet determination in her beautiful face.

'Then let's go. Time is running out.'

Together they stepped out over the two bodies, leaving the dead Higgins to eternity.

3

Hertz took out his set of stainless steel false teeth, noting how hollow-cheeked and old he looked in the mirror, and started to scrub them with a nail-brush under the running water.

On the bed, sleeper, clad only in skimpy underpants, exhibiting his perfect, muscular body in that way of his which Hertz had begun to hate in the last few days that they had spent together, was cleaning his pistol, slightly oiling the 9mm slugs before replacing them carefully in the magazine.

Hertz studied his face as he scrubbed the teeth, which replaced those he had lost in the years after his flight from Minsk when undernourishment had turned him into the toothless, skinny old man he was now, motivated only by the hatred of a world which had turned him into an outsider. A Jew after all, in spite of his lack of religion, cut off from the gentiles by his nose, his hair, his oriental cast of features, just as much as if he went around in the medieval clothing, complete with kiss curls and prayer shawl, of those from the heart of the ghetto.

The sleeper was a tough proposition. There was something brutal, even cruel, about the packed muscles of the shoulders, and his fingers, long and strangely splayed at the tips, looked as if they might tear a man apart without too much strain. What if he went ahead with the plan suggested to him by the strange couple from the Haganah, or whatever they called their organization? He would have to tackle the sleeper. His companion was loyal to the cause, there was no doubt about that. Like so many of those who lived outside Russia, the Soviet Fatherland was a second Rome, a paradise on earth. If they knew anything about the corruption, the cruelty, the cancerous nature of Soviet society, they conveniently forgot it, or found some easy excuse. The sleeper would never believe that there could be anything wrong in the U S S R. He would try to stop him.

Somehow the other man seemed to be aware of Hertz's scrutiny of him in the mirror, for suddenly he said in that easy un-Russian manner of his: 'You're a Jew, aren't you, Hertz?'

Hertz paused in his task, the water dripping down over his teeth and hand. 'As a matter of fact I am. Why do you ask?'

The sleeper took his time. He slipped the final cartridge in the magazine, snapped it back into the pistol's butt with professional ease and clicked on safety. 'Oh, I don't know. I suppose I like to know as much as I can about the person I'm teamed up with.'

'I'm a Russian first and then a Jew,' Hertz said a little testily, still holding the grotesque set of teeth in his hand.

'Hm.' The sleeper's comment could have meant anything, or nothing. Was it that of someone accepting the fact without further discussion, or were there hidden depths to it? Hertz found himself looking at his own face in the mirror, as if he were attempting to find his own reaction there. Why should he be concerned about being named a Jew after all these years since he had fled from Minsk?

'How did you get into the organization?' the sleeper said, holding up the pistol and closing one eye to squint along the barrel. 'I mean your kind,' he left the rest of the sentence unsaid.

'What do you mean – *my kind*?' Hertz asked, finishing the task of cleaning his teeth and slipping them back in his mouth. He frowned at his image in the fly-blown mirror as if he were not very pleased with it.

The sleeper seemed satisfied with the sight. He put the pistol in its holster. 'I have been away too long from the

Soviet Homeland to know what the situation is there, but in America, they always say that the Jews are too smart to enter the Services where there's danger – they're too busy making money.'

Hertz looked at him aghast. Did he really mean what he had just said, or was it some sort of cruel joke, an attempt to get him angry? The sleeper's face revealed nothing, and with his next question he changed the subject completely, as if he were not aware that he had insulted Hertz. 'What is the drill tonight, Hertz?'

Hertz pulled himself together swiftly. Anyone looking at him at that moment would not have been aware of the hate that had just crept into his heart and steeled it. There was nothing visible on his face to indicate that the sleeper's casual words had made up his mind for him; he had come to his decision, whatever the outcome.

'We shall take a small squad of infantry from the 150th Rifle Division with us,' he began the briefing, amazed at his own calm, for he had just decided to kill Bormann. . . .

Now, as the oily yellow and red flames that had charred the bodies of the Goebbels so that Goebbels himself lay shrunk to the size of a real dwarf, one hand raised in a horrible blackened claw, began to die, the order echoed down the gloomy damp entrance to the bunker. *'Gruppe Mohnke – vorwärts!'*

The tall burly S S general buckled on his helmet and started for the entrance, followed by Hitler's adjutant, Guensche. Behind him, came the rest of the group, which included the Führer's secretaries and his personal cook.

They emerged into a lunar landscape. The once-proud government area was now a waste of brick rubble, blanketed with a pall of brown smoke, electrified every now and again by the violent scarlet flash of a shell burst or the icy, silver light of a Very flare.

But the first group had little time to consider the changed face of Berlin, which most of them had last seen a week before. Already a slow Russian machine-gun was beginning to fire at them. The tracer zipped through the smoke. Slugs started to howl from the walls all around them. Mohnke cursed angrily. Things were going wrong right from the start. He bellowed an order above the crackle of small arms fire. One by one, his group crawled through a narrow hole in the wall of the wrecked Reich Chancellery, near the corner of the Wilhelmstrasse and Vossstrasse, and pelted at irregular intervals in small groups of two or three across the two hundred yards to the burning Hotel Kaiser-hof.

Mohnke, his chest heaving with the unusual exercise, counted them as they skidded to a stop in the ruin, the men panting, the women for the most part frightened out of their wits by the gauntlet of fire they had just run. They were all there. He had not suffered one casualty. 'All right, follow me, and keep a distance of five metres between each individual. There might be snipers down there.'

Hurriedly, they began to descend the dark, slippery, debris-littered steps of the Berlin *U-Bahn*.*

The first group of escapers were on their way.

'They've gone . . . they've gone . . . they've gone . . .' the shouts announcing the news that the first group had disappeared echoed and re-echoed down the corridors of the bunker. Most of those left were too drunk by now to hear, but those of the next group, Kempka's, began to pull on their equipment. Erich Kempka himself, dressed now in the uniform of a colonel of the Armed S S, pulled on his helmet and slung his machine pistol across his chest. 'Follow me,' he commanded huskily and together with his group, he started to elbow his way through the drunks.

'Good luck,' Bormann shouted after him.

Kempka gave him a last contemptuous look, but said nothing.

Bormann shrugged and walked across to his secretary,

* Underground.

Else Krueger, his new jackboots creaking noisily on the concrete. He took the girl's hand and for a moment he seemed unable to say anything.

'*Reichsleiter?*' 'Kruegerchen', little Krueger, as everyone in the office called her, asked surprised. Had emotion crept even into his hard heart at last, she wondered.

'Well then, good-bye,' he said slowly. 'I don't think there's much sense in it. I'll try, but I don't think I'll get through.'

The secretary looked at her boss critically. If 'M B', as she had always called Bormann behind his back in the office, didn't think there was a chance of getting through, why had he filled his left pocket with that favourite salami sausage of his and placed his collection of pornographic photos in the other? They didn't seem the actions of a man who was about to leave this world, she told herself. She gave a slight shrug. 'All the best. . . . We'll be thinking of you.'

'Thank you.' Bormann turned. Kruegerchen was staying in the bunker. She would spread the news that her boss hadn't expected to live. That news would finally reach the western allies and would probably prevent them looking for him until the time that the Ivans decided he should be resurrected from the dead. In spite of his inner tension and fear, he smiled as he walked back slowly to his own group.

Dr Naumann looked at his watch. It was ten minutes to ten on the night of 1 May, 1945. At ten o'clock precisely the third group would make its break-out attempt. He loosened the flap of his pistol holster and, wishing that he could urinate again, though he knew it was only a matter of nerves, called, 'All right, Naumann Group start to form up in your positions – *now!*'

'The Spree?' Mallory shouted above the roar of the Russian barrage.

Ilona shaded her eyes against the glare of the flames. 'Yes, that's the Weidendamm Bridge and those are the ruins of the Admiral Palace Theatre over there on the other side, I think,' she added, telling herself that she was no longer sure about anything in the city in which she had been born and spent all her life.

A machine-gun chattered suddenly nearby. *'Duck!'* Mallory yelled and pulled her down.

On the other side of the Spree, clearly outlined by the flames of the burning buildings everywhere, a group of S S men ran straight into the fire of a Russian machine-gun positioned on their side of the river. Wild, obscene curses flung from their gaping mouths; man after man went down, bowled over by that murderous fire, faces upturned towards a merciless Heaven, hands clawing the air as if they were trying to climb an invisible ladder. In seconds the S S platoon had been transformed into a heap of bloody bodies, most of them already dead before they hit the ground, lying there like broken toys abandoned by some careless child. Ilona stifled her cry of fear and Mallory pressed her hand hard, as they crouched there in the rubble. 'Well, now we know where the Russian front line is,' he whispered into her right ear.

She nodded, visibly controlling her fear. He pressed her hand ever harder and she said, 'Don't worry, Mike. I'll be all right. But do you think we'll ever be able to find anyone in this confusion?'

'I think so. If we can get across that damned river,' he stared grimly at the German tank barrier at the far end of the Weidendamm Bridge, with the bodies of Russian infantrymen lying everywhere on the cobbles in front of it, as if they had made an all-out assault upon it and failed at the last moment, 'and get into the area of the Chancellery, we'll find him. My guess is that there'll be a kind of no-man's land out there. On the only road he can take to the Russian positions around the Reichstag, we'll intercept him and . . .' he left the rest of his sentence unfinished.

Ilona fought her fear. In the blood-red light of a sudden flare, ascending over the river, dragging its crimson shadow across the water behind it, she stared at the man she now knew she loved. 'Have you ever killed a man, Mike?'

'A few.'

'What's it like?'

To Mallory, it didn't seem a strange question at that moment. Life in the dying capital was cheap that May night. 'I've not thought much about it before, Ilona,' he answered, his eyes searching the churning blood-red water that barred their way. 'It seemed then that one killed to survive. Tonight I kill a man to stop all this ever happening again. Then . . .' he paused, wondering if he dared envisage a future without bloodshed, 'then it's the last time for me.'

The Russian machine-gun had stopped firing and the flare was dying on the river with a subdued hiss. Ilona sprang to her feet, enthused with new energy. 'Come on, Mike,' she urged. 'We've got to find a way to get across!'

The stench of the tunnel hit Hertz in the face like a physical blow. He winced. The ancient German holding the hissing carbide lamp grinned, showing a mouthful of blackened stumps. 'Just the honest stink of shit,' he croaked, staring around at the two civilians and the little patrol of Russian infantrymen, each one with round-barrelled tommy-gun slung across his bemedalled chest. 'They closed it up in '33 after that van Lubbe affair,' he chuckled again. 'He was one of your lot, wasn't he?'

The sleeper wrinkled his nose in disgust. It seemed to him at that moment that their German guide might well be right. The tunnel stank as if it had been closed since the days of the Dutch crazy man, van Lubbe, who had been accused by the Fascists of setting fire to the Reichstag in 1933. 'Oh, come on,' he said impatiently, 'let's get on with it.'

The German hooked his lantern to his leather belt and with surprising speed for such an old man began to descend the dripping iron ladder into the nauseous tunnel, great swinging shadows rocking back and forth on the walls as he disappeared. Hertz drew a deep breath of the smoke-filled air and followed.

Zhukov himself had decided upon this route. Somehow or other in the confusion of the embattled capital, the Red Army had managed to find the ancient, slightly cracked German who had worked in Berlin's underground sanitation service for forty years before the war. Now the pensioner was to guide them beneath the estimated German frontline in the Reichstag area so that they would be able to meet the fleeing German politician in the area beyond, believed to be held only lightly by the enemy. 'You're too precious, Hertz,' the gravel-voiced army commander had rasped into the phone. 'Can't let some suicidal Fritz take your hide, can we? Get there safely and bring out the damned Fritz the same way. And say a good word for me to Comrade Beria when the secret police come to arrest me after the war when Old Leather Face starts to clean up the Red Army again like in '38.' Zhukov had chuckled throatily and rammed down the receiver, leaving Hertz to frown at the dead telephone and ask himself: 'Is a country where its heroes are frightened of being arrested by their own authorities worth fighting for?'

The old German could not be hurried, although the stench was murderous. Swinging his carbide lamp from side to side on the white, caked dripping walls of the tunnel, he plodded on at a steady, deliberate pace as if he had all the time in the world. Now, in this strange underground world, there was no sound save the hollow tread of their boots and the asthmatic breathing of their guide, whose wheezing lungs hissed like cracked bellows. Down here there was nothing to indicate the ferocious battle taking place above their heads. Once, they were startled by a gigantic shadow ahead, trembling in the glaring white light of the carbide lamp. One of the riflemen gasped audibly. The old man chuckled. He clapped his free hand against the side of his leather jacket. The shadow disappeared immediately in a soft scuffle of clawed feet. 'A rat,' the guide explained. 'Lot of 'em down here. Before the war in my day they were skinnier. But since the bombing and fighting, they've got nice and fat.' He grinned inanely at them. 'Lot of human grub for them up top, ain't there?'

Hertz shuddered and the sleeper said, 'Get on with it, you old fool!'

They marched on in silence. Five minutes passed. Ten. Without the old man, Hertz told himself, they would have been lost long ago. There were tunnels branching off in every direction at regular intervals, but the German seemed to know exactly which way they had to go.

'Unter den Linden,' the old man announced and paused for a rest after fifteen minutes. He pointed to an iron ladder secured to the wall and leading up to the surface. 'Back in the twenties when I was a young lad, I'd be up that at least twice a week when the ganger wasn't about. You see them days, the whores waiting for the rich gents coming home from the ministries didn't use to wear drawers. Quicker that way, I suppose. Surprising the things I've seen standing on that ladder looking up.' He guffawed with feeble pleasure at the memory of his ancient lecheries.

'Hurry up,' the sleeper snapped. 'Which way now?'

'Turn right here and down the Wilhelmstrasse. There are a lot of exits up there though. You'll have to tell me exactly where you want to surface, gentlemen.'

Before the sleeper could consider, Hertz spoke. He had already made up his mind that they would surface before the corner with the Vossstrasse. In the no-man's land which existed there, as he knew from the 150th Rifle Division's senior Intelligence officer, he would have a better chance of carrying out his task and disappearing. The Haganah people had promised him that they would take care of him once he reached the western suburb of Schoeneberg. According to them, they had an underground railway which would take him through Russian-occupied Germany, across the Elbe and from displaced person camp to displaced person camp until he reached Italy, where a freighter in their service, hired to smuggle Jews into British-mandated Palestine, would land him at a lonely spot on the coast not far from Haifa. Palestine – what would it be like? he mused.

'Junction of Vossstrasse and the Wilhelmstrasse,' the old man mused and rubbed his unshaven white chin making a sound like sandpaper. 'Yer know yer can get a bad headache popping up yer turnip just there? Lot of fighting going on about there, according to all reports.'

'Let me worry about that, old man,' Hertz snapped.

The sleeper stared at the other agent in some surprise. He had never heard the little Yid speak so decisively before. He shrugged and put it down to nerves. But he merely said, 'Let's get the hell out of this place.'

They marched on.

Kempka cursed. He had managed to get his group as far as the bank of the River Spree beyond the Friedrich-strasse Station. But just as they had been about to make an attempt to cross they had been hit by a severe Russian artillery barrage and had split up, with most of them running for the shelter of the nearby Admiral Palace Theatre.

Now he was alone, cut off from the rest by a Russian machine-gun located on the other bank of the river which had pinned him down while the others had fled in panic. Dodging from door to door, he edged his way to the Weidendamm Bridge where the anti-tank barrier, he could see in the red glare, was manned by SS troops. Taking a chance he pelted across the cobbled road, littered with the bodies of dead German soldiers and civilians. The men at the barrier swung round in alarm at the noise, for the sound of firing had died away again now, save for the dry crack of a sniper's rifle.

'Friend!' he gasped. 'Friend!'

The weary, begrimed SS troopers, most of them teen-aged boys, relaxed the pressure of their fingers on their triggers. He skidded to a stop, chest heaving, and leant

211

weakly against one of the cement blocks which made up the barrier.

Very formally, the NCO in charge of the defenders reported in the German fashion, even clicking his heels together as if he were on the parade ground at some SS training barracks in Paderborn or Sennelager. 'One NCO, two soldiers, first class, and ten men, eight casualties, sir.'

Kempka weakly touched his hand to his helmet. Did they really take him for a soldier? He was only a better-class chauffeur who had been given his colonelcy because Hitler had taken a shine to him. 'What's the situation, Oberscharführer?' he gasped. 'Can one get across?'

'Not a chance, sir.' He indicated the bonfire burning steadily on the other side of the Spree, its flickering flames magnifying silhouettes to gigantic size on the shattered walls of the ruined houses on both sides of the street that led to the bridge. 'They've got that going so that their snipers can pick off anybody who makes an attempt to cross the bridge. The shitty Ivans are parked on both sides of the road. A death trap.'

'Thanks,' Kempka said, trying to conceal his disappointment from the boy. He'd have to find another way to cross the Spree. Turning, he made his dangerous way back to the doorway of the Admiralspalast where what was left of his group who hadn't tried to find an escape route on their own were sheltering. 'No good,' he snapped laconically. 'The Ivans dominate the Weidendamm Bridge. We've had it there.'

Time passed. At his lookout post at the doorway of the Admiralspalast, Kempka strained his eyes against the glowing darkness, waiting for an opportune moment to make another dash for the anti-tank barrier and the expected gauntlet of Russian fire which would meet him when he and his people attempted to cross the bridge. Abruptly his heart missed a beat.

A small group of uniformed figures, strung out in single file and hugging whatever shadow was cast by the ruined houses, were making their way cautiously in his direction.

Kempka crooked his finger around the trigger of his machine pistol. A cold trail of fear traced its way down the small of his back. Were they Russians who had crossed the Spree? Abruptly he relaxed. He had recognized the uniform of the first man. It was *Wehrmacht*. He called to them as loudly as he dared. They started, stopped in alarm, obviously recognized the caller and hurried in the direction of the Admiralspalast.

Now as they came closer, he recognized them all by the dull, red glow from the Russian bonfire on the other side of the river. In front, there was Bormann in his SS general's uniform. Behind him came Naumann, Stumpfegger, Schwaegermann, Baur, Hitler's pilot, and the one-armed Hitler Youth leader, Axmann. They greeted each other as if they had not seen one another for years, then Kempka briefed them on the situation on the Weidendamm Bridge.

Bormann seemed bored or apathetic; his eyes wandered continually off, not in the direction of the river they were discussing, but back to the way they had just come. Naumann, the leader of the group, was very attentive. He suggested that the only way to force the Russian line was by tanks.

Kempka shook his head firmly. 'Tanks, Herr Doktor? Quite out of the question. There isn't a German tank left in the whole of Berlin!' He had hardly made his pronouncement when the escapers crowded into the doorway heard the rusty rattle of metal tracks and the harsh squeaking of huge brakes that heralded the approach of tanks.

Fearfully, they pressed themselves into the shadows, m.ps at the ready. The first gigantic tank swung round the corner squarely with a massive rumble of its engine in very low gear. Kempka breathed out a sigh of relief. The tank was not an Ivan T-34 as he had anticipated it would be; it was a German Tiger armed with a great overhanging 88mm cannon! It seemed almost too good to be true. Next instant another appeared, and another. Thereafter three

213

half-tracks swung into view, escorted on both sides by heavily armed infantrymen.

Kempka, happier than he had been for years, hesitated no longer. He ran into the street in front of the lead tank, waving his arms frantically and shouting for the driver to stop.

'Who are you . . . and who is in charge?' he cried as the first tank rumbled to a stop, its long cannon hanging above his helmeted head.

'Obersturmführer Hansen!' a voice called from the glowing darkness.

'Hier Obersturmbannführer Kempka. What's your objective?'

Quickly Hansen, a begrimed young man without a helmet, told him they were a section of the Nordland Division. The three half-tracks were piled high with their wounded. They were determined not to leave them behind for the Ivans; they were going to break out with the tanks in the lead.

Kempka absorbed the information. 'We'll join you,' he said. 'Up there the Ivans have a fortified position beyond the tank barrier. Your Mark VIs* will rout the Russians and give us cover as far as the Ziegelstrasse. After that, it's every man for himself. *Klar*?'

'Klar, Obersturmbannführer,' Hansen sang out, cheerfully.

Swiftly the survivors of Kempka's and Naumann's groups joined the weary youthful SS panzer grenadiers, who were forming up in a *Traube*, a grape, behind the Tigers, snapping home fresh magazines into their m.ps, checking the detonators of their stick grenades, loosening their pistols in the holsters ready for instant action.

Kempka's eye fell on Bormann, who was half crouched behind Naumann. The Reichsleiter looked frightened, very frightened indeed. Kempka nodded to himself with ap-

---

* Designation for the Tiger tank.

214

proval. The fat swine deserved everything that might be coming to him. Then, he concentrated on the way ahead.

Cautiously the first 'grape' moved off, Kempka, Stumpfegger, Bormann and Naumann, fringed by S S men, bent in fearful anticipation just behind the metallic giant, which stank of diesel fumes, its long hooded cannon swinging slowly from side to side like the snout of some primeval monster seeking out its prey.

They cleared the barrier. None of the S S men guarding it made an attempt to join them. Obviously they thought the break-out attempt was doomed to failure. Kempka felt the little hairs at the back of his neck stand erect with fear. They were approaching the first of the houses occupied by the Ivans. His flesh cringed. He could already feel the hot steel of the first sniper's bullet burrowing into his naked flesh.

Now they were almost parallel with the first house ruin. Still no Ivan fire. No angry shout of alarm. No bullet. Perhaps they were going to get away with it. The Tiger's engines roared. On both sides of the Prominenten, the S S troopers flashed apprehensive looks at the upper storeys of the ruins, jagged-edged and windowless, the walls bathed a blood-red hue. Now they were nearly past the house.

The darkness was torn apart rudely. Tracer zig-zagged alarmingly across the street. The S S troopers flung themselves down. Rifles started to crack on all sides. In an instant the night was hideous and frightening with the deadly music of war. A harsh, frightening explosion ripped the air out of Kempka's lungs. Directly in front of him the Tiger shuddered to a stop. For what seemed an age it trembled violently, as if by a tremendous wind. A violet-yellow light shot up from its right side. Kempka screamed out loud, more with fear than pain, as Dr Stumpfegger slammed into him, propelled sidewards by the explosion. Just before everything went black before his eyes, Kempka had one last terrible sight of Bormann and Naumann being raised high into the air by some huge invisible hand.

215

Then he hit the ground and lapsed into unconsciousness. Bormann *must* be dead!

Now the rats were everywhere. Perhaps it was due to the fighting above their heads, Hertz didn't know. All he knew was that wherever the old man flashed its light, the loathsome long-tailed, brown creatures were to be seen, fleeing instantly the carbide lamp illuminated them, but under their feet again as soon as darkness returned.

'*Boshe moi!*' the sleeper cursed in Russian, 'horrible bastards, aren't they!'

Hertz didn't reply, but he told himself that the sleeper was getting jumpy. The long trek through the maze of stinking tunnels had unnerved him. It was all to the good.

Two minutes later the old man held up his hand for them to stop. There was a moment's silence broken only by the slither of the rats and the harsh wheezing of their guide's lungs. 'Vossstrasse,' the old man announced finally. 'In the old days before the first war when everyone still had a nag, the hoss piss used to pour down that hole there by the litre . . .'

'Oh, shut up,' the sleeper snapped irritably. 'Is this it?'

The old man looked at him, head cocked to one side. 'Is the gentleman getting a little nervous?' he asked, using the old-fashioned third person form of address with which a superior was approached. 'Does the high-born gent –' He stopped abruptly.

The sleeper's hand had dropped to his pistol and even the old man's cracked brain realized that the Russian wouldn't hesitate to fire; the blaze in his eyes was lethal.

Next to the sleeper, Hertz was pleased. The sleeper's nerves were really cracking. Quietly, he asked: 'Is this where we go up?'

'Yes, sir,' their guide answered with sudden politeness.

'Thank you.' Hertz turned to the bandy-legged, pock-marked sergeant in charge of the soldiers. 'Ivanov, you go first.'

216

Ivanov licked his parched lips apprehensively, but he said nothing. Slinging his tommy-gun, he began to clamber up the ladder, the old man illuminating his path with his hissing lantern. A few seconds later, he disappeared into the chamber above. The waiting men could hear him moving something or other, then his head reappeared through the hole. 'The Fritzes must have put up some sort of barrier between here and the manhole cover. I've cleared enough away for us to get through, Comrade Hertz.'

'Good work, Sergeant. All right, stand by, we're coming up. You German, stay here.' He indicated that one of the soldiers should remain below and guard him, telling himself that if and when the little group returned that way, it would be minus two of its members, the sleeper – and himself.

One by one they started to climb the slippery ladder to the surface. Just under the dripping manhole cover, the pock-marked sergeant waited. Hertz, completely in charge now, nodded. Cautiously the N C O began to raise the heavy metal lid. He heaved and abruptly the lid clattered noisily on the cobbles of the road above.

'Freeze!' sleeper rapped.

A harsh silver beam of light cut the glowing red darkness. They pressed themselves against the sides of the shaft. Hertz hardly dared breathe. The light flashed over them and came back to rest on the sergeant just as he had pushed his helmeted head above the surface to check what was going on. It was a fatal mistake. Before he could duck, the stick grenade rolled to a halt a metre in front of his horrified gaze. It exploded the next instant. His headless body slithered down the shaft, while his head, complete with helmet, rolled into the nearby gutter like an abandoned football.

'Come on!' Hertz yelled and, kicking the dead sergeant's torso out of the way, heaved himself up and out. The sleeper followed, firing from the hip as he dived for cover. Someone screamed in pain and a wild burst of machine-gun fire scythed the street, blue angry sparks spurting up from the cobbles. A soldier went down, writhing with pain, his stomach ripped open. Another stopped in mid-stride, pawed the air with pain-racked claws, and hit the ground, face forward. Hertz hit the nearest ruin, rolled over, just as a grenade exploded in a flash of purple flame, and came up firing. The sleeper hurtled through the air and landed with a gasp next to him. The Red Army men did not react as quickly as the two agents. The last burst of Fritz machine-gun fire caught them as they made their dash for the cover of the ruins. They were galvanized into violent, electric action, slapped back and forth by the vicious slugs, hurtled round and round by the impact at such close range, until finally they were ripped to red shreds by the cruel bullets.

Hertz looked at the sleeper, nostrils full of the cloying smell of hot blood. He could see just how violently the other man's hand, holding the pistol, was trembling. The sight gave him more confidence in the outcome of his self-imposed task. 'Come on,' he cried above the loud echoing silence which had followed the last burst of m.g. fire, 'let's get the hell out of here – *quick*!'

Knowing that it would be only a matter of seconds before the Fritzes left their positions in the ruins at the corner of Vossstrasse and began combing the area for survivors, the sleeper needed no urging. Rising hastily, he started to run after Hertz. Now there were only two of them to receive Reichsleiter Martin Bormann.

His nostrils still full of the acrid smoke of the explosion which had destroyed the Tiger, Kempka opened his eyes slowly. His head ached like hell and somewhere he could hear flames crackling. But he couldn't see anything.

Several times he blinked his eyes, but nothing happened. Panicking, he rubbed them hard. Still nothing was visible save a series of bright, yellow and red stars which

218

shot by his eyeballs in a crazy, frustrating pattern. *'Um Gottes Willen!'* he sobbed. *'Ich bin blind. . . . Blind!'*

Frantically, he ran his hands over his body. But they could find no wound. Nowhere was there the warm frightening dampness of his own blood. He seemed to be all right. But what had happened to his sight? In spite of the fact that he was verging on panic and couldn't see a damn thing, Kempka knew he must get away from the spot where he lay at present. For all he knew he lay in full view of the Ivan snipers, illuminated by the light of the burning Tiger, which had to be very close by.

Kempka started to crawl back the way he had come, guessing the right direction by the fact that the heat on his face was now making itself felt on his back; hence he had to be crawling away from the wrecked Tiger. For about forty metres, he crawled on his hands and knees, wincing and yelping every time the soft flesh of his hands was cut by the razor-sharp shards of shrapnel which lay everywhere. Then he struck something which he couldn't clamber over. He guessed it would be the tank barrier. Confused and panicked, he felt his way along it until his hands touched the rougher surface of what he judged to be one of the two walls between which the barrier had been erected. He started to grope his way along the wall, feeling the cement of the concrete drums of the barricade rubbing against his other shoulder and indicating that he was passing through the barrier.

Now vague shadows, getting clearer by the instant, began to materialize before his eyes. His sight was returning. Weakly, he clambered to his feet. A figure loomed up out of the grey gloom. 'Beetz,' a voice announced, 'Georg Beetz, the Chief's pilot.'

Kempka recognized the voice. It was that of Hitler's second pilot. 'I've been hit in the head,' the other man said.

'Me, too. Can't see very well at the moment.'

For what seemed an eternity, the two men clung to each

other like lost children; then Beetz said weakly, 'There's no way out. All of them, except the two of us who tried to break through, bought it. Look . . .' he pointed a trembling finger back at the way Kempka had crawled.

With difficulty the ex-chauffeur could see the vague outlines of a fat man clad in a long greatcoat sprawled out in the gutter, his helmet rolled to one side, beyond him other bodies piled up behind the wrecked Tiger. 'Who is it?' he asked.

'Bormann. He bought it like all the rest.'

Supporting one another the best they could, the two survivors of the Weidendamm Bridge break-out staggered back to the Admiralspalast, convinced that there was no way through the Russian ring of steel drawn around the centre of the capital, and that Martin Bormann was dead.

4

But Martin Bormann was not yet dead.

He had come to, his head splitting, to find himself pinned down by a heavy weight. For a moment or two, he was too dazed to reason why he couldn't move. Then he recoiled with horror. A headless panzer grenadier was lying across his chest, the blood still pouring from a huge gaping wound in the neck. With all his strength he had heaved the corpse from him and risen to one knee.

He was alone, save for the dead, who lay everywhere. The Russian fire had ceased and the only immediate sound was the crackle of flames licking up around the burning Tiger and the steady gurgle of the dead man's blood down the gutters and into the drain. His first inclination was to turn and run back the way he had come. Only with difficulty did Bormann resist the temptation. At last he was alone, he reasoned. This was the chance he had been looking for ever since he had left the bunker with that swine Naumann's group. He could cover his tracks and work his way back to the area of the rendezvous.

Hastily he took off his blood-soaked greatcoat and, wrinkling his nose with repugnance, draped it around the shoulders of the headless corpse. Thereafter, he had ripped off his sole decoration, the Blood Order, and his badges of rank as a general in the Armed SS. Now there would be nothing to distinguish him from an ordinary SS trooper; and when the time came to clean up the battlefield, they would find the headless body with his greatcoat on it and assume it was him. Grinning in spite of his fear and inner tension he had turned and had been about to make off when he had remembered. He had cursed and forced himself to touch the monstrosity, removing the soldier's paybook and personal papers and replacing them by his own Ausweis and two letters from his current mistress, Manja Behrens. The searchers would find the pornographic pictures, mostly of well-known UFA movie stars, too, and draw the appropriate conclusions. It was a pity to have to abandon them, but he had told himself his cover was more important.

That had been fifteen minutes before. Now he was stealing through the red gloom of an increasingly silent city centre like a grey ghost. Waiting each time for a whiff of smoke or a cloud to obscure the moon which was beginning to rise before he made a dash for the next patch of shadow. Time and time again he tripped and fell on debris so that the knees of his breeches were soon ripped and his soft hands were cut and sore. But he did not notice the pain. For the time being, the Russian barrage had stopped and he was getting steadily nearer to his objective.

Hastily Mallory started to pull on his shirt. Opposite him, crouched behind the cover of the wall which bordered the Spree, Ilona did the same. The crossing of the river had not been difficult, save for the horror of the corpses which floated along it everywhere. Twice a burst of machine-gun fire had hissed across the surface of the body-littered water and Mallory had started with alarm. Had they been discovered? But they were random bursts, not fired at them.

Finished dressing, Mallory took stock of the situation, taking in the strange alarming noises on all sides and the dry snap of snipers' rifles. He realized that time was running out. They had to get to the anticipated rendezvous soon if they were going to stop Bormann. 'Are you ready?' he snapped.

'Just a moment,' Ilona answered, putting on the rest of her damp clothes and throwing back her wet hair. 'Now.'

'All right let's go – and stick close to me, Ilona. Do what I do, and no hesitation.'

'*Jawohl*, Herr General,' she said and gave him a mock salute.

He grinned briefly. An instant later they moved off.

Ahead of them loomed up the nineteenth-century bulk of the Lehrter Station. Mallory guessed that it would already be in Russian hands and so they left the railway embankment before it ran into the station itself. With luck, he reasoned, the two of them could work their way around the place, dodging from one shattered train to another until they were clear of the station.

Tripping and cursing over the buckled lines, doubling from one shattered locomotive to another, some of them still bearing the proud legend, *Räder Rollen Fuer Den Sieg*,* they made good progress, leaving the station to their left.

Now there was little noise save the dry crack of a sniper's rifle and the hot hiss of yet another flare sailing into the sky over what was left of the German positions. The Russians, it was obvious, were not going to lose any more lives this night; tomorrow the Germans would walk out of their defences with their arms raised in surrender. By dawn it would be all over.

Suddenly Mallory froze and held up his arm to stop the girl. She gasped. Directly in front of them camped out between the rails around a small bonfire, there were half a dozen Russian soldiers. They had walked right into a Russian outpost!

'Come on,' Mallory hissed, making a snap decision, 'play it nice and easy. They've seen us.'

Already the nearest Russian was waving a bottle at them, his face gleaming in the ruddy light of the bonfire, as if it were covered with grease. '*Voina kaputt . . . voina kaputt!*' he called in drunken happiness. 'War over!'

Silently releasing the safety of the Schmeisser slung over

* Wheels roll for victory.

223

his shoulder, Mallory and the girl walked slowly out of the shadows into the circle of light cast by the flickering flames of the fire. Behind him, Ilona did the same. Mallory could feel her tension, but he knew he could rely upon her.

The nearest Russian proferred his bottle, his slant eyes rolling drunkenly. 'Drink, German,' he said in broken German, slurring the words, 'you drink –' He broke off suddenly, his gaze abruptly focussing on the machine pistol over Mallory's shoulder. 'German, why you —' He never finished his question.

In one and the same gesture, Mallory slipped the m.p. from his shoulder and fired. The wild burst caught the Russians completely by surprise. They flew to all sides, dropping their bottles. One splintered into the fire. With a great *Hoosh*, the alcohol exploded. In that same instant Mallory pushed Ilona to one side. Not a moment too soon. Crouched on one shattered knee, a stocky Russian gave them a full burst from his tommy-gun. He didn't get a second chance. Mallory pressed his trigger again, and the Russian slammed against the side of one of the goods wagons.

'Come on!' Mallory yelled.

The German girl needed no urging. Together they ran forward out of the light cast by the bonfire. From a shed to their right, a light machine-gun had started up. Whoever manned it wasn't drunk; he was firing his weapon in short professional bursts. The slugs zipped all around the two running figures, clanging off the iron sides of the shattered locomotives. Mallory cursed. They'd never pass the lone gunner; he had the whole damn yard to their front covered.

'*Down!*' he commanded and dived for cover behind a wrecked coal tender, his ears full of the howl of the slugs striking the metal just above his head.

Ilona fell down next to him. 'What now?' she panted, trying to regain her breath.

Mallory sought around for a way out, his face grim.

Time was running out. He couldn't let the lone Russian stop them now. 'I've got to get that bastard with the machine-gun,' he answered.

'How?'

'Do you know how to fire that thing?'

She nodded.

'All right, when I say so – fire.'

'You will be careful, Mike?'

'I will.' He pressed her arm for an instant. 'Don't worry, Ilona, I want to live. Now I've got something to live for. All right – *now*!'

In the same moment that she pressed the trigger of her Schmeisser and sent a stream of tracer zig-zagging through the darkness towards the engine shed, Mallory was up and running like he had never run before. He hit the metal wall a flash before the machine-gunner had recovered from his surprise and turned his weapon on him. He crouched there for a second, searching for a way into the place. He spotted it. A shattered window some five yards away. He didn't hesitate. Summoning up all his strength, he dashed forward and threw himself through the window. Cat-like he landed on his feet and was running again. Crouched next to the door, the Russian heard the clatter of his boots. He swung his weapon round. Now he couldn't miss. But luck was still on Mallory's side. In the same instant that the Russian pressed his trigger, Mallory's feet went from beneath him and he found himself sliding head-long.

For a moment, he lay there stunned, his face in a pool of engine grease, the tracer hissing harmlessly above his head. But only for a moment. He knew his life depended upon a quick recovery. He dived forward for the cover of what looked like a pile of boogie wheels. Bullets whanged off the metal. Furiously Mallory wiped the grease from his hands. He dare not miss this time.

Then it happened. The m.g. stopped with frightening suddenness. Mallory chanced a look from behind his cover.

225

The Russian was jerking furiously at the cocking handle of his machine-gun. He had a stoppage. Mallory swallowed hard and took careful aim. He fired in the same moment that the Russian cleared his weapon. He screamed. His dead finger clenched on the trigger and as he slumped forward, his m.g. made a brief catherine-wheel of tracer before it shook itself free from his nerveless grasp and clattered harmlessly to the shed floor. The way ahead was free once more.

The petrol tanker detonated with appalling violence. Flame erupted into the sky. Great belching clouds of oily black smoke followed. Bormann, his chest heaving with the impossible effort, recoiled and pressed his sweating hands against the wall behind his back as if to prevent himself from falling. Eyes wide with horror, he watched transfixed as the roaring wall of burning petrol started towards him.

The second explosion which showered the area all around him with white-hot debris awoke him to his danger. He gasped with fear. Would he never get through to the waiting Ivans? Which way was he to turn now? A thousand-and-one fearful questions raced through his brain. What must he do?

The all-consuming wall of flame came ever closer. He could already feel its searing heat, as it spread out engulfing the remaining walls on both sides of the street, turning them a dull-glowing purple in an instant. He swung round and started to run back the way he had come.

From the direction of the bunker came the smash and crash of the last battle. The Stalin organs and Russian multiple mortars were firing all out. The fiery red rockets fell on the bunker with a frenzied rush like a flight of angry hornets. Great spouts of earth and rubble flew into the air. Debris rained down on his helmet and struck him hard blows on his shoulders. The bunker wouldn't hold out much longer.

Bormann skidded to a stop. What was he doing? He was

running back to a certain death. Those green and red flares hissing into the burning sky ahead were frantic pleas for help that was no longer forthcoming. Only violent death lay in store for the defenders and anyone else who ventured in that direction. He had to find a way through to the waiting Russians. *He had to!*

Crouched in a shattered doorway with death all around him, his chest heaving with both fear and exertion, Martin Bormann forced himself to make a plan, think clearly. Somehow or other he had to pass the barrier of flame formed by that damned burning petrol bowser. That was the only way to the Russians. And he had to do it soon.

'Where in three devils' names is he?' Hertz cursed, as the two of them crouched in the cover of the brick rubble observing the corner where the two roads intersected. 'He should have been here thirty minutes ago.' He flung another glance at the glowing green dial of his wrist-watch.

The sleeper looked at him contemptuously. 'Losing your nerve?' he queried. 'Moscow said you were a good man, but then with your race . . .' he shrugged and left the rest of his sentence unsaid.

Hertz said nothing. He had understood well enough, but at this moment, he had no intention of quarrelling with the sleeper. The final showdown would come soon enough as it was. Instead, he eased himself back a little to the rear of their hiding place so that he was to the blond giant's right and rear.

The sleeper sniggered and Hertz could sense that he interpreted the movement as fear. 'Don't worry, friend,' he said to himself grimly, 'I've never been less scared in all my life.'

Now he knew exactly what he would do. He would kill the sleeper first and then the Fritz. He narrowed his left eye and squinted through the right one at the approximate spot at the back of the sleeper's cropped blond head where a slug would ensure instant death.

Hertz felt the goose-pimples begin to start up along his spine. Suddenly, his mouth was very dry and he felt that hellish incapacitating nausea which he knew stemmed only from fear. He could even smell its sick odour.

To his front the sleeper grinned. The little Kike was scared, shit scared: the stink of his fear was in the air. At that particular moment, he told himself, he would not give a wooden nickel for the Kike's chances of raising his pistol and firing it, if any trouble started.

The sleeper was happy, in spite of the fact that his heart was beating faster, perhaps with excitement (he told himself). Once this job was done, he could return to his Soviet Homeland at last. The director had promised him that. There would be a medal in it for him, too. Perhaps the Hero of the Soviet Union? He frowned seriously at the red-glowing gloom ahead of their hiding place. He deserved it, after all. God, the years he had spent as a sleeper! Now all that was over. He could take his rightful place in Soviet society, as a respected, honoured Party member. But first there was this business with the Fritz.

He peered at the ruins to his front. Where the devil was Bormann? He cursed softly to himself, hardly aware he was doing so in English. 'Where the hell is the guy?'

'Here,' Mallory gasped, taking in the place in a flash, 'here's as good a place as any.'

Gratefully she stopped running, her chest heaving with the exertion, and leaned weakly against what was left of a brick wall. 'Why?'

'Because we can cover the corner by the light of that burning gas main over there. It's as light as day there. Whether he takes the left or right fork, you'll be able to identify him all right.'

She nodded and sat down.

He did the same, taking a seat on a pile of brick rubble, and unslung the Schmeisser.

For a few moments there was silence between them, as

he took out the machine pistol's long m. checked it carefully, before firmly ramming it ᴸ more.

For a while Mallory's mind raced as he consider᷈ problems ahead of him, alone in the middle of a ba᷈ field, with every man's hand against him. Could he pull ᷈ off under these conditions? Then he calmed himself, knowing that he must keep a clear head. The next half hour would affect the course of history, albeit the secret one, of Europe, perhaps even the world. He had to keep calm.

For what seemed a long time, the two of them crouched there in a heavy silence, broken only by the regular thump of the heavy guns to their front and the chatter of automatic weapons. To Mallory, staring at the crossroads, illuminated by the flaring light of the broken gas main, everything was as it should be, as it had been planned so long before in London. Yet he could not shake off a growing sense of unreality, of illusion, as if he were a spectator at some play, which held no meaning for him. He remembered that time in Prague when they had killed Heydrich. He had been the back-up man for the two Czech paras Gabcik and Kubis, who were going to do the actual killing. It had all been like a dream. The big Mercedes had seemed to make no noise as it had come swinging round the hairpin bend. Kubis's screamed warning had been soundless too. As had the explosion of the grenade which had wrecked the back of Heydrich's car and had brought it to a skidding halt. And then suddenly the dreamlike quality of that moment had vanished. All had been noise, confusion, violence and he had been running away from the scene of the slaughter chased by the 'man with the iron heart', as Hitler had called him at the funeral oration, firing, firing until he had crumpled unconscious to the suddenly blood-stained cobbles. Then the dream had become a nightmare.

Would it be the same this time? Mallory sighed heavily. For six years he had been trained to repress his imagination and subject it to reason. Now he was aware of the strangeness of his emotions and was at a loss to account for it. Was it just tiredness?

'Mike, you'll kill him when he comes?' Ilona asked softly, seeming somehow to read his mind at that moment.

'Yes,' he answered laconically.

'And then it's over?' Her emphasis was strange. Were her words a question or statement of fact?

'It's over,' he said with more firmness than he felt. 'I'll have absolved my debt to England.'

'You won't be going back to your own country?'

'With you, I won't be able to go back.' He grinned at her, but his eyes did not light up. 'Officially you're an enemy alien.' He hesitated. Should he tell her the real truth? What would she say if she knew what was going through his mind at that moment? *They* were expendable, C had said. And hadn't he been right, with poor Paddy and Higgins both dead? But wasn't *he* too? Could C allow him to live *if* and *when* he had killed Bormann, with the knowledge that one day it might come out that England had ordered the killing? Hadn't that been the very reason why they had used the two Czechs to kill Heydrich in Prague instead of native S I S agents? And hadn't C been a very relieved man, according to what Fred had said later, when he had heard from Czechoslovakia that all the Czechs involved had been 'liquidated' in the S S shoot-out?

'Anyway, Ilona, my type is finished in England. No one will want to know me in my old regiment, I'm sure.' He forced a smile. 'I'm finished one way or another.' He felt a cold finger of fear trace its way down his spine as he said the words.

'I see. But where will you go?'

'*We!*' he corrected her. 'There are other countries than Germany and England. The world is wide. All I know, Ilona, is that when this is over, we'll make a run for it.' He dismissed the uncertain future and concentrated on the even more uncertain present.

230

'Now let's forget that. Dear Mr Bormann can't be far away now.'

They settled in to wait.

Not fifty metres away, Hertz slipped the safety catch off his pistol, hands wet with sweat. To his front, the sleeper merely yawned, as if he hadn't a care in the world.

Bormann yelped with pain, as the nails were ripped off from his right hand by the rough brick. Blood streamed down his fat paw. But in spite of the excruciating pain, he kept on clawing at the fallen rubble which blocked the way out of the bombed cellar into the next one. Above him, the burning petrol bowser still roared like a stricken monster. Twice he had tried to brave the wall of flame but each time he had been driven back, his eyebrows singed, his coat stinking of burning cloth. In the end, desperate to reach the rendezvous in time, he had hit upon the solution. If he couldn't get through above at street level, he would manage below the surface. The cellars were the only way.

Now he had been clawing frantically at the brick rubble which barred his way for nearly an hour, knowing that time was running out, his face coated in dust, his body lathered in sweat, working like he had never worked since those days as a young man on that remote farm in Mecklenburg. But he was making progress. To his right, he could make out a faint glimpse of grey light coming through the pile of bricks. It *had* to be the other cellar!

Ignoring the agony of his bleeding, ripped hand, he clawed ever more bricks loose, praying to a God he hadn't believed in for years – although his pious *Mutti* had named him after the Great Luther himself – that he wouldn't start a fall. The hole started to grow larger and it held. Larger still. The light grew stronger. It indicated that the other cellar was not blocked. Once he was through the hole, he would be away. The sweat streaming down his crimson face, his fat chest heaving, mouth open and gaping like that of a stranded fish, he continued his frantic labour.

And then finally it was large enough to admit his gross bulk. Gingerly, very gingerly, as if he were mounting a pile of eggs, he grasped a fallen girder jutting out above the hole and heaved himself upwards. Carefully he inserted one booted foot. The other followed. The strain on his arms was tremendous. A purple vein ticked alarmingly at his temple. He could feel his heart beating furiously. *Grosse Kacke am Christbaum!* What if he had a heart attack now?

He lowered himself with the tenderness of a lover and prayed that the bricks would hold. They did. He breathed a sigh of relief and for a long moment was unable to move; as if he dared not risk the action that might collapse his last escape route.

He pulled himself together and, levering his bulk up on his hands, swung his legs up and out of the hole. With the last of his strength, he pushed himself forward. In the same instant that the hole collapsed with a roar and slither of falling brick rubble, he hit the solid cement floor of the other cellar with a satisfying smack of his steel-shod boots, and even as he tumbled into a gasping sweating untidy heap on to it, his heart leapt with joy. The steps that led out of the new cellar were free of obstruction, with the street clearly visible ahead. He could start running again. Now he would make it!

'There's somebody coming, Mike,' Ilona whispered abruptly. Mallory tensed, feeling Ilona's heart thumping suddenly with tension, his head cocked to one side to try to make out the noise, separate it from the gunfire.

He had it: the crisp yet somehow hesitant sound of heavy military boots coming down the road, stamping over the debris which littered the cobbles everywhere.

'Look!' Ilona whispered.

Mallory followed the direction of her outstretched hand.

232

A figure had detached itself from the dark shadows of the wall to the right. It stopped there, seemingly afraid of the light cast by the burning gas main.

'Is it him?' Mallory whispered, his throat suddenly dry, his finger searching and finding the trigger of the Schmeisser.

'I can't see him clearly enough.'

Nothing moved. Mallory could hear his own heart thumping in his ears. *Was it him?* He could stand the strain no longer. Clicking off the safety catch with what seemed to him a tremendous noise, he whispered in the girl's ear, 'Call his name. . . . Call him out, Ilona. It might work.'

She nodded her understanding. Cupping her trembling hands around her mouth, she called in a voice that was hardly recognizable as her own, 'Bormann. . . . Reichsleiter Bormann. . . . *Sind Sie da?*'

Mallory could see the dark figure of the hesitant man start. Did that mean it was their man? He started to raise the Schmeisser. Still the dark figure did not come into the circle of yellow light cast by the hissing gas flame.

'For God's sake, Ilona, try again,' Mallory hissed desperately, feeling the finger curled around the trigger break out in a damp sweat; the tension was almost unbearable.

Ilona forgot her own fear. Abruptly, she was angry at the shadow for his obstinacy, his silence, the fact that he was making them risk their lives. 'Reichsleiter Bormann . . . if you are he, come out at once. . . . We're friends. Please,' there was iron in her voice now, '*at once!*'

The harsh words had their effect. Slowly, very slowly, as if he were still not quite sure that he was doing the right thing, the man who had been standing tensely in the shadows for what seemed an age emerged and stood there, framed by the glowing eerie yellow light.

Mallory stared at him: a fat, undersized man in a shabby, dust-covered *Wehrmacht* overcoat that reached down to his booted ankles, an ordinary steel helmet on his head. Was this the man who had been the most powerful man, next to Hitler himself; who had had the power of life and death over eighty million Germans and three times that number of conquered Europeans – the second most mighty man in Occupied Europe? 'Well?' he hissed, while a hundred yards away the little man stared into the outer darkness like an overweight owl, trying to make out the position of his interlocutor. 'Is it *him*?'

Slowly Ilona opened her mouth, 'Yes,' she began slowly, 'it's him all right. . . . It's Martin Bormann.'

Mallory didn't hesitate. He jammed the steel butt of the Schmeisser tightly into his right shoulder and, expelling his pent-up breath slowly, directed the muzzle until the fat man appeared in the centre of his sight, neatly dissected by the crosslines. Gently, he started to squeeze the trigger.

'*Hold it there,*' a very familiar voice cut the night silence icily. 'Just hold it there, Major Mallory. . . . And you, Fräulein, watch that pistol!'

Mallory let the Schmeisser fall with a clatter to the bricks.

5

'So it's Comrade Piludski.'

'Yes, dear old Paddy Piludski in person . . . surprise, surprise, eh, Major Mallory?'

Mallory stared aghast at the transformed American captain, dressed now in the baggy breeches and earth-coloured tunic of a Red Army officer, his broad chest covered with cheap red enamel Russian medals.

'The last person you expected here, eh, Mallory?' Piludski sneered, savouring his moment of triumph, as he towered above them on the heap of rubble, pistol in his big unwavering hand, while Bormann, Mallory and Ilona stared at him, frozen into shocked immobility. At that moment, he was complete master of the situation.

'But how . . .' Mallory stuttered foolishly, not even able to end his sentence, he was so completely surprised by Piludski's sudden resurrection from the dead. 'I mean . . . who . . . who are you really?'

Piludski shrugged and relaxed his grip on the pistol for a moment, but only for a moment. He knew he would have to kill the Englishman soon. Mallory had not been so decadent and hidebound as he had first supposed he would be. In spite of all the difficulties and the trap they had set for him, he had made the rendezvous. Now he was in at the kill after all; only it would be his death, not Bormann's. Forbidding enemies of Moscow such as Mallory had to be liquidated.

'Who am I?' he echoed, looking down at a crestfallen Mallory from his commanding position at the top of the heap of rubble. 'I guess you might say I'm a kind of substitute, the man from the bleachers as the late and un-lamented ex-member of the Pittsburg Steelers might have said.'

Mallory did not know what a 'man from the bleachers' was and who the 'Pittsburg Steelers' were, but he guessed that the references meant the real Piludski was dead. 'Are you an American at least?' he demanded, playing for time, knowing instinctively he was not going to get out of this one alive and knowing too that if the man opposite killed him, he would kill Ilona as well.

Piludski pursed his lips, as if he were considering the question seriously. Then he said: 'What does it matter? But if it gives you any comfort, Major Mallory, I'll tell you this.' His voice hardened and there was a sudden fervour in his face as he stood there, clearly illuminated by the blaze of the gas main. 'I'm an internationalist, with an allegiance to no country and to every one. If I have a mother country at all then,' his voice broke for an instant, 'it is the Russian Communist Party.' He threw back his brutal, muscle-packed shoulders proudly.

'But how can your Communist Party do a deal with that man?' With a jerk of his thumb, Mallory indicated an im-mobile Bormann, who was watching the strange scene being played out in the smoking ruins with a look of in-comprehension on his broad dirty face. 'You know how he and the rest of the Nazis persecuted your own Party mem-bers throughout the thirties after Hitler's takeover of power? The Nazis put them into the concentration camps by the thousand, long before they started on the Jews –' Mallory broke off hopelessly; he knew he was not getting through to the other man.

Piludski's handsome, cruel face showed nothing but triumph; he did not even seem to be listening to the Eng-lishman's words.

But Hertz was. His English was not very good and he had not understood much of what the Englishman, who had turned up at the rendezvous so surprisingly, had said.

236

But the word 'Jew' had registered. Of course Bormann was as responsible as the rest; he was a *Schreibtischtäter* * as the Germans said, if nothing else. He looked at the sleeper's broad back, licked his parched lips, and felt the pistol weighing down his hand like a ton weight. Should he? *Could he?*

Piludski looked away from Mallory to the waiting Bormann. 'Herr Bormann,' he said in his fluent German, 'please come forward. We are friends. We are the ones sent to bring you back to our headquarters. You are quite safe with us now. Come, please.'

'Piludski!' Mallory cried desperately.

'Aw, knock it off,' Piludski snarled. 'Don't ya realize you're at the wrong ball game, buddy? You limeys are finished. We're calling the play now.'

Bormann came forward slowly, his heavy shoulders slumped in relief, a smile beginning to cross his dirty fat face. He had done it. He could stop running at last.

Hertz watched the Fritz advance, a strange feeling creeping over him like the icy spread of an anaesthetic at the dentist's, deadening the body of pain, fear and emotion, but sharpening the wit. At last he was completely unafraid. More, he knew with the clarity of a sudden vision just exactly what he should do.

He stared at the fat Fritz's self-satisfied smile and then at the sleeper's proud stiff brutal back and felt cold hatred. The two of them at that moment represented all he had fought against ever since he had first joined Beria's secret police so long before. Now he realized why. They symbolized that over confident *goy* (he used the Jewish word consciously), superciliousness. A racial memory? Hertz didn't know. All he knew in that instant, his skinny little body held in the sway of that hatred, was that he must kill the two of them as an act of revenge.

Bormann came nearer. They could see him quite clearly

---

* Literally a 'writing-desk criminal', i.e. one who gives his criminal orders from behind a desk.

now as he waddled closer, his confidence growing by the instant. Now he was again the old Reichsleiter, Hitler's 'grey eminence', full of his power and sexual prowess.

Hertz sought and found the thermite grenade he had secreted in his left pocket in case of an emergency. If he killed the sleeper first, the Fritz might be able to make a break for it in the ensuing confusion. If he did it the other way, the sleeper would surely kill him; he had no illusions about that. The sleeper was a dangerous man indeed. Hurriedly he pulled out the pin and pressed the lever down hard, still keeping the grenade hidden in his pocket. Even as he did so, he was amazed at his own icy calm.

Bormann was perhaps a dozen metres away now. Already he was beginning to look at the girl, his greedy little pig's eyes following the lines of her figure appreciatively.

Hertz swallowed hard and brought out the grenade. Opposite him the Englishman's eyes widened as he saw the movement. Hertz's eyes flared. Would the Englishman think he was going to kill him and the girl? Would he cry out in alarm? Gently Hertz shook his head from side to side and raised the pistol in his right hand. Silently he brought it up so that its muzzle was directed at the centre of the unsuspecting sleeper's skull.

Now Bormann was only six metres away. The sleeper started to lower his pistol in order to accept the Fritz's already outstretched fat paw. Hertz's skinny face contorted with disgust. How could anyone accept that Judas hand? He stretched his right arm to its fullest extent, as if he were back on the Moscow range, his pistol sight full of the sleeper's blond head. Bormann stopped abruptly, the greasy smile gone from his fat dirty face. He opened his mouth, as if he were about to shout, but nothing came out. Hertz didn't give him a second chance. He fired and in the same instant threw the thermite grenade. The sleeper screamed shrilly as the back of his head disintegrated, showering the rubble with a gory red spray.

Mallory pushed the girl to the ground in the very same

238

moment that the thermite grenade exploded at Bormann's feet. In a flash the Reichsleiter's body was showered with a myriad pellets of phosphorus. They ignited at once. Bormann screamed, high and hysterical like a woman, as his clothes caught fire. Desperately he beat at the white flames with his pudgy hands. To no avail. The greedy flames rose higher, wreathing his chest in their terrifying incandescence.

'*Um Gottes Willen!*' Ilona cried in horror.

'Don't look!' Mallory ordered savagely and forced her face deep into his chest. Next to him Piludski's virtually headless corpse had sunk to its knees in the rubble as if he were praying, although the traitor must already be dead. He quickly looked at the other man, the one with the gleaming stainless steel teeth and burning eyes. He stood there, pistol lowered carelessly, watching the death scene emotionlessly, as if it had nothing to do with him.

Bormann was on his knees now, completely engulfed by flames, but amazingly he was crawling, crawling away from them the way he had come, screaming agonizingly, trailing the glaring, cruel white light behind him, but crawling all the same.

Mallory looked on in awe. How could the German do it? His whole body was eaten up by the flames. How could he do it?

But he did, meaningless sounds emerging from the burning lips, the flesh dripping off the charred bones in great black bubbling strips, one horrible claw reaching forward after another, taking him forward with infinite terrible slowness.

Then that horrifying obscenity had vanished around the corner and, pushing the headless figure of the sleeper to the ground, the man with the stainless steel teeth had sprung forward and was screaming, 'Come . . . come with me. . . . It's all over. . . . Quick. . . .'

Mallory awoke with a start as the first golden stream of sunlight poked its way through the dusty window of the barn. Somewhere a cock crowed. Slowly he turned in the hay, trying to make as little noise as possible. Ilona was still asleep. He nodded his satisfaction. Let her sleep a little longer. She was going to need all her strength in the days to come.

He remembered that last hectic night with the strange little Russian urging them to ever greater speed as they fled from the centre of the burning capital, running up and down the maze of shattered, smoke-shrouded streets, until finally he had brought them to the edge of the city. There he had shown his special pass to the drunken Red Army, still celebrating May Day and their victory, and slipped them through the Russian lines. The little man's English had not been very good, but he had tried, flashing one of those metallic smiles of his. 'Bad time to come, Englishman, for you – me. Now I run. You run!' And with that he had disappeared, vanishing as mysteriously as he had appeared.

'Now I run. You run!' Mallory repeated the words softly to himself. The Russian had not known just how right he had been. For a moment, he considered what they should do. His assets were a thousand dollars, a gun, and six years of experience in the war of shadows. He had contacts in the 'underground' all over Europe. But he'd have to be careful. C would not want someone with his knowledge alive. C had an exceedingly long arm, but there was always South America. Perhaps – Next to him Ilona stirred in the straw and was awake at once. Somehow she seemed to sense what he was thinking. 'It is time to go, Mike?'

He nodded, rising to his feet and brushing away the straw bits. It was a beautiful May morning outside. She got up and followed him outside. Suddenly on impulse, she seized his hand. 'Mike, we've got a chance, haven't we?'

He didn't reply immediately, then he forced a smile. 'It's going to be a long haul. But a chance we've got. Come on.'

240

Like two children finally released from a hated school, they started to walk westwards, leaving the dead city on the burning horizon behind them. Their walk quickened until they were running, as if the devil himself were after them. *Running, running, running....*

Epilogue

A small grey man in a big grey room.

That was how the visitor, who in twenty years' time would be one of the country's leading historians, had always thought of him. As Miss Pettigrew ushered him in, he looked around the room which he had last seen two years before when he had had his bust-up with C and transferred to the Services Intelligence.

It hadn't changed much. There was grey dust everywhere. Perhaps it was some trick of the weak November sunshine, but it almost seemed as if there were a patina of dust on C's thin grey hair. The historian was not an imaginative man, but at that particular moment he had a sensation as if C were already half dead and crumbling to dust.

He dismissed the macabre thought and accepted the wave of the cold, claw-like grey hand to take a chair, wondering why he had been sent for in the first place.

C took his time. 'Congratulations on your commendation,' he began. 'You deserved it.'

'Thank you, sir,' the historian replied non-committally, frowning at C through his horn-rimmed glasses.

'I expect you'll be leaving the Forces soon, eh?' C said.

'Yes, sir. My college wants me back. I'm hoping for a senior fellowship this time.'

'Excellent,' C smiled, showing his grey false teeth. 'That is my information too.'

'*Damn!*' the historian cursed to himself. C seemed to have his finger in every pie. How did he know about his old college's proposed election? Aloud he said, 'You sent for me, sir?'

By way of an answer, C passed him a piece of paper. 'Please read this.'

The historian adjusted his horn-rims and stared at the official-looking paper, headed 'Form of Notice', and 'Take Notice'. He began to read:

Martin Bormann is charged with having committed Crimes against Peace, War Crimes, Crimes against Humanity, all as particularly set forth in an indictment which has been lodged with this Tribunal. This indictment is available at the Palace of Justice, Nuremberg, Germany.

If Martin Bormann appears, he is entitled to be heard in person or by counsel.

If he fails to appear, he may be tried in his absence, commencing 20 November, 1945....

His trained eye skipped over the rest of the indictment. 'The Nuremberg War Crimes Trial?' he queried.

C nodded. 'Yes, that damnfooled trial our American allies and that little squirt of a new P M of ours, *Major*,' he emphasized the word maliciously, 'Clement Attlee have insisted upon. Naturally Herr Bormann will not oblige by appearing.' He rubbed his head. What appeared to be grey snow – dandruff – fluttered to his skinny shoulders.

'Why?' the historian asked, wondering what all this was about. 'Is he dead then?'

'Yes, we know it, but do the Russians?'

'But there has been nothing of Bormann's death in the papers, sir?'

C did not seem to hear the question. 'We in London would like to keep the idea going that Bormann is alive and on the run somewhere or other.'

'Why sir?' the historian asked.

'Why?' C paused. 'Let us assume that originally the Russians themselves had wanted to use our dead Hun friend for their own political purposes. Let us also assume that they are now very fearful that the knowledge of that purpose may become public property. Then it would suit our purpose here to let them keep believing that Bormann is still alive, somewhere in the West, where at a convenient time he could be trotted out to display to the world that Uncle Joe was prepared to co-operate with a notorious Nazi.'

In spite of his deep-seated dislike of C, the historian was impressed. 'Political blackmail?'

'Exactly.'

'But how do you know this – about the Russians and the fact that Bormann is dead, sir?'

C suddenly recalled Mallory standing in front of him in this same office only six months before, and felt a twinge of doubt. Had the sad-eyed major really killed Bormann? What if his own cunning rebounded upon him and Bormann were really still alive? And where was Mallory himself? For half a year, agents all over Europe had been trying to find him. He knew too much. He couldn't be allowed to live. Yet he seemed to have disappeared off the face of the globe. But perhaps, he consoled himself, he, too, was dead like Piludski and Higgins (his agents had established their deaths quickly enough). Berlin had been full of unidentified corpses that summer. Abruptly he became aware that the lanky historian was watching him. 'I know this because I ordered Bormann to be killed,' he said solemnly. 'Now,' he was his usual businesslike self again. 'What do I want you to do?'

'Please?' the historian answered weakly.

'They say, great men can't die,' C announced to the lanky historian, whose career, unknown to him, the S I S was already beginning to shape for the rest of his life. 'Whether they are famous, or infamous, the public will not let them be taken away in a wooden box, buried and forgotten in the due course of time – as is the fate of most of us. In this past century, men such as Marshal Ney, Czar Nicholas, Field Marshal Kitchener – oh, half a dozen such chaps – have been reported as having escaped death by

245

some miracle or other and lived on in some suitably remote part of the globe.'

The historian nodded. On the wall, the old-fashioned Ministry of Works clock ticked away the minutes of their life with metallic inexorability.

'In short,' C droned on, 'the man-in-the-street wants desperately to believe that his lost idol is still living. Now, he leaned forward, his faded eyes suddenly animated, 'you and I are going to satisfy that hunger for immortality. We are going to create a legend – the legend of a running Martin Bormann. He is still a comparatively young man – forty-five, I believe – and he can be a thorn in the Bolshies' flesh for ever, as far as I am concerned.'

The historian saw from the look on C's grey face that the thought he might be fooling the world long after he himself was dead gave him great pleasure. 'But sir, I cannot participate in –'

'Regard it as a kind of hoax,' C urged. 'They tell me that you pride yourself on being something of a prankster. There will be compensations, of course, great ones. High academic honours, a chair, a title in due course, if you wish.' C's eyes bored into the bespectacled historian's face winningly.

'But how am I to, er . . . give you this legend, sir?' he asked a little helplessly.

'It is all planned. You will go to Occupied Germany as the British official historian. There you will establish that the deaths of the Nazi leaders actually took place. With one exception. In due course, you will publish your results in a book on the subject, which will appear under the imprint of your college. One of the Prominenten, you will write, escaped –'

'Martin Bormann?'

C nodded. 'The future is yours now. All doors will be opened to you, but give me my legend, give me Bormann, running for all time. . . .'

*   *   *

Thus, the legend of the running man was created in a dusty grey office in a building off St James's, which has long since been pulled down. The hunt for Martin Bormann became one of the greatest manhunts of all time. For twenty-seven years he was sought on all five continents, hunted by the S I S, C I A, Mossad, K G B and half a dozen minor Intelligence services. Sighted time and time again, 1945 in Upper Austria, '47 in Egypt, two years later in Chile, '52 in India, a decade later in Spain, '64 back in Chile, '72 in Brazil, he always seemed to be one jump ahead of his pursuers: running, running, running, as that grey-faced, long-forgotten spymaster had wanted so long before. Until one day in the summer of 1972, a tall, bespectacled editor from the German magazine *Stern*, finally convinced the German authorities that a shattered skull, found not more than two hundred yards away from the spot where Bormann had been seen last nearly three decades before, was that very person. What was left of the missing Reichsleiter was placed in a cardboard box, tied with string, and deposited in the Frankfurt state prosecutor's archives, where it rests to this day. The running man had stopped running at last.

Towards the end of that glorious summer of 1972, a tall, lean man, who had still the bearing of an ex-regular army officer about him, in spite of his snow-white hair, spectacles and wrinkled, bronzed face, read the tiny notice, headlined 'Bormann Found', on the fifth page of the *Sydney Herald*. He read it slowly and three times before he finally was able to absorb the information.

Stiffly he turned and called back to the farmhouse, a typical, sun-bleached 'outback' wooden structure. 'Eye!'

She opened the swing door, covered with the typical fly-screen, drying her hands on the kitchen towel. 'What is it, cobber?' she cried. Once the 'cobber' had been a private joke, but now it seemed perfectly normal to use the Australian word.

He looked at her a moment. Her blonde hair was salt and pepper and she was heavier than she had once been, but that was due to the children. 'What do you know?' he asked in that accent which fooled most Australians.

'What?'

'He's officially dead – Bormann is.'

Oh, is that all,' she said, a little irritated, and went in again to tend to her oven – the grandchildren were to come up-country from the coast that day – leaving him squinting in the sun, the *Sydney Herald* hanging purposely from his strong brown farmer's hands. . . .

For those who are interested in such things, the following historical characters made their appearance in this book

'*Fred*'=Group Captain Frederick Winterbotham, code name 'Zero C', Chief of Air Intelligence, 1929–1945.

'*C*'=Major-General Sir Stewart ('Stew') Menzies, Head of the Secret Intelligence Service, 1939–1955. Died 1968.

'*Kim*' or the '*Stutterer!*'=Harold 'Kim' Philby, senior member of the S I S 1940–1962 (?)

'*Big Bill*'=General William Donovan, head of the Office of Strategic Services, forerunner of the C I A, 1942–1945. Sometimes known as 'Wild Bill'. Died 1959.

'*Old Leather Face*'=Joseph Stalin, Soviet Dictator, 1924–1953.

'*The historian*'=Sir Hugh Trevor-Roper, Regius Professor of Modern History, University of Oxford.